A. N. Steïnberg is an American who divides her time between London, New York, and her permanent home in St Louis, Missouri. She has had a varied and interesting career as a radio presenter, a boutique owner and a counsellor at a crisis centre. She has published short stories but MANROOT is her first novel, and she has recently completed her second, which will also be available from Headline.

# Manroot

## A. N. Steinberg

HEADLINE
REVIEW

First published in 1994
by HEADLINE BOOK PUBLISHING

First published in paperback in 1994
by HEADLINE BOOK PUBLISHING

A HEADLINE REVIEW paperback

10 9 8 7 6 5 4 3 2 1

ISBN 0 7472 4501 0

Printed and bound in Great Britain by
Cox & Wyman Ltd, Reading, Berks

HEADLINE BOOK PUBLISHING
A division of Hodder Headline PLC
338 Euston Road
London NW1 3BH

To the dear ones,
those who believed and those who did not;
the Gaffer, Tracy Tolkien, Marc Steinberg,
Todd Steinberg, Lisa Barry and Simon Tolkien.

And the second string;
Nicholas Ruell Tolkien.

# PROLOGUE

Those who travel the river road in the season when the trees are bare can see, on the left near Kiefer Creek, an old rustic cabin. The woman is there every evening just before dusk, sitting in her customary chair on the porch, staring into the dark woods as if they hold some needed answer. Her constant companion, a cat, moves slowly around and around her chair, circling on its long leather lead. The animal is too large to be an ordinary cat. Its shabby gray-brown coat with a vague suggestion of stripes and its nervous tufted ears hint at bobcat lineage. Nothing about the animal is pure; it seems a mutation.

Her rigid posture is a contrast to the animal's nervous movements. He circles with his lead until it becomes hopelessly tangled; frustrated, a growl begins deep in his throat and the angrily twitching tail signals to the woman. She readies the thick towel in her lap, for she is never sure where he will strike – her cheek, her hand, her ankle – any part of her with which he can connect.

The attack, though anticipated, contains an element of surprise. They struggle, a confusion of lead and towel; she tries to contain the sound of her pain as he tears at her flesh. In moments the struggle is over and his claws are made immobile by the rough fabric. Wound tightly now, she holds the cat tenderly to her bosom, and hums softly in his ear to quiet him.

His strange opaque eyes look up into hers with the anger of a thousand betrayals, and in the soft twilight

1

mist, she cries, her tears dropping into his outraged face, matting the fur. He is lulled by the soft hypnotic motion of her rocking and he seems to doze, subdued, as she places him in the wicker cage; but through the cracks he watches. She sits wearily in her chair, humming, and from her pocket she brings forth the salve and smears it into her fresh wounds.

Like agate marbles of gray-green, his eyes glint through his wicker prison. He envies her the tears that run freely down her cheeks. All is quiet now – just the wood sounds and the woman's weeping.

It is a solitary place. The old ones who pass it look with nostalgia at the swatch of wilderness surrounding the woman and the cabin. The property, like her, is from another time; only she and the woods seem to remain unchanged.

On occasion, to pierce the solitude, children come to spy on her, and those among them who feel brave enough, dare to shag rocks that ping off the cabin or fall on to the porch. Still, she pays no mind to them, and children and adults alike give her a wide berth – the privacy allowed to those thought to be crazy.

Up the road the old swimming pool is now a camp for handicapped children. It was donated, like the rest of the property, by the Judge's son. Next to it, just east of the cabin some 200 yards up the hill, the mansion that was once called Hilltop, the Judge's home, is now an institute for the blind. In the will, when the house was donated, there was a lifetime provision for Bruce, the blind man, who had been charitably housed in the Judge's mansion back in the old days.

Bruce comes on Tuesday afternoons to the cabin to visit. A rope tacked from tree to tree is his lead. He comes promptly at 2 p.m., and this routine is their calendar and clock. In the endless days, it marks time for both of them.

The snapping of twigs, and soft curses, announce his arrival. He stumbles onto the porch with his arms waving;

she resists the urge to assist him as he shuffles slowly in the direction of the rocking chair that awaits him. Her voice seems rusty with disuse as she greets him. His own is far too loud as he belts out his, 'Hello, Katherine.'

In the way of clumsy heavy men, he plops into the chair, and there is a look of surprise on his face as if he didn't expect to reach his destination at all.

He begins rocking his body, moving back and forth from the waist until he realizes anew that the chair will do that for him. The rungs creak on the old chair as he rocks. Bruce is a big man; above the blunt square face he has a shock of thick, tousled beige hair, and his eyes are wide, vacant and blue, no different from when he could see. He follows her movements with his body, his head cocked towards the sound as she brings refreshments – lemonade or tea, hot or cold depending on the weather, served with the thick oatmeal cookies that are his favorite.

They eat in silence; his hand, uncertain, reaches out to the snack tray. He stuffs the cookies into his mouth whole, crumbs dropping down the front of his shirt. Noisily, he slurps the liquid, and she refills his mug and plate two or three times until he burps loudly and sits back into the chair contentedly.

Any unexpected noise startles him and she can see his fear.

'He's not out here; he's in the cage inside the cabin,' she reassures him.

Bruce has a great distrust of animals. 'Momma said I must be careful.'

'I know – we must all be careful.'

They sit in silence for a while, then she asks him the usual question. 'Bruce, how was your week?'

His forehead knits, deep lines crease as he tries to remember. 'Oh, yes' – first he lists the triumphs – 'I found the button in the Friday-night game. I won a quiz, and made ten corn brooms. And then, and then . . .' his face furrows trying to remember. Sometimes he repeats his triumphs from the previous week or the week before, then he turns the coin over in his mind to the other side of existence to complaints, large and small. He rocks the chair fast. His voice quivers with indignation. 'Sarah took my seat near the radio at the spooky story; the aide made me take a shower and the water was too cold.'

Katherine nods. She is patient in her giving – she listens, she *really* listens. He cannot see her nod, but he hears her cluck of sympathy. She is his sounding board, sharing his triumph, and like a sponge she takes the pain of his daily life, while he fills her up like a well.

Soon they fall silent. The chair moves slowly now.

Like a child he coaxes: 'Now tell me a story. Maybe two – please.'

'Yes, maybe two.' She sits back and a look descends on her brown oval face. Her eyes turn towards the woods and she seems far away.

'Oh please,' he begs.

'Yes, Bruce. I'm thinking which one to tell you – one you've not heard before.'

'It's OK – I like to hear 'em over.'

She leans back, shuffling in her mind the myths from her grandmother, and the books, the many books that William gave her. When she chooses, like a skilled dressmaker she alters the story so it creates good; she lends him hope, and with the telling coaxes him to believe. She is a marvelous storyteller – her words rise and fall in her mellow, pleasant voice. And inside the cabin, the cat also listens and is lulled with the magic. Fairy princes, swans, good, evil, belief in the impossible . . . hers is a mother's voice telling lies: there is always hope and there is nothing to fear.

Afterwards, they listen to the south wind rustling in the trees and both sit silently for a moment, caught in the spell of the story. Then the sound of clinking dishes tells him he must go and he rises reluctantly from the chair.

'Next Tuesday at two,' he says loudly. 'See, I remember.'

'Of course you do. Goodbye, Bruce.' She will put her voice away until then.

She watches him walk unsteadily up the hill, and the spell of myth and magic is broken. His rope twangs against the tree trunks, and the cat in the cabin hurls himself against the sides of his prison, his reality.

The wind changes, and smoke from the factory a mile west drifts through, fouling the purity of the woods. This was Tom and Hannah Brunner's parcel of land. How many years had it been since they sold the land and moved on? Katherine can't remember, but a pang of loneliness clutches at her, and below her ribcage, she aches. Her whole life has been spent alone – or almost her whole life.

Secrets – they were what kept her separate and apart. She could not even tell Ryan for he would curse her, pronounce her mad, or at best he would not believe her. No one would!

He was her only other visitor. When he came the locals strained and rubbernecked and found numerous reasons to drive by and gawk at the limousine with tinted windows that was parked on the rocky driveway for several hours, once or twice a year. Even the old-timers weren't sure who it was that came to visit her, but they knew it was one of the Judge's sons. The gossips said that one son had died and the other was famous, and they knew there was still some connection with the woman. Some said she was the old nursemaid, or maybe a poor relation. They all knew that she had been involved with the Reardons in the old days.

It was on starry, still nights when the anxiety would come to Katherine. It crept slowly like a fog, slithered up the quilt, crept under her eyelids until she sat bolt upright in the bed with fear closing her throat and her heart hammering wildly. She would leap up, fling open the door and pad barefoot across the boards to look at the stars.

A. N. Steinberg

She searched for the one, the one Me Maw had told her about. The star that had hung low and brilliant that night in Gallup, New Mexico, when she was born. The star that was still up there ... She felt kinship and fear for the child being born somewhere tonight, under this same dark star. She felt with the unknown child, who sought the damp darkness only to scream with fright at the light as he entered the world. How many others like her had been born under an unfortunate star?

# CHAPTER 1

This particular section of road was called The Crossroads. No one remembers who gave it this name or why, for the roads did not cross but ran parallel to each other, verging ever inward until they met. Others claimed, without knowing for certain, that it was the waters which contributed to its name. The bodies of water, like the roads, ran parallel to each other, until at one point they merged, and like capricious children parted again, and it was difficult in certain places to identify which was Kiefer Creek and which the Meramec River.

The largest body of water was the river snaking its way through the Missouri foothills called the Ozarks, twisting and turning to accommodate the hills, covered in pin oak and scrub oak and huge rocks where the gray mineral galena sparkled, masquerading as something precious. To the novice it seemed that these slopes were rich with silver! Wildflowers and flowering trees grew in profusions of pinks and purples, dotting the landscape. Occasionally the earth parted in sinkholes and caves created by the limestone and soluable carbocate rocks. The land housed many animals; squirrels scratched among the leaves and scaled the trees, leaping from one branch to another gathering nuts, while below, rabbits dozed in their burrows, and all manner of birds called to each other. The thicket concealed creatures common to the Ozark foothills – deer, possum, raccoon, and small red foxes, and a few bobcats still roamed, not yet threatened by the creeping civilization. The land was very beautiful, the river was not! At one time the Meramec River had been a navigable body of water for early Spanish and French explorers. It was named after an Indian tribe who used it often. It could only be admired for its persistence, its muddy, greenish-brown swirling water that never seemed at peace, gushing ever southward to wear itself out in eventually nameless waters.

On the river bank, here at The Crossroads, abandoned scaffolding and equipment lay rusting in the early May sun like skeletons of prehistoric creatures. The debris was left behind years ago, when dredging for silica became no longer profitable. The river, like a chameleon, changed her colors when the industry left. Small ramshackle club-houses were built on her steep banks, and entrepreneurs were contracted to dump tons of sand on one barren bank to create an artificial beach; the large stone house on the hill was converted into an hotel.

Then a local man digging a well for his clubhouse struck instead an underground spring, and curiously enough, the spring was salt water! A geologist studied the phenomenon and documented its source as the Gulf of Mexico, some 1500 miles south! The owner abandoned the well and built instead a public swimming pool, naming it 'Castlewood' after the town. The salt water was touted for its therapeutic properties, and customers came in droves from the city to float, to play and swim in the miraculous pool.

The pool at Castlewood was just the tourist attraction that the area needed. The trains leaving St Louis on a Friday afternoon were full of all manner of people coming down to spend the weekend there. Families came to swim in the pool, boat, or fish in the river. Single men came alone to fish, play poker and drink. Castlewood acquired a reputation as a place where drinks were always available, so even during the years of Prohibition, whiskey flowed as freely at Castlewood as the nearby waters.

Young couples in love came to swim in the pool of miracles, and to dance on the deck nearby, swaying under the paper lanterns far into the summer night.

A cortège of single women came, with silk dresses and painted faces, and those without occupations stayed, clinging to the jukeboxes and staking out territories which they fought fiercely to protect. They were always there, waiting to lead a drunken stranger into a cloistered bedroom, and Castlewood soon became known as a place where 'anything goes'.

In 1939 a lot of people passed that way, to pause, maybe to work, in one of the establishments there for a few months until they could afford to move on, looking for something more permanent. Times were hard; it was a way of life for many, the wandering!

They came that spring, passing over the wooden bridge of the river. He appeared to be a tall man, for he was slim and sinewy, but he wasn't – he was only 5' 7" or so. He was dressed in a faded blue cotton shirt, tucked into tweed trousers that were far too heavy for the warm May temperature. The thick belt that held up his trousers had been moved over twice to another fresh-made hole in the leather, showing that at one time he had carried a lot more weight. His black shoes turned over badly at the heels, hinting at better times. Like the trousers, his wool socks were winter wear and the numerous darnings the girl had sewn made him limp with new-made blisters.

His stained hat covered thick, curly, salt-and-pepper-colored hair. He had been a handsome man once, although his forty-eight years now showed plainly on his lined, wind-burned face. The skin around his sunken cheeks was faintly spiderwebbed from too many whiskeys, downed over too many years. His eyes, once a brilliant blue, had faded to a formless color much like the shirt he wore.

His eyes watered now in the soft wind as the couple

walked. In his right hand he carried a cardboard suitcase covered with souvenir decals from the many towns between Gallup, New Mexico and Missouri, mostly stolen from bus stations and cheap hotels. He wetted his lips, as he thought that there might be whiskey, right down the road, and he checked his pocket to reassure himself that the last silver dollar was still there!

The girl with him walked a step or two behind. She was as tall as the man and her long legs could easily have outdistanced him, but in respect for him as her father, she lagged a little behind. There was no clear resemblance between them. It was as if his seed had only modified her Indian features. Her skin was dusty rose-brown, a lovely color. Her face was long and angular, with a heart-shaped chin, her eyes large and liquid, dark brown. Her aquiline nose was reminiscent of a fine racehorse, and her full lips covered perfect, rather large white teeth. Her body was slender and agile; she had small breasts set high on her long torso, unlike the soft cow-like appearance of many mature Navajo women. Her straight hair, parted in the middle, was a warm brown with hints of auburn. She wore a white cotton dress that was too high-waisted for her, and she carried worn white sandals while her flat brown feet padded on the dusty road. Instead of the suitcase that he carried, her few belongings were rolled into a black and white Indian rug tied together with a cord that rested easily on her shoulder. Her neck, in harmony with her body, was long and slender, yet two tendons protruded from the smoothness of her skin – marks of a long acquaintance with worry. In her small, perfectly-shaped ears, turquoise nugget earrings had grown long ago into the flesh.

She was called Katherine. Although her father felt that the name did not really suit her, he could not think of another that did. 'Kack' was easier – it was a nickname her mother had given her, was it seven or eight years ago? He wasn't sure, for the days, the seasons, the towns

10

had become a blur since he had left his wife dying in a hospital ward in Santa Fe. He had abandoned her, for he did not know what else to do. It was after he had taught her to drink, and she took to it with such zeal that he became alarmed. On more than one occasion she had lost the little girl and returned home drunk, not remembering where she had left her.

It was when work was slow for him that his wife, Mama Rose he called her, had consented to do the unthinkable; she had agreed to weave a forbidden rug. Her mother had come and wept and pleaded, trying to dissuade her, for the Navajo believe that to weave the forbidden rug is to lose your sanity and your soul.

Mama Rose closed her ears to this talk and for her white client she began. It was a difficult chore, for while her hands had once been steady and sure, now they trembled, dreaming of liquor. She worked, frustrated and crying, and as the rug neared completion, bringing the money so close, she felt her throat quiver with craving, and her stomach churn with want for the liquor that would bring peace. Convinced that her soul was already damned, Mama Rose talked of myths and legends while she wove and told her daughter to beware.

Rose finished the rug, and with the last stitch, she stuck her finger and it bled for three days. She believed now that the curse was real!

With her pay, she and her husband spent many endless nights in dim bars with blaring jukeboxes and tinsel laughter. It was later in the daylight when the money was gone that she saw them, scorpions crawling everywhere. It was then that she tried to kill the child. Jesse took her screaming and cursing to the hospital ward and with no money to pay left her there, convinced as she was, that she had lost her sanity and, if it existed, her soul. They had wandered, his daughter and he, was it six years or seven years since then? He couldn't remember. They went

11

from town to town, doing odd jobs here and there. He had taught the girl to read, and she was quick. His daughter had not been a troublesome child and she had grown into a quiet, solemn woman, given to daydreams and imaginings which he ignored as he could not be sure if she was crazy or merely different. He knew and conveyed to her that it was safer to be quiet, to speak only when spoken to, and never, never to share the magic she often spoke about. She used to tell him about the dream sleep and how it told her things. She spoke of trees and rivers that had souls, and he hushed her, and sometimes when he was sober, he wondered what would become of her.

He cursed the old woman, the grandmother, for her craziness which he was certain had been borrowed by the child.

Pausing now at The Crossroads, at the far side of the bridge, he sat on a wooden stump, removed his stained hat, and with a dirty handkerchief wiped his forehead and mopped his neck. Like a man who was always aiming but who never reached his mark, he sighed.

'Sign says it's the Meramec River,' he said aloud. It was not their destination. Someone on the road had told them of work in St Louis on the levee of the mighty Mississippi River. This spot was thirty-five miles short of the mark. She nodded and he watched her lips moving slightly as she too read the sign.

'Damn sure ain't . . . don't look like the Mississippi,' he commented sourly as he stood, unbuttoned his trousers and urinated into the muddy water. She averted her gaze until he spoke again.

'Damn sure ain't,' he repeated, disgusted.

'Maybe it's not much further?' she commented.

Ignoring her remark, he looked about at the trees and hills and spied the huge stone building ahead, a painted sign rocking back and forth in the wind. 'Looks like a hotel.'

She nodded, agreeing with him as she sat rubbing her

bare feet. Even though she was tired from the many miles they had walked that day, she felt a lift from the beauty of the place. The gentle hills around them were brilliant with color, wild redbud trees still wore the bright purple blossoms of spring and the dogwoods, while smaller, were heavy with tiny flowers of the gentlest pink. Higher up on the ridges stood tall oaks and elms with their straight trunks, in nature's arrangement more perfect than an artist's canvas. It was mid-afternoon and the sun was unseasonably warm for May.

Following her eyes, Jesse commented, 'Oaks ... best trees in the country. Why, when I was logging—' He stopped mid-sentence, realizing she knew better and too tired to continue the fabrication. He pointed toward the hotel. 'We'll try for work there.' He hitched up his trousers purposefully, put his hat back on his head, replaced the handkerchief in his pocket and set off again, hoping with all his heart that they sold whiskey.

In the small, homey hotel they were told to go round the back and ask for Frieda. As they reached the cobblestone yard, they heard a shrill voice cursing violently at someone, and came upon a confusion of people and sounds. Under the shade of a huge tree stood a mammoth iron kettle held up by a tripod; glowing embers hissed beneath it, and a woman, rather handsome, stout with flaming red hair and face to match, was chasing a man with a curious long L-shaped stick.

'You dumb bastard, I said no pine,' she shrieked as she swung the stick at the man, who dropped his armload of logs to protect his face. 'Oh, you're stupid as a jackass, you are. I should have known better than to hire me a dummy!' she raged.

As she yelled, he turned and ran off in terror into the thick woods.

'Bruce, come back here!' she hollered at his retreating back, knowing he wouldn't.

She turned toward them then and started when she saw

13

Jesse and Katherine standing there holding their bundles. Forgetting her rage, she looked them over from head to toe, noticing that the girl's sandals were on the wrong feet. Katherine looked down and realizing her mistake, blushed crimson.

'Well, what do you want? You can see I'm busy.'

Jesse issued what he hoped was a friendly smile. 'The man at the desk said—'

She didn't let him finish. 'You know pinewood from the others?'

'Yes, ma'am,' he lied.

'The woodsheds back there – get me some small kindling right quick. *Not* pine,' she ordered.

He picked up a piece to aid him, and soon found that sniffing helped him make the right choice.

In his absence, the woman turned to Katherine and held out the stick. 'Here, girl, stir . . . the paddle-side down in the kettle, like this.'

Timidly, Katherine took the paddle from her and stirred the pot evenly to keep the mixture from burning. Watching the girl for a minute, she spoke aloud, though really to herself. 'Damn dummy. With chasing him around, I could have broken that paddle – cypress wood. I don't know where I could have got another one . . . cypress don't grow around here.'

'Yes, ma'am,' Katherine murmured.

Satisfied that the right wood was being fetched and the girl was stirring properly, the woman left to fetch more spices from the kitchen. When she returned, Jesse appeared, laden with sticks. She took the wood, and piece by piece carefully placed it under the kettle. 'Can't let the wood touch the bottom of the kettle or it'll ruin the apple butter.'

From her apron pocket, she retrieved several cinnamon sticks and dropped them in the middle of the bubbling mixture. 'Now stir faster, girl. Faster. I'm making this batch out of last year's dried apples, and it can be tricky.

That's better, but not quite it.' Again rushing off to the kitchen, she returned with a smallish crock. She poured some thick syrup into the kettle and watched it bubble. 'Sorghum . . . it needed more sorghum. It's tricky working with dried apples instead of fresh.'

The woman circled the pot again, sniffing loudly. Reaching over, she removed the wooden spoon from Katherine's hand, took a bit of the apple butter, blew on it and finally touched it to her lips. 'That's it,' she said confidently. 'That's right . . . now I've got the best darn apple butter in Castlewood, if I say so myself.'

They stood in silence as Katherine continued stirring the bubbling mixture. Sweat formed on her forehead from the effort. Frieda watched carefully, occasionally nodding her head to indicate that everything was OK.

Once again tasting the mixture, she pronounced it 'done.' Handing Jesse two large quilted pot-holders, she told him to bring in the kettle.

They followed her into the kitchen. Jesse's neck bulged as he maneuvered the heavy, scalding pot. She indicated a low porcelain table. 'Put it there . . . it needs to cool.'

The kitchen was spotless, large and bright. A black wood stove took up an entire corner of the room, and on the wall above it hung bright copper pots of various sizes. The bottom half of the walls were wood painted apple-green, and the top half was papered, in a busy design of trellis with ivy leaves winding through that made the room seem like a covered garden. On the window-sills clay pots of herbs thrived, filling the air with a thick spicy scent. The table was oblong and spread with a cloth of immaculate white linen. The chairs were covered by seat cushions tied to the rungs, and on the back of each chair was a carefully applied decal of fuzzy yellow ducks splashing happily in a puddle. The linoleum shone brightly with numerous waxings and its pattern was one of a real wood floor. You could feel the woman's pride in the kitchen; she ruled here. Firmly she placed her hands on her ample hips.

'Now,' she said, looking from one to the other. 'What do you want?'

'Work,' answered Jesse, fighting his urge to say too much.

She gave him a piercing glance. 'We do need a handyman – it's almost the season. Last handyman we had just took off, that's why I was using the dummy, but we don't need any maids,' and she looked toward Katherine.

'That's all right, ma'am.' Jesse spoke up eagerly. 'That's my girl Katherine. You'll get two for the price of one,' and he listed his skills rapidly, lying through his teeth.

Frieda looked from him to her sternly. Her heart softened as a mother who had lost her only child. She was drawn to the girl. She studied Jesse's face carefully. She had seen his kind before – he was a drifter, she'd bet her life on it. She knew the answer before she asked the question, which she put in the form of a statement. 'We don't tolerate a drinking handyman round here.'

Watching the girl, she saw her eyes drop to the floor.

The smell of something burning forced her decision. 'Forgot the biscuits on account of that dummy.' She drew open the stove and brought out the trays to cool. The biscuits were far darker than she would have liked.

'Wait here,' she commanded, and left them standing in the kitchen.

'Bitch,' he muttered softly at her retreating back. 'Redheaded, smart-aleck bitch.'

Katherine, like someone who was used to being turned away, still held her bundle, reluctant to put it down.

In a few minutes, the woman reappeared. 'Mr Taylor, he's the owner, he said it's OK. It's five dollars a week, room and board, but we can't be paying for any maids.'

Jesse nodded his consent and Frieda went on pushing her luck. 'Well, long as the girl's here, she can help me in the kitchen, so's she might learn in case he decides to hire a maid.'

'Yes, ma'am,' Katherine agreed, liking the prospect.

Frieda smiled at the girl, feeling she had a bargain in her that would be offset with the father.

She led them through to the back, to show them the room that would be theirs. It was beneath the lattices of the back porch that led to the guestrooms.

Theirs was a small room containing two iron beds. It had wallpaper depicting oversized roses that had once been brilliant red, long since faded to an agreeable pink. The floor was covered with a floral rug, and around the edges, worn linoleum peeked out. A massive wardrobe stood in one corner, next to a matching tigerwood dresser that gleamed with the industry of a former occupant's hand-rubbed wax. The mirror above it, while clear, was cracked evenly from one lower corner to the opposite upper corner. The doily on the dresser was starched to a parchment consistency and its fluted edges stood up in graceful curves. The table between the beds had a matching doily, and square in the middle sat a radio.

Frieda caught Katherine's glance. 'It works. The owner of that radio drowned in the river two summers ago, so now it's part of the furnishings and it's up to me to see that it stays here.' They could not help but grasp her meaning.

She plumped the pillows. 'Real clean we are here, you don't need to be 'fraid of no bugs. Pillows are down, real good sleepin', not like some of the pillows you get today ... stuffed with chicken feathers ... pert near put your eyes out. This room's almost as nice as the guests',' she said with pride.

Then, like a woman who has forgotten her manners in front of company, she said, 'Oh, I'm Frieda Broom.' She caught the man's smirk and felt the need to go on. 'Good Christian name it is, too.' She waited for him to share the same information.

'I'm Jesse Sheahan. My friends call me Jess – and this here's my girl Katherine.'

She nodded, satisfied. 'Work starts around five. I'll need

the wood-basket filled, and then I'll need help in the kitchen. We serve the guests at eight . . .'course, it's light right now, season starts heavy in June.' They all nodded in a curious unison. She left them, closing the door softly.

'Oh Papa, Papa!' Katherine gushed, her face pink with excitement. 'It's beautiful! Let's stay here forever.' She ran around the room with unaccustomed gaiety, opening drawers, looking into the wardrobe and finding some old magazines there. She grabbed a couple and sat in the armchair carefully turning the pages, drinking in the sight of beautiful dresses as she studied the advertisements as if they were priceless works of art.

He stood at the sink splashing water on his face and running a broken pink plastic comb through his hair.

'Going out, honey, to see what's around here.'

They both knew he was going to spend their last silver dollar.

After looking at both magazines twice, Katherine neatly laid them aside and began unwrapping her bundle. Her two spare dresses she hung in the wardrobe; her cotton nightgown was clean, as she had washed it in a sparkling creek only two days ago. Among her meager possessions was the tattered God's eye Mama Rose and she had made a long time ago; she placed it on the dresser. The twigs were intact and the yarn had started to unravel in only one place. It was the only thing she possessed from her mother – that and the turquoise nugget earrings in her ears. From the bundle she took out a faded Sunday-school card with a picture of Jesus, which had been given to her at a church in Gallup years ago. The remembrance of that Sunday, the sound of the organ and the stern nun who taught at the church school telling her and the other Indian children that they must give up their heathen ways, was not a pleasant memory. Yet Katherine was afraid to throw the battered card away. It was her father's religion and she kept it for his sake.

After settling her things she put away her father's belongings, brushing his worn clothes carefully.

She took off her dusty dress and, using the basin, she dipped the wash-rag in the luxurious hot water and washed herself clean with the fragrant soap she found there – Camay. She had seen this very soap in the magazines. She replaced the bar, regretting that so much of it was now gone.

Pulling down the white chenille spread, she climbed into bed, weary with the many miles they had walked today. Remembering, she got up and knelt by the bed and mumbled her father's prayers, rushing over the words, not feeling the meaning at all. He had taught her the 'Our Father' when she was very small, and she said it every night no matter where they slept, but to her it was merely a superstition she kept for his sake. She tumbled over the words rapidly until they became one long, unintelligible sound. Climbing back into bed, she quickly reached the place between sleep and wakefulness, then she heard it – soft strains of music coming up from the river. She shivered with exhaustion and happiness. As the strangers danced under the lanterns and stars at Castlewood, she slept. She never heard her father come in, even though he stumbled, bumped into the furniture, cursed loudly and finally fell into bed, fully dressed. He snored loudly and before morning he had soiled his clothes.

# CHAPTER 2

They learned the work, Katherine doing hers well.
Secretly she did some of her father's chores, too, so they
would be allowed to stay. Frieda took to the girl in her
rough way; not knowing how to express her affection she
was often gruff. Her words to another person might have
given offense but Katherine, who had not known the
company of other women, took none even when the older
woman compared her unfavorably with her lost daughter, Anna.

Over shelling the peas or peeling the potatoes, this close
kitchen work often promoted talk of the lost Anna.

Frieda was a well-kept woman for her age, her figure
large and ample, not really fat, just large and raw-boned.
Her best feature was her naturally curly hair, the once-
brilliant red now kept bright by a henna rinse to cover
the grey. She pretended even to herself that it was a
treatment like hot oil, not really an alteration of the truth.
After all, the package bragged that Egyptian women used
it, perhaps even Cleopatra had . . . it was a shampoo, a
treatment, not a dye.

Her cheeks needed no rouge as they were often red
from the stove in the kitchen, but she liberally applied
color to her full lips; a major portion of her small check
was spent on cosmetics of various kinds. On Mondays
when there wasn't much kitchen work Frieda often
painted her nails a brilliant red and wore rhinestone rings
that turned her fingers green. Katherine had never seen

her without the large pair of gold cameo earrings that dangled from her ears as a permanent adornment. They must have been a gift or an heirloom as they were far too expensive for her to have bought them out of her salary. Her eyes were large, piercing blue and rather cold. She had learned about the world a long time ago and the way that it worked.

On Monday afternoon Katherine followed Frieda's leisurely pace. With the weekend over and the rooms vacated and cleaned, they had only to prepare supper for the staff of five. As they worked, the snap of the peas broke the silence between them. Frieda cleared her throat once or twice, which was her way of introducing talk of some kind.

'No, my Anna would never have been in this kitchen the way you are. She wasn't cut out for this sort of menial work.'

Katherine nodded in agreement.

'No, not my Anna. She's probably sitting in a fine parlor somewhere.'

'She is?' Katherine blurted out, for up until now, reference to Anna had always been in the past tense, as if she had died in some romantic, tragic manner.

Frieda threw her a withering look, and Katherine stared down into the bowl of shelled peas. Satisfied that there would be no more interruptions, Frieda continued: 'No, maybe not a parlor, maybe they couldn't let her go. She could be sitting on an emerald-green lawn somewhere, her arms heavy with gold bracelets. He could be singing to her . . . love songs, probably.'

She grew silent, enjoying the pictures in her mind. After a time, she continued her monologue.

'But if that's where she is, the King must have chosen her to be his Queen. How marvelous, Anna so fair . . . imagine her as Queen of the Gypsies. Yes, if she's still with them, then surely they must have chosen her to be their Queen.'

Katherine's hands shook with anxiety; she bit her lip hard to still the questions that flooded her mind and imagination.

The clock ticked, the stove sputtered, and in her private reverie Frieda was still. She would tell it in her own way, in her own time.

Frieda rose and put a pan of water on the stove, retrieved the bowl from Katherine, and the water again sputtered as she tipped in the peas. From the boiling kettle she poured two cups of sassafras tea, added three heaped teaspoons of dark honey to her cup, and stirred it slowly.

She took a sip then looked at Katherine, an unnamed anger in her face. 'She was a beauty, beautiful baby she was,' and she peered at the girl unkindly. 'Not dark like you. No, she wasn't dark – her skin was like polished ivory, so white, so fair. Anna's hair curled around my little finger ... her hair wasn't straight like yours. The ringlets, golden like burnished brass, it hurt your eyes to look at that crop of hair in the sunlight, and her eyes ... so blue, like the sky on a summer day. She was a beautiful child, my Anna. That's why I lost her.'

Frieda's eyes misted and she drew up the corner of her apron; wiping her eyes, then blowing into the cloth she cleared her nose. Katherine took no offense at the unkind words. She knew instinctively that this was like the times Papa was drunk and said cruel things. Some deep pain within the older woman ached so, that she took comfort in saying these things to Katherine.

She continued, her voice a monotone, 'But what's a mother to do? It's a mother's sorrow that she was born so special. They couldn't help it, I know that ... they couldn't help stealing my baby.' Frieda leaned across the table and clutched Katherine's hand as she imparted the information. 'It was the gypsies. They do that – they steal very special children.'

Katherine squeezed the older woman's hand. 'I'm sorry.

Oh Frieda, I'm so sorry,' she said. Tears brimmed in her eyes.

Frieda pulled her hand away and said roughly, 'No sorrier than I.' Then her face crumpled and she began weeping quietly again.

In an attempt to console the woman, Katherine committed the gravest error. 'They're awful, those gypsies. We saw them once in their camp drinking wine and dancing. My father said they were dirty, so dirty, their minds always plotting things . . . awful things.'

Whatever else Katherine planned on saying was frozen in her throat as Frieda looked up, her mascara smeared with tears. She leaned toward Katherine, her eyes blazing with fury and she hissed at the girl: 'No, no! Those that stole my Anna were different. It was the caravan of the King. They sat on velvet cushions – drank their wine from golden goblets, and the music . . . their violins sang with voices like angels. They camped behind our house in the woods, the house I used to live in. They saw Anna where I laid her in the sun on a snowy blanket . . . and they were dazzled.' Her head shook with remembering. 'Oh, I snatched her away many times when I saw them creeping in the bushes, their eyes feasting on my baby's beauty. Oh no, they wanted her to marry their prince. I saw him – a dark handsome child, carried around in a carved chair. It was them that stole her and in her place they left these earrings.' She raised her hands to feel them now. She nodded, affirming the tale, rose wearily and went to the stove to stir the pots.

Katherine shook with horror and fascination at the telling, and that night she barely ate her supper. In bed she shivered and could not decide whether it was horror or joy that she felt at Anna's destiny. She got out of bed twice, mumbled the 'Our Father', and fell asleep thinking that she was safe, for she was not beautiful and Frieda had told her she was too dark.

The summer went by in a series of easy days and long

nights. She heard tales from the maid, Sally, of dancing and men who gave her presents, and how they loved her. Sally often coaxed her to come along to Castlewood, but Katherine would not go. Instead, she sat on the hill and listened to the music, watching the shadows in the distance of couples around the pool dancing close, under paper lanterns.

Her father went there every Saturday. Combing his hair into a pompadour, he set off to the clubhouse and played cards and drank; many times he came home smelling of cheap perfume.

It was a night in August when she first heard it. The moon was full – an orange ball against the sky. Katherine lay in the tall grass on the hill and found Ursa Major. She traced Orion's belt and she was happy in a vague way. It came at first as a low wail, eerie, calling, crying, seeking its place. She knew . . . Me Maw had told her of it – it was the 'Oh mu'. She had never heard its cry, but she remembered her grandmother's words . . .

When she was a child in Gallup, Katherine had loved staying with her grandmother. The adobe house at the edge of town was small and intimate, with windows that opened out onto a vast space. In the distance she could see Window Rock. It looked like the entrance to the world. She was happy roaming in the yard and running around the rocks, the dust rising as she played with the sticks that became her companions. She chased lizards, wanting to feel, just for a moment, their coolness squirming in her small brown hand.

It was here in this very house a long time ago that she had awoken at dawn as the morning star rose and a cock crowed in the darkness, and she had felt it to be magic. She had crawled into Me Maw's bed to tell her of it and the old woman held her, shivering and rocking, murmuring against her silken hair, the ancient words spoken in the Navajo tongue.

On that particular day she had been given permission to play with the colorful maracas from Laredo, brought here by her grandfather whom she didn't remember. She skipped outside in the blowing dust and tried to make music, and eventually the sun set over the rocks into a purple twilight and she smelled the cooking of corn cakes. In the wind she felt an unknown excitement, and seeing a clump of tumbleweeds spinning in the dusk, she began spinning with it. She spun around and around, the world passing her by, again and again, her head swimming dizzily. The scene rotated wildly about her – house, rocks, purple sky ... visited again and again in her mad whirling.

Finally, unable to keep her balance any longer, she lurched and fell laughing to the hard earth. The bush scratched her cheek and when the ground stopped spinning, she saw a large hare, not two feet from her, poised, ready to leap away. Instead he stretched toward her, his nose twitching, and from under the soft fur, his throat worked. She heard a soft peal of sound . . . something she had never heard before.

The hare turned and hopped away. Katherine ran screaming with excitement to the house, knocking over a bundle of dried herbs in the doorway, scattering them across the floor.

'Me Maw! Me Maw! Oh, Me Maw — '

Her grandmother opened her arms to catch the frantic child and held her against her ample bosom. A small fire played shadows on the wall, and she tried to calm the child.

Katherine whispered into the old woman's ear.

The corn cakes on the table were forgotten. While her grandmother found a clean cotton rag, she put a bottle to heat on the stove.

'Perhaps it's a small mosquito buzzing in your ear,' she said, reassuring the child.

Katherine allowed the old woman to put the sweet oil in her ears.

'Me Maw, it wasn't a mosquito. I don't hear anything now.'

The old woman held her close, wishing to protect her. She said solemnly, 'The rabbit is small and insignificant, always before it – temptation. Its life runs rapidly across the land, it gives birth to more than one and it lives in silence. Only in the moment of its death can it squeal in protest. It knows that it is better not to tell!' She rocked the child, who believed she was telling another story.

'But Me Maw,' she interrupted. 'It said it very clear. It spoke to me. I understood it!'

'Yes, child, tell me again. What did it say?'

'It said, "*You are one of the ones who knows*".'

The woman shivered and embraced the child tightly for, like all her people, she believed the hare was the totem and the child had been born under an unlucky star ...

'It is a gift, Katherine,' she said, calling her by her given name. 'It would be better if you could, to give it back, but that is not possible.'

So instead, from that day on, she began to teach the child the magic!

Now, leaving the Oh mu, Katherine rose and ran stumbling back to their room in the hotel. She must not sleep. She bolted the door. She worried about her father, for often he drank too much and slept somewhere on the road. It was too dark; she could never find him.

She worried about Frieda. She knew she could never explain the danger to her, but she must try.

She knocked loudly on Frieda's door, and finally it was answered. The older woman was wide awake; her hair was mussed and she wore a filmy black gown. 'What is it?' she snapped.

'That sound,' Katherine blurted out. 'It's the Oh mu.'

Behind Frieda she could hear the creak of bedsprings and a man's voice saying, 'What is it, Frieda?'

It was Mr Taylor. Frieda thought, What's the difference?

Now she knows how the world works. Women do what they must. Jobs all season were hard to find.

The air split with the shrill whistle from the firehouse.

'It's nothing,' Frieda yawned. 'Go back to bed. It's only the siren from the firehouse – it means someone has drowned in the river.'

But it was not the sound of the siren that Katherine meant, for it had come well before the shrill whistle. Back in bed, the girl stayed awake until she saw the first light of dawn.

From that night on, Katherine looked at the river with new eyes. It was deceptive, narrow, swift, and now that she heard how many it had claimed with its sinkholes and whirlpools, she felt fear.

# CHAPTER 3

Katherine sensed her father's restlessness; Jesse grew lazy in his work and she did what she could. They saved no money, as he took his pay on Saturday and did not return till late Sunday night. She hoped fiercely that he would not make them move on. She had grown comfortable, and for the first time in years she felt safe. She enjoyed the older woman's brusque attention. She giggled with the maid Sally and listened to her stories of dancing and loving under the moon at Castlewood.

Sally, like her father, was lazy and often instead of cleaning the rooms Katherine would find her reading *True Confessions*.

Finished with her end of the hall, Katherine opened the door to Room 11 and found Sally comfortably stretched out on the love seat. 'Sshh! Don't let the ole slave-driver know,' she cautioned. Katherine shut the door quietly and went over to the girl. Sally held up a magazine. 'This story was sizzling, I can tell you. You should read it.'

Katherine took the magazine that was offered, and Sally stretched like a lazy cat. 'I guess my love life's as exciting as those stories. Why, I bet I could write a couple.'

Katherine nodded and smiled, wondering if Sally's stories about all the men who were in love with her were really true.

'Who do you like – from the guests, I mean?' Sally asked.

'I don't really know any of them.'

'I didn't mean you have to know 'em, but we do learn a lot about them from their rooms – the tips, the ones that swat your fannie.'

'No one's ever done that to me,' Katherine said.

'I guess not – you're so stuck up. Come on, which one do you like? I'll tell first,' Sally offered. She lay back on the sofa. 'I bet you could guess anyway. I like Justin, you know the one, that traveling salesman, the real handsome one with the mustache. He gave me a bottle of perfume, free of charge.' Sally looked dreamy as she thought of him, and the magazines slipped to the floor. Her fingers caressed her cheek in a thoughtful way, remembering the touch of his hands.

'Justin is so sophisticated. I like a man who knows his way around, and he does. Know what I mean?'

Katherine nodded, not knowing at all what she meant. Sally continued, 'I like his shaving stuff. Smells nice, he does, not like the farmhands around here stinkin' of manure.' She closed her eyes remembering last night. 'It's something about his manner – cocky-like. He knows what women like to hear. He's always goin' on about my figure. He's crazy about blonde hair. I told him mine's natural . . . he thinks I should be in the pictures . . . maybe I should!' The thought of Justin created a dreamy look on her face and what she was thinking about now she kept private. Shortly she sat up and continued listing Justin's attributes. 'He dresses sharp – why, in that plaid suit he's a regular Clark Gable. And that cute little curl fallin' over his forehead just gets to me. He's got a wink on him that melts me to jelly. Why, I've been mad as blazes at him then he winks at me with those big brown eyes and I starts to giggle and we make up. He's about the handsomest man I ever seen. That smooth dark skin and his hair shimmering with that hair tonic, and his mustache tickling me when we kiss.'

Katherine blushed a deep red.

'I'm lucky,' Sally murmured. 'He's telling me all the

30

time how much he loves me. Now you've gotta tell. Who do you like? With all the men that come and go there must be somebody.'

Katherine tried denying it.

'Oh, come on,' Sally coaxed. 'Even if you haven't done anything there must be someone you're sweet on, someone you daydream about. Truth is, I thought about Justin lots, way before we got together.'

Reaching up, Sally took Katherine's hand and pulled her down on the love seat next to her. 'You gotta tell.'

Katherine enjoyed their silly talk. She always felt warm and touched, as if they were sisters.

'Well,' she gulped. 'I hadn't really thought about it.'

'Liar, liar, pants on fire, sure you've thought about it! All girls are lookin' to fall in love.'

The word 'love' made Katherine's blush deepen. She felt hot and embarrassed, and she had to deny the word love. 'Nothing to do with love,' she started haltingly, 'but as far as men go, I think the Judge is the nicest.'

'The Judge!' Sally squealed, holding her stomach as she giggled hysterically and finally rolled off the couch. 'The Honorable Judge William Reardon!'

'Ssh,' Katherine hushed her, instantly regretting her confidence.

Sally sat up. 'I'm not laughing at you, honey. You've got good taste. The Judge is a little old for you but there's still fire under those ashes, I can tell you! Why, he's traipsing them women from the Eagle's Nest up to his room at least every other weekend.'

'I didn't mean like that,' Katherine protested. 'I mean, he seems a real gentleman. Anyway, he's married.'

'That don't make no difference,' Sally scoffed. 'Well, girl, you do have taste. He's rich enough, the richest man in the county, and I guess he's sort of handsome for an older man.' She stared at Katherine as if seeing her for the first time. 'I bet he'd give you a tumble if you fixed yourself up a little.'

'Oh Sally, stop it. You're mixing up what I said . . . I just meant he's nice.' But Katherine knew the other girl would be teasing her from now on.

'I'm good with make-up and hairstyles – let me try something.'

'All right, but this has nothing to do with what I said about the Judge,' Katherine insisted.

In her room Sally seated Katherine at the vanity table. In minutes the room filled with the smell of pressed hair. She used the curling irons on Katherine's auburn hair until it fluffed out around her face attractively. 'Make-up – you need a little make-up.' Sally powdered and applied rouge and lipstick until Katherine seemed totally transformed. The older girl stepped back and surveyed her handiwork. 'Not bad, not bad at all. You'd be a real knockout if you'd let me fix your eyebrows; they're too thick.'

'I don't see anything wrong with them.'

'Not stylish enough. I could pluck 'em for you?'

'No, no,' Katherine protested.

'You really should think about it. Why, them movie stars shave their eyebrows right off, and draw them where they want 'em.'

'They do? Why would they do that?'

''Cause it makes your eyes look bigger,' Sally announced. 'God, you don't know nothin'. How do you expect to get the Judge?'

This last statement was too much for Katherine to bear and in a voice quite unlike her normal one she said sharply, 'I don't! I never said anything of the kind!'

Sally just laughed, aware of what such protest meant. She stepped back again admiring her creation, then picked up an eyebrow pencil. 'It's a shame I can't pluck them,' she shrugged, 'but never mind!'

She tipped the mascara brush in the glass of water and rubbed it back and forth over the cake of mascara until satisfied.

'Now, look up towards the ceiling,' she instructed.

Katherine blinked as the brush touched her lashes. 'No, keep looking up, or you'll smear it,' her friend warned. Katherine tried to do as she was told, but again and again the approaching brush made her flinch.

'Oh well, I guess your lashes are dark enough,' Sally sighed, and taking the corner of her white apron, she spat on the edge and wiped away the streaks.

Then she stepped back, hands on hips, her head cocked to one side and said, 'I could have been a beautician, you know. My ma always said I had a talent for it. You can look now.'

Katherine swiveled the stool around and faced the mirror. Before her sat a perfect stranger and she felt goose bumps rise on her neck. She wasn't sure if this was due to Me Maw's warnings about mirrors, or the fact that in the glass was a dark reflection so strange, so alien to her, that it was possible to believe that the mirror had stolen the real Katherine and had replaced her with this one. The face that stared back seemed like the ones she had seen in the magazines. Timidly, she raised her hand to touch the fluffy waves, soft as duck's down. She pursed her lips, and they felt cool and slick as satin. Her heart began to race; she was afraid of this strange woman in the glass.

'You're a knockout, a true knockout!' Sally said softly, secretly amazed at the transformation she had wrought. As she looked at Katherine in the glass a thought stole in swiftly: 'What about Justin?' She shook her head and said aloud, 'It's too much of a change – maybe you shouldn't.'

They heard Frieda calling impatiently up the stairs. Katherine jumped up from the stool and tried smoothing her hair.

'I'll go,' Sally offered.

Grateful, Katherine slipped down to her room. In the gloom she looked once again into the mirror, and the crack split her face in two, making it grotesque. She thought of the fun-house mirror that time when her father had taken her to a carnival in Topeka. She hadn't liked the mirror then; she didn't like looking in the mirror now.

She ran water in the sink, washed her hair to smoothness again and scrubbed her face till it stung. The tangles in her hair made her eyes smart as she combed every strand straight. But the strange haunting face in the mirror stayed clearly etched in her mind's eye.

When Katherine went to bed, strange scents still clung to her; the tang of perfumed cosmetics was pleasant. She had trouble sleeping; now that she had mentioned to Sally that she thought the Judge was special, he came clearly into her mind. The tawny lock of unruly hair reminded her of the wheatfields of Kansas. She pictured his clear, blue-gray eyes; she thought of them as kind, honest eyes. Every impression she had had of him came clearly to her. She hugged these impressions close and finally she fell asleep and he came in the dream, smiling with stalks of wheat waving behind him in the brilliant noonday sun. She felt the warmth of a body beside hers. It was hard to separate the dream from the real sensation. A hand, hard and calloused, squeezed her breast. She was breathing hard . . . the dream, his face smiling, it didn't make sense for the hand snaking up between her legs and the fingers like steel prying her apart was far from pleasant. The stench of stale whiskey overcame her like an ominous cloud. It was pushing at her, trying to enter, fingers hard as steel creating pain awakened her.

'Mama Rose, be good to your daddy.' His voice was hoarse with passion.

Understanding descended. 'Papa! No, Papa, it's me,' she screamed.

'Call me your daddy, your big strong daddy.' His arms were forcing and twisting, pulling at her, his body thrust full up against her.

With her elbow she aimed for his Adam's apple, and she pushed with all her might. She heard him falling to

34

the floor. She reached for the lamp and the room bloomed with light. He was lying there naked, his manhood full. He blinked up at her.

Katherine gathered her nightgown up tight around her, and cowered in the furthest corner of the bed. She shivered. He hadn't done it since they came here.

The light was between them – it felt like a ray of protection. For months now she had been able to sleep soundly. It was over – it was behind them. No longer did she clench her teeth in her sleep, dreading his touch, his demons. In the woods, in the wheatfields, when they slept rough . . . she never knew when he would fall on her drunkenly, hurting, always hurting her – the smell of whiskey making her faint, his rough fingers pinching her breasts, doing that – always doing that. When she was little it hurt so much that for days afterwards, the pain, when they walked, was unbearable.

'No,' then she had begged. 'Please don't.' But he had whispered wetly in her ear, 'It's 'cause I love you, baby.' She never understood why his loving her had to hurt.

It was after the time in Kansas, in the wheatfields, when she had been so sick, curled up, her stomach on fire with pain, followed by some sort of magical release, when her period came on strong and the blood flowed. Then he had looked scared and worried, and by the moonlight, she saw him scratching at the earth, burying something. She was so very tired, she slept.

After that night, he never climbed on again, pushing and pushing. It was then he made her do the other thing. He had said, 'I'm your father. If you love me, you'll do as I say.' She couldn't refuse, for he was her daddy – and she must love him, for she had no one else.

Now, he rose drunkenly, fell into bed, and covered himself. It was the woman. She could tell the woman, he thought.

Katherine turned out the light and crawled back under the bedclothes, listening to the sound of him pulling at himself. She could not sleep until she heard his loud snores.

It was over, of that she was sure; it would never happen again. She didn't understand what had changed, but she was safe. He would be angry with her, certainly, but it didn't matter for she was safe.

After that night, Jesse seemed to do even less work and Katherine grew used to covering for him. The weekdays were slow now, for it was autumn and the season had ended. Sally stayed on working carelessly and chattering about her many boyfriends, of whom Justin was still her favorite. Frieda enjoyed Katherine's quiet company and serious attitude, so she taught the girl about cooking and canning and gathering useful plants. Katherine had a natural bent for the plants. She knew herbs without knowing how, she brewed up mixtures in the kitchen and Frieda encouraged her, for through trial and error Katherine's mixtures worked. She had concocted a salve that eased backache, another for corns, and she was what Frieda called a 'natural with the healin'.

The woman talked about the preserves they would put up this autumn, and during the week, when things were slow, they enjoyed outings into the woods.

'There's plenty of free food around if you know what to look for. A body wouldn't starve if you know what to get and where to go get it,' Frieda bragged.

Katherine's mind spun with the unfamiliar plants that Frieda talked about – the river haws, cattails, Jerusalem artichokes and basswood. 'Katherine, come September we'll go sang-hunting,' Frieda promised.

'I don't know anything about hunting,' Katherine answered. 'I couldn't kill an animal.'

'No, silly, it's not an animal. Sang is the manroot – ginseng. Never mind for now.'

One slow autumn day Frieda produced some large burlap sacks.

'Is this for the sang-hunt?' Katherine asked eagerly.

'No, it's a little too early for the manroot, but there's lots of other things we can harvest now.'

Sally begged off saying she always got poison ivy, so they went, just the two of them, through the trees to a wild, unkempt meadow.

'There ...' Frieda pointed to a group of scattered sun-flowers that towered, some as high as twelve feet. 'It's a little early, they're best in late fall, but they'll do.' A covey of blackbirds took flight as they approached the giant flowers.

'We're not after the seeds. Let the birds have them.' She took her small spade, dug into the earth, and toppled the plant. 'It's the roots we're after. Breadroot, my mama used to call it. Some call it Jerusalem artichoke.'

Katherine watched her clip the large knobby root that looked very much like a potato; and soon their sacks grew heavy.

'That's enough,' Frieda said. 'We've only got five to feed tonight. Now for some onions.' They walked a long distance before they noticed the sharp smell of wild onions. They pulled only a few and moved on, Frieda's eyes rapidly scanning the trees, bushes and meadows to see if she could find anything familiar. She looked for birds, and in the distance spotted some, diving and circling and landing.

'Could be a grove, with all those birds around,' she said, walking briskly toward the thicket. Katherine struggled to keep up, carrying both sacks, as well as the spade and shears. As they approached the grove Frieda spied it, a small tree with narrow leaves growing in clumps. 'We're in luck. These are plums,' she announced. 'Chickasaw plums ... Indians planted these trees a long time ago. They can be found in lots of places in these woods.'

Katherine smiled and felt a special pride for the Indians who had planted here so long ago. She glowed as they pulled the branches down, and picked the yellowish plums that the birds had left.

They walked back slowly; Katherine guessed at the plants that were useful, trying out her innate skill. Often she stopped to pick a leaf, and rolling it between her fingers and sniffing it, she gingerly guessed at its use. She had an instinctive feel for the medicinal properties of plants.

'You're good,' the older woman said. 'Some's got it, the knowing, and I reckon you do.'

Katherine flushed with pleasure for she was so unused to compliments.

That night they worked eagerly in the kitchen and Katherine followed the older woman's methods faithfully, her mind crammed full of the recipes she had already learned.

Unpacking the sunflower roots, Frieda said, 'We'll bake 'em – they'll be good with roast pork. 'Course, we can boil 'em or bake 'em, but I think baked for now, and some time when we get enough of the root, we can pickle 'em.' They scrubbed the roots clean, sliced them thin and layered them in a flat pan with finely cut onions, scattering a light covering of grated cheese over the top.

After putting the casserole in the oven, Frieda turned her attention to the chickasaw plums. Washing them carefully, she handed Katherine a large plum and bit into one herself.

'Sweetest plums ever. Wild plums are the best, you can make most anything out of them – catsup, cobbler, pudding, jam, sauce, pickles . . . just about anything. Anna liked pudding best – so let's make pudding,' Frieda decided.

They pitted the plums, filled the pot with water to cover the fruit, then sat relaxing with tea while the fruit simmered fragrantly.

Katherine so hoped the reference to Anna might be the preamble to another story, but Frieda seemed to have forgotten as she gathered the necessary ingredients for the pudding – a cup of sugar, four tablespoons of butter and one egg. She mixed the ingredients vigorously with the beater until the mixture was a thick cream. To this she added one cup of milk, two cups of flour and two teaspoons of baking powder. The boiled plums were arranged in a baking pan, and the mixture was poured over them. Frieda spat on the stove trying to judge the heat. She lifted the iron plate and added two small logs before putting the dessert in the oven to bake. 'Log-basket wasn't filled this morning,' she said, 'and it was empty a couple of days last week.'

Katherine squirmed. Frieda must know, even though Katherine had always hurried to do her father's chores early. She looked at the girl. 'He's gone, hasn't he?'

# CHAPTER 4

Pacing the room at night, Katherine would run to the window whenever she heard a strange noise. 'Papa, is that you?' was her eternal question. She felt terror at being left totally alone. It was his tongue, his glib ways that had always managed to find them work. Alone, she would be tongue-tied – no one would hire her. The season had been over for some time; she knew Frieda had not told Mr Taylor that the handyman was gone. He stopped their wages in October, assuming that Frieda had let them go.

Finally, Frieda called in the sheriff, who took a Missing Persons report. His manner was cold and unconcerned. 'Lots of men run off,' was his comment to the girl. 'Times is hard.' Then, seeing the anguish in her eyes, he softened his words with hope that neither of them believed. 'Maybe he'll come back.'

'The river?' Katherine said. It was a whisper of a question.

'Oh, that's a treacherous river, all right. You say he's been gone two weeks? He'd be up by now if he was in the river.' He rubbed the stubble of his beard. ''Course, if a body's caught on a branch...' Katherine knew why Papa had left. Lying in the dark with him in the next bed was no worse than knowing he was gone forever. He would not come back for her. In his sober moments, he was afraid of himself.

Frieda finally told Mr Taylor, who came down and looked at the girl. 'We can't pay wages in the winter,' he said, yet his eyes flickered over her, measuring her body.

Frieda knew that look and it brought home her deepest worries. She feared the time when he would notice that she had grown old and not want her any more, although it had not happened yet. Their arrangement had been going on for years. Neither of them pretended it was a love affair. It was after Anna that she had come here; her prudent ways had saved him money, her willing arms had sealed the bargain. He came to Frieda maybe two or three times a month when his wife slept.

'She's slow,' Frieda told Mr Taylor. 'Slow and very strange, with those Indian ways, but the girl is a big help and it doesn't cost much to let her stay in the room.' She pleaded for Katherine, yet instinct made her protect what was hers. 'Smells, too, but she's a good enough worker.'

'All right,' he agreed.

For the heavy work, they hired Bruce on a part-time basis. Although he was slow, his work certainly rivaled Jesse's leisurely pace.

Bruce was a boy of twenty-six, who lived three clubhouses away from the hotel. Rumor said he was kicked by a horse when he was six years old, and his powers of reason were left on the horse's hoof. He was a big man, but so harmless and timid that it was difficult to think of him as a man at all; most folk referred to him as 'the boy' or 'the dummy'. His powerful shoulders could easily hoist and carry the heaviest logs, and his arms, which were far too long in proportion to his thick chest, gave him the appearance of a gentle ape. His shirt more often than not buttoned up the wrong way, and when he could, he removed the tight shoes that someone had given him, and walked barefoot. He obeyed Frieda when he could; he worked well enough when he understood what was needed. He adored Katherine.

The days were slow and easy, but Katherine grew pale and drawn, for she had heard it again in the night – the Oh mu. It made her wonder, could her father be down there in the dark water, caught on a branch like the sheriff said?

No. In her heart she knew he was off somewhere drinking in some dim bar, and she said a number of 'Our Fathers' for him.

Katherine kept busy and Frieda took to a mad housecleaning spree.

They knew Sally would be leaving soon, as there was no more paid work available, so Frieda left the two girls alone to talk, to dream, to do whatever young girls do – she didn't really remember. She took on the chore of cleaning out all the guestrooms' closets. Collecting an assortment of things left and forgotten by a series of paid-for women, she brought the bag to Katherine's room saying, 'If it were your birthday, I should like to give you a present . . . It's not much, but here.' She handed her the bag.

'I don't know when my birthday is. Papa said I was born in the summer, but I don't know the exact day.'

'Well, then, make it today – October the second. Now open it,' she said gruffly. Frieda sat on the unoccupied bed in Katherine's room, feeling uncomfortable. She wasn't used to being tender.

Katherine gave a small 'Oh!' and 'Ah!' as she drew each item out of the sack: a string of imitation pearls, an ivory comb, bits of ribbon, satin and velvet, half-empty perfume bottles and a pair of red satin garters. The thing she loved most was the shimmery red Valentine box; its ribbon was somewhat crumpled but the inside of the box still smelled of chocolate.

'I'll keep all these things in this beautiful box,' Katherine said. She felt an urge to rise, throw her arms around Frieda's neck and kiss her cheek.

Almost as if guessing her thoughts, Frieda stood. 'It's late,' she said. 'We have to get up early, and Sally needs help with her packing. She'll be leaving in a week or so.'

Frieda hurried out of the door; she felt like crying. The

girl was so grateful for any little thing. It made her think of Anna, and for the first time she lay in bed and thought of her daughter – not the preposterous stories she made up, but the truth, the real truth about Anna. And she wept far into the night for her lost child.

Katherine went to the dresser drawer, and from under the carefully folded pillowcases she brought out the other items she wanted to keep in the heart-shaped box. Ever since she had admitted to Sally that Judge Reardon was her favorite, it had unleashed something that had slept deep inside of her. She now took notice of everything in the Judge's room, and when he departed on Saturdays she searched for bits and pieces of him. It didn't matter that on the Fridays when he arrived he always put out a framed picture on his bedside table of a smiling blonde woman who must be his wife.

While cleaning up, Katherine collected a cigarette from the ashtray, a handkerchief – lipstick-stained, with the initials W. R. – and a tiny gold shirt stud that, ordinarily, she would have turned in. She even kept two sandy-colored strands of hair that she found on his pillow.

Now as she stared at these relics of him, it seemed to her like some sort of magic rite that she performed without knowing how.

# CHAPTER 5

Working alone in the kitchen, Katherine scrubbed it clean.
Looking up at the calendar, she knew tomorrow was
Friday. The Judge was one of the few people who stopped
here regularly, even now, in late autumn. Perhaps it was
telling Sally that had started it all, for now her thoughts
of the Judge were like a fever that stayed with her. Last
Friday when she took him his bourbon and spring water,
she had noticed it for the first time, the birthmark. It was
on his right hand, so clear and vivid that she had almost
dropped the tray. He had smiled at her nervousness,
called her 'my dear', and given her a silver dollar for a tip.

Katherine slept restlessly; she dreamed of the Oh mu
and heard its moan of agony echoing in her sleep. She
dreamed of Papa floating in the muddy river, caught and
held under by a treacherous branch, his eyes vacant pools
staring upward through the water. It was so real that in
the morning when the siren from the firehouse once again
split the air, she rushed into the kitchen where Frieda was
telling Bruce, 'You be careful . . . another one's gone and
gave herself to the river. It was a suicide, a painted woman
from the Eagle's Nest . . .' Frieda shivered as she told the
story the way that she had heard it from the postman.
The woman in the night had cut her wrists but the dying
was too slow, so she ran from the clubhouse, perched
only for a moment on the railing, then jumped headlong
into the cold water.

Katherine moved slowly this morning. Frieda fussed at

her, but knowing the girl had never been lazy, she thought the drowning must have upset her or maybe she was coming down with something.

The guests were all gone. They only expected one tonight – Judge Reardon. They'd have time to go into the woods today, hunting for herbs and the manroot. But Frieda went alone as the girl looked a bit too peaked.

Alone, Katherine cleaned the rooms again; it took no time, for they were already clean. She lingered in number 8, the Judge's room.

She knew a lot about him now, and she felt a very real presence that he left in the room. She knew intimate things about him – like the size of his shirts, the smell of his aftershave, which side of the bed he slept on, how he preferred his coffee, the brand of cigarettes that he smoked . . . numerous details about him that she had collected bit by bit, saving them in her mind and in her dreams, like pennies to be spent at a later date.

He knew nothing of her, dusting his dresser, straightening the bed after he had risen. He was not aware that while he was out, she pressed his shirts to her lips, inhaling his aroma, and sat on the bed in the same crevices his body had made over the years that he had slept here. Now she knew with the wisdom and instinct of centuries, she knew that what would be, would be.

Last week for the first time she had seen it, the birthmark, on his right hand. It was paler than the surrounding skin, crescent-shaped like a slice of the moon, and within its outline, unmistakable, a perfect five-pointed star. She knew its shape by heart, as just above her right breast she had its identical replica.

The Navajo blood flowed strongly in her veins, with all its beliefs in the signs, even though her father had tried vainly to smother these strange alien traits. Since her childhood she had believed that she could speak to animals, and she could find herbs hiding under any rock and knew exactly what they would cure.

She stayed dreaming in the Judge's room until she heard Frieda calling her. The woman had returned from the woods, carrying a full burlap sack.

'You should have come today . . . I found it . . . the time is ripe, and you're much quicker than I. You would have climbed the higher spots where it grows.'

Placing the sack on the table, she pulled out one root. 'It's perfect . . . it's prime, probably ten or fifteen years old.' She held the root up to the light. Its torso similar but lighter in color than a carrot, with no hint of orange, just tannish-brown, the root seemed to have two arms, two legs and a fine network of tendrils. It appeared to be a miniature figure of a headless man.

'What is it?' Katherine questioned as she stared at the unusual root.

'It's the manroot!'

'The manroot,' Katherine repeated, liking the sound of the word and feeling it described the plant perfectly. 'It seems as if it could contain magic?' she said, as she gingerly touched it with a timid finger.

'Oh, they say it does. It works wonders. The Orientals prize its properties – to them it is also the love root. It does many things, cures most anything that ails you. For me it lines my pockets – Bailey's general store pays about four dollars a pound.' Emptying the sack on the counter, Frieda explained, 'You can't let it get damp – it ruins the root.' She began taking them out, examining and inspecting and drying each root with a clean dish-towel.

'They're not all like this one, that's special. Some don't come with the likeness of arms and legs, some just look like a pale carrot . . . but the old ones, the very special ones do. Here, Katherine – take it, it's yours.'

They sat at the table and by habit Katherine helped her.

'If you weren't such a lazy girl, you could have come with me today. When these are dry, I'm sure Bailey's will be paying twenty dollars or so for the batch.'

'Twenty dollars?'

'Yes, ma'am!' She knew the girl wasn't lazy; it was her way of trying to shake her out of the listlessness. 'Put on the kettle, Katherine. I'll slip a little of the root in it. That will perk you up.'

They drank the tea, and Frieda continued drying the root. She did a rare thing, she hummed as she dried the fine tendrils.

'It takes time for the manroot to grow. You shouldn't harvest a root less than seven years old, and you must always plant the seed when you harvest – each red berry has two seeds – not deep, just under the leaves. It's a sin . . . to harvest and not plant the seed,' she said solemnly.

Katherine watched the clock. 'I better put on my uniform. The Judge . . .'

'No need to. When I was coming in, he was headed for the Eagle's Nest. He told me he wouldn't be wanting any supper.'

Katherine's face fell with disappointment.

In previous gossip from Frieda, Katherine had learned that the Judge lived twenty miles up the road with a wife who was said to be fragile since the births of her two stillborn sons. There was not much in these parts that the Judge did not own; he was rich, well-liked, respected, and known to be a fair man. Remarkably young to be a Judge, no one faulted him for his tendencies to card-playing, drinking whiskey, and relieving himself with the local women. A lesser man with these leanings would be called no account, but he was, after all, the Judge, and this title brought with it a tendency to look at vices as virtues.

It was just another Friday. Destiny waited for her; she felt it close, closer than it had ever been.

The hotel was quiet. There were no guests and the only person staying was the Judge, who would be out late.

Katherine played the radio softly, dancing about the room, pretending she was at Castlewood waltzing under the lanterns with him. She put the perfect manroot in the

Valentine box with her other things. After midnight when he rang, Katherine shook the sleep from herself when she realized the bell from Room 8 was ringing.

She owned no robe, and the persistent ringing threatened to wake Mr Taylor. She flew up to the Judge's room and knocked timidly, aware that her hair was down, and she was in her nightgown. It was plain enough – white cotton, sturdy and sensible.

He opened the door to her. He seemed surprised.

'I'm sorry, sir, everyone is asleep,' she said, not really knowing how to apologize for her attire.

He blinked at her, his hair ruffled, his shirt-tail out; she had never seen him like this.

'You're new?'

'No, sir, I'm Katherine. It was late, I didn't have time to put on the uniform.'

He nodded and leaned forward studying her face. 'Come in.' She did so but left the door open.

'Sit down,' he said. She could tell he was very drunk. She sat timidly in the vanity chair. He paced the floor unsteadily, running his fingers through his hair. 'It's my head . . . I have a headache that won't stop. I thought maybe you had something in the kitchen.'

He kept pacing. 'I went out tonight, trying to forget. I've drunk a lot . . . it doesn't stop . . . my head hurts so.'

'Sir, I could go look, or — ' She wondered if she should chance it – maybe he would laugh. 'My grandmother had a remedy that always worked.'

He stopped pacing. 'Yes? What is it?'

'Well,' she said, 'if you rub your thumbs vigorously for a few minutes, it has something to do with the blood flow . . . if that didn't work then a leaf of boiled cabbage on the forehead never failed.'

He smiled and stopped. 'Well, try it.' He pulled up a chair in front of her and held out his thumbs.

She blushed. She hadn't meant that she should rub his thumbs, but he was there across from her, waiting.

A. N. Steinberg

She reached forward, and with a firm grip clasped his thumbs and rubbed vigorously, while he leaned back and shut his eyes. She alternated between each thumb. It seemed natural to her to be touching him.

'Do you know what it's like to play God?' he asked abruptly.

Startled, she didn't know if he was really talking to her, but she replied, 'No, sir, I don't.'

'Well, I do, and it's not pleasant, not pleasant at all ... Today I've sent a man to the gas chamber – well, not me personally, but the jury.'

'I'm sorry, sir,' she said quietly.

'Stop saying "sir" – my name's William. The Judge ... sir ... that's somebody else. I don't feel like a judge right now. I never wanted to be a judge.' He opened his eyes and she drew back.

'Do you know what it feels like to judge other people?'

'No, si — ' She stopped herself. 'No, I don't.'

He looked down at her hands. 'Don't stop. By God, I think it helps!' He closed his eyes once more and held out his thumbs to her. The house was quiet. Somewhere a nightbird called; the ticking of the clock in the hall kept time in its steady rhythm, and Katherine felt the sound of their breathing in tune.

His face looked so young. He seemed to have relaxed, and every so often he issued a deep sigh.

After about ten minutes he opened his eyes. 'By God, it did it. Or maybe it's just that I didn't look forward to a cabbage leaf on my head.' They both laughed.

'Do you have any more of those old remedies from Granny?'

'Yes, sir, lots of them.'

'I told you my name is William.' He looked at her intently. 'I'm sorry to have awakened you, but I was very troubled. Tell me, Kathy, what do you do when you're troubled?'

His calling her Kathy instead of Katherine sent a shiver

through her. No one had ever called her that.

'Well, sometimes I go and sit by the river and watch the water, or I look at the stars to find Ursus Minor, or Major, or the Pleiades.'

'That's wonderful. I used to do that when I was a boy . . .' He seemed to be far away, remembering.

Abruptly he rose, went to the French doors, opened them and stepped out on to the porch. 'Show me,' he said loudly.

Afraid of waking anyone she hurriedly went out to the porch after him. The cold night was brilliant with stars.

'There,' he said, 'the Big Dipper. It makes the world seem constant.' She nodded, agreeing with him. 'And look, the little guy is up there, too.'

She smiled at his silly reference to the Little Dipper.

'Now the rings of Saturn, or Halley's Comet – that would be something to see,' he said, feeling a new excitement. Those were the sort of things that had thrilled him as a boy.

He looked toward her. Her upturned face, bathed in starlight, glowed.

'Orion,' she said softly, and he looked in the direction of her gaze.

'You like astronomy!'

'Yes,' she agreed.

'You seem to know a lot about it.'

'No, not really, just the things my mother and grandmother showed me. I don't know about the comet or the other circles – the — ' She stopped, not remembering what he had called it.

'Rings of Saturn,' he said.

They both looked back up to the night sky. She shivered in her thin cotton gown. Just then a falling star fell, leaving a trail through the velvet sky.

'Did you make a wish?' he teased; it was the sort of thing he would have said to a child.

'No,' she lied.

In their silence he felt the old numbness begin. His eyes misted and he mourned for the other William, the one he had lost, the one who would have wished on a star. This one, the one who was left, had no idea what to wish for.

An unfamiliar anger rose within him. He felt stupid – he had allowed the mask to slip. What was he doing standing out here in the middle of the night with an ignorant hotel maid discussing the heavens?

'That's all. I don't require anything else,' he said sharply.

Katherine started. His abruptness made her stumble as she re-entered the room.

'Goodnight, sir,' she managed to mumble.

'Wait,' he said. He came into the room, avoided looking at her, fumbled in the pocket of his coat, and held out the silver dollar to her.

She shrank back from him, and he saw her face. Where it had been eager and open, it was now closed with hurt. He was not a cruel man; he felt he had hurt enough people in his life, and a small kindness would cost him nothing.

On impulse, he reached for the strong brown hand, and he bent forward, kissed her palm, which smelled of fresh lemon, and placed the silver dollar there, the gesture an apology.

Seeing the hurt look on her face an idea came to him; he wanted to please her. 'Would you like a book on astronomy? I think you should have one, since you enjoy the stars so much. I'll bring you one next week. Goodnight, Kathy. Thank you.'

*Kathy.* She kept the name in her mind; she felt it suited her well.

When she awoke on Saturday, he had already gone; his key hung in the kitchen. Frieda prepared the sacks. Today they were going out to gather wild fruits for herbs or teas. The mason jars were lined up on the sideboard, indicating how sure they were of finding ample things to preserve.

'Mr Taylor's real partial to maypops. There's a spot where I used to find a whole hedgerow of 'em ... and this morning there was a frost right before sun-up. I'm sure we'll find plenty.'

Frieda brought out a large wool cape for the girl, who she knew didn't own a coat. 'It's OK to keep it,' she offered. 'It belonged to the maid before Sally – she left it.'

Grateful, Katherine took the cape and they started out on the beautiful cold sunny morning.

Frieda enjoyed talking, Katherine liked listening, so they made a comfortable pair.

'In New Mexico we didn't have any maypops,' Katherine volunteered. 'What are they like?'

'Well, they go by a lot of different names. Some call them the passion flower, as they have the stickers like the nails of Jesus when He was crucified, but most call 'em wild apricots, or grandilla. I call 'em maypops. Now, keep a close eye.'

Katherine didn't know what to look for, so she just followed Frieda, enjoying the beautiful morning.

'Do you suppose you could call me Kathy?'

'Why, child, I suppose I could. I never knew you'd want to be called that, but probably as not I'd forget as I'm used to saying Katherine by now.'

The woods were alive with small creatures, skittering among the fallen leaves searching for nuts and berries as the feel of winter was here. In a grove of bushes Frieda spotted them. 'There they are – the maypops!' They went to the thicket where the vine grew ten to twelve feet high, climbing over another bush. Just a few showy lavender flowers were left; on the rest of the vine the flowers had already turned to fruit. The wild apricots, about the size of an egg, had turned yellow from the frost, but some were still pulpy yellow-green. 'Try for the yellow ones,' Frieda instructed.

They pulled and yanked on the vines and searched among the three-lobed indented leaves for the maypops.

They had soon filled their sacks. 'That's enough,' Frieda said. 'Let's save room. I'm really needin' some swamp rose.'

They turned direction and headed towards the river.

Enjoying her role as teacher, Frieda instructed: 'You can usually find swamp rose by creeks or rivers ... We still have a little left in jelly. I'm thinking we need it this winter for the teas.'

Katherine loved Missouri and the abundant fields and woods, so different from the wind-blown, barren landscape where she had grown up. She felt the wonder of nature here, it was so generous. She followed Frieda eagerly; she had already learned so much, and as they walked Frieda told her of the uses for swamp rose. It was used to make tea, jam, jelly, soup – and rose sugar. She talked of how, in the spring, they'd find the roses and dip the petals in whiskey and batter and fry them, then coat them in sugar ... a true delicacy. On the banks of Kiefer Creek they saw the rosebushes which grew to about six feet. The leaves were dry from the recent frost, but the rosehips were plentiful – the small, ball-like fruit left where the fragrant roses had been. They filled their sacks and, well satisfied with their day, they started back.

'There,' Frieda pointed. 'But we don't have room. There, that's the ginseng – the manroot. Why, when I was a girl, my daddy used to go sang-hunting every fall, and he even tried growing it as a crop, but the cultivated isn't as good as the wild. The buyers ... they don't hardly want the cultivated.' She paused and knelt down. 'You can tell it, it's different to any other plant. See how gold the leaves look? There ain't anything in the world that has that color. Look, Katherine – study it so's you'll know it. It grows in dark places like this ... manroot don't like the sun. It never grows taller than two feet and it has a cluster of five leaves.' Frieda touched the leaves with a wonder. 'Some folks when I was little dreamed of making a fortune with it. My daddy knew a man that did. He hunted and hunted, pert near cleared out all the hollows and they said he moved to a big house in Chicago.'

'It sounds like treasure-hunting!'

'Oh it is, child. It is.'

They enjoyed the crisp, cold October afternoon. Katherine felt a quiet happiness, for the beauty of the Missouri landscape always made her heart quicken. They walked slowly now, their sacks heavy.

Slightly out of breath, Frieda stopped and looked around. 'I suppose we could take a short cut.' She glanced down at her stout stockings and reasoned she was wearing her old shoes; mud couldn't hurt them any.

'I know one that'll save us about a quarter of a mile,' she suggested and Katherine followed her, leaving the worn path as they cut through the woods. They went slower, as they had to avoid treading on the wildflowers and the rocks.

'Oh my!' Katherine looked down and saw the lovely violets crushed beneath her feet.

'What is it?' Frieda asked, stopping and putting down her sack.

'I've crushed them,' Katherine said, gesturing at the tiny flowers.

'It's OK; they're hardy. They'll spring back up in no time.'

Katherine knelt down and gently coaxed the leaves up. 'My mother loved violets,' she said quietly. 'She had some once in a big pot on the window, but they died. Sun was too hot in New Mexico.'

Katherine's reference to her mother made Frieda pause. She pushed away her impatience.

'Violets like the damp – they'll be OK.'

Unwilling to leave her destruction, Katherine asked, 'Maybe I could take 'em – nurse 'em back?'

'OK, but it's getting late,' Frieda said, handing her the small trowel.

They were glad to get back to the warmth of the kitchen.

55

Mr Taylor and the Missus were in St Louis for the day and since the Judge had left and the women didn't have to cook, they prepared sandwiches of cheese on thick bread with strawberry jam, and ate the fresh mulberries that Bruce had picked yesterday from the bushes behind the orchard.

Frieda separated the apricots into two separate piles. 'These we'll make jelly with, and these we'll dry for crystallized apricots.'

They peeled the maypops, cut them in half and took out the seed. Frieda prepared a pot with water, and from the icebox she took out the lime Mr Taylor had brought her from St Louis. She squeezed the lime juice into the pot and added the sliced maypops. 'That's all we do for now. We let them stand for twelve hours, then we boil them in weak alum water, then reboil in clear. We drain them, put in white sugar, three-quarters of a pound for each pound of apricots. We let them stand again . . . boil them one more time, flavor with ginger root and dry 'em. It takes two days. Crystallized apricots is one of Mr Taylor's favorites.'

They prepared the second group using the seeds as well as the pulp. After boiling the maypops for thirty minutes, they strained them through cheesecloth, then reboiled them, adding one pint of sugar to each pint of juice, until the mixture jelled. Then they cooled it and sealed it into jars with wax on top.

Katherine broke the tip of her pencil and with her teeth she nibbled the wood until she had a new lead . . . for she was busy writing; she had copied down every recipe of Frieda's since she had been here. This was very flattering to the older woman.

'You just sit, child. Them rosehips is nothing to it.' Frieda dropped the plump knobs into boiling water, and covered the pot. 'Now tomorrow we strain it, bring it to a boil and add two tablespoons of vinegar. Then we bottle it. It's a good tonic for just about anything!'

Katherine closed her notebook. 'Monday I'm going to Bailey's general store. I need another book – this one's full.'

'Well, it's no good wasting money. Notebook'll probably cost you a dime,' Frieda warned, and she looked through the tablet, searching it for a blank page.

'I know, but I've got a silver dollar.'

'You do? Where did you get a silver dollar?' Frieda asked, a worried frown coming over her face.

'The Judge . . . he tipped me a dollar.'

'Hum,' Frieda warned. 'Nothing in this world is free. Mind you watch him. He's handsome and young enough – who'd think of him as a Judge? Yes, you watch him. I dare say you're lucky none of them men has grabbed you yet and slung you across their bed and had their way with you.'

'No, the Judge isn't like that. He wouldn't do nothing like that,' Katherine protested.

'Oh no? You've seen them fancy women he's brought here – he's no saint, he's just like the others. I know about men like him. I was a young girl once, a working maid like you, and I've seen enough of them, those fancy men. They don't need to sling a girl in their beds, oh no. The only weapon they need to ruin you is their golden tongue . . . it glides smooth as honey.'

Katherine was surprised at her anger, but Frieda could only remember Anna and know that what she said was true.

'Not me,' Katherine assured her. 'That would never happen to me.'

Frieda laughed. 'You're a child in a woman's body . . . you'll see. I tell you – mind yourself, and don't listen to no golden tongue. I suppose your father's never told you about men?'

Katherine flushed at the mention of his name. Yes, in a way, Jesse had told her about men.

That night, the girl could not sleep. She needed to tell

someone of the wonder that had been the Judge. She had touched his fingers; he had told her private things; he had kissed her palm. She went over every detail in her mind again and again. '*Call me William.*' She didn't dare, but now, alone, she could say it, to hear how it sounded. '*William . . . William.*' She whispered his name over and over in the dark. She turned and tossed in her bed. She remembered his words, '*What do you do when you're troubled?*'

It was too far, and too late, and too cold for her to walk to The Crossroads and sit by the river, but she could go out and look at the stars.

She threw the cape over her shoulders and went out into the yard and the clear autumn sky. The cold barely touched her, as her body raged with an unknown fever.

She walked to the mound, the hay-covered hill, where she lay down and searched the sky. Very faintly, she made out Taurus the Bull and there were her favorites . . . the Seven Sisters. She squinted her eyes and saw things; she loved them, that cluster. She imagined these daughters of Atlas to be beautiful girls glittering there in white, running across the dark skies to meet their lovers.

Her hand touched her breast. She remembered the birthmark. She smoothed her hand near it, caressingly. Would he someday see the birthmark and marvel that hers matched his? The touch of her fingers made her nipple harden and she closed her eyes tightly and conjured up his face, his eyes stark blue and his smile . . . God, how she loved it. It seemed that her imagination brought him here, and her hand now touching the mound of Venus . . . it was him . . . it was her . . . doing a shameful thing. *It was him . . .* Her breath caught in her throat and she ran back into her room, knelt and said three 'Hail Marys.'

# CHAPTER 6

The violets had started a new interest for Katherine. The patch of earth eight feet by ten outside her window had been a hard, uncared-for, unsightly piece of ground in front of the ashpit. The trash men, always careless, left it littered. With Frieda's permission, Katherine cleared it, dug it up, fertilized it with leaves, and after planting the first violet, she now spent her free time searching the woods for other wildflowers.

'Silly,' Frieda pronounced it, 'all that work. Them plants are good for nothing – can't eat 'em, nor use 'em for medicine.' But she watched with interest as the plot was transformed.

To Katherine, this rectangle of earth was an anchor. In beauty, it connected her to the place. The feel of the rich earth as she dug and planted, gave her happiness. Frieda's reference to her green thumb made her feel pleased.

She had created beauty out of nothing. Early in the morning, the garden was the first thing she saw. It refreshed her. The blooms of the flowers attracted bees and butterflies, and a small hummingbird was seen often drinking the nectar. It was a wild unplanned garden, and she ignored Frieda's advice: 'You should plant 'em in rows – neat-like.'

She'd nod, then continue planting just as nature would, at random – and if seeds fell, and new plants sprung out,

59

that was OK; she felt she must let them live the same as they had in the untouched woods. Her garden, her flowers, they were free. She would not make them prisoners in clay pots or neat unnatural rows.

After supper, when the dishes were cleared and the guests had gone, Frieda released her and Katherine set out, when there was still daylight left. Taking a sack and a small trowel, she made for the woods. When tired she would rest on a fallen log or rock and listen to the chatter of the birds as they prepared for nightfall. Used to her now, squirrels leapt from branch to branch overhead, and through the underbrush, she saw the rabbits, with their soft, cautious tread. Occasionally, a small green garter snake would slither across her path, and turtles draw in their shells, to slowly re-emerge, watching her with curiosity. She disturbed nothing, she was part of the fabric of life in the woods. She belonged!

She found the plant by the stream; it was different from any she already had. Its furry leaves, and the brilliant purple satin of its flower was like none she had seen before or gathered. Carefully, she dug the trowel deep, and lifted the clod of earth, noticing that the leaves did not shudder. She had gone deep enough; a fat earthworm – cut in half by the trowel – dropped to the ground and disappeared under the leaves to regenerate itself.

Cradling the plant in her apron, she made her way back. In the west the sky was red with sunset and she hurried, for she did not wish to deny the plant. It was so special; she would plant it right away. She knelt at the corner of her plot and began digging.

'Rhododendron,' she heard a voice call down to her.

She glanced up and saw Judge Reardon looking over the balcony.

'I don't know what it's called,' she answered.

'Rhododendron,' he repeated. On his weekend visits he had noticed the barren patch being transformed. Now he knew whose garden it was. That girl – the maid – the strange one who liked the stars.

Idly he watched her motions. 'No!' he shouted. 'That's wrong – not in that corner.'

She looked up, her hand shielding her eyes from the setting sun. 'What?'

It was ridiculous, shouting directions like this. He came down the steps.

She sat back on her haunches and looked up at him.

'Not in that corner. It doesn't like the sun – it must be in shade.'

He dropped to his knees and took the plant from her. Small clods of earth fell unheeded on to his fresh gabardine trousers. He held the plant up – rotated it in his hands, admiring its healthy perfection.

In a low voice he began, ' "In the spring I found the rhododendron hiding its blooms under the — " There's a poem written about it, you know. I had to memorize it in the fifth grade. I didn't realize I still remembered it,' he grinned.

The plant was special. She knew it, feeling a kinship with the unknown poet.

'Wrong corner.' He rose and went to the other side, cleared a space. 'Trowel?'

She handed it to him.

He pushed up the sleeves of the immaculate white shirt and began digging in the rich earth. 'Pebbles – a handful. It should be well drained.'

He waited patiently as she searched the yard and came back with a handful. He hollowed the hole and filled it with pebbles, sprinkling the dirt liberally.

She watched as he lovingly patted the earth around the settled plant.

'It should do well here,' he said. He gazed at her garden, and below she could just hear him listing verbally the plants he recognized. 'Verbena, alyssum. This one's rhododendron.'

'Thank you,' she said. 'I didn't know what it was. I

61

really don't know what half of them are called, but I like growing 'em anyway.'

In the dusk he seemed younger. A lock of hair had fallen over his forehead, a streak of dirt lay across his cheek. With sudden realization, he looked down at his hands.

'I'll get you a wet cloth,' she offered. Beyond her the door to her room was still open.

She entered the darkness, reached for the light switch. In the basin she ran warm water over the cloth. When she turned, she saw him standing in the doorway, one arm up on the frame, looking about the room. She put the damp cloth down and with an unspoken invitation, moved away from the sink.

He entered the room, went to the sink and lathered up his hands again and again until they were clean. In the manner of men, he scooped water in his palms and splashed his face, finishing with a cold rinse that made him issue a 'Brrr, Brrr,' sound.

She held out the towel and he buried his face in it; the scent of warm sunshine, fresh lemons and a faint tinge of natural flowers assailed him, and he felt a pang of nostalgia. The smell made him think of running through a field of sunflowers, coming home to a warm kitchen redolent with fresh lemon as his mother's pies baked in the oven, the feel of her arms, her lips in his hair. 'I love you, William – you're my good boy.' He hadn't been lonely then – the emptiness was full then.

He stared over at Katherine. What was it about her that dredged up these childhood memories?

She stood near the door, uncomfortable with his presence here.

He looked at the dresser; in the injured glass he saw that his face was clean. He picked up the 'God's eye'. 'Hey, this one's great! I remember making these in Boy Scouts. I was clumsy as hell, it took me two or three tries to make one and even then it was always lopsided. I forget now how we made them.'

She stepped closer and took the 'God's eye' from him. 'It's simple. My mother and I used to make them back in Gallup. She sold them as Indian souvenirs. First you find two twigs and tie them together to form a cross, then you take a piece of yarn and wind it round and round until you can tie it off at the end. The you take more yarn, a different color this time, and do the same thing, winding and changing colors until it's done.'

He reached for it and held it up. 'It looks like a small kite.' He pointed to the middle of the triangle. 'Your "God's eye" – it's red, scary. I'd hate to think that God's eyes are red,' he teased. She blushed with embarrassment and he laid it back carefully on the dresser.

Next he saw the card, with Jesus. 'Are you Catholic?' he asked.

'No, but my father was.'

'I am,' he said. 'Don't go to church much; though. Don't go to church at all.'

Again this faded card brought back the scent of incense, the feel of the starched cloth of the alter-boy apron scratching his neck. For so many years he hadn't thought of those things.

He saw the carefully clipped article on the dresser. *Reader's Digest: Know your stars.*

'I promised you a book about stars. I haven't forgotten,' he lied. He straightened up and felt the urge to run from this room, away from this strange girl. She, too, seemed reluctant, pulling back as he passed her and made his way back up the stairs.

Careful, he must be careful, he thought. What would people think? His friends – his professional friends, those that talked of nothing but laws and bills and stock options, and his other friends – fair-weather friends, those he drank with, played cards with . . . to those he was the Judge, a cardboard caricature of someone, this person Judge William Reardon. What would they think of a friendship with a half-breed Indian servant? They could understand a drunken one-night-stand with her, but could they fathom the warmth of standing next to her in awe of the stars, or the joy of working in the soil planting a wild shrub?

He had forgotten to tell her: he had a greenhouse. Foolish, he was being foolish. It was near his birthday. He was approaching fifty. It made him examine his life, and he found it wanting.

The next morning she found his cuff-link among the flowers – in small diamonds, his initials W. R.. She put it in the heart-shaped box, not knowing or caring for its value, but it, too, added to the parts of him she now possessed.

With patience and fear, she waited, for she knew before he did, that they belonged to each other!

# CHAPTER 7

William came to Castlewood the next week as usual. After showering and shaving he rang for bourbon and spring water.

He would give the girl the book and be done with it. He had said he would bring her a book; being a man of his word he had done so.

But this slow slithering friendship that was beginning with her would have to stop. It made no sense.

Shortly after ringing, there was a soft knock on the door. In answer to his, 'Come in,' she stepped inside.

Holding the tray unsteadily, she walked across and put it on the night-stand, knocking over Elizabeth's picture.

He came out of the bathroom to see the blonde maid standing there. Her jaw moved as she chewed her gum, waiting for her tip.

'I thought—' He stopped in mid-sentence and reached for a coin which he put in her waiting palm. 'Thank you,' he said curtly.

In twenty-five minutes he tried again, ringing for more spring water. Again the strong blonde brought the water, still chewing frantically on her gum.

Just before she shut the door he said, 'Wait.' She stepped back in the room, her face slack now; surprise had stopped her chewing motion.

Embarrassed, without looking at her, he said softly, 'The other one, Kathy—'

'Oh yes, sir,' she chirped, and ran noisily downstairs. Breathless, she found Katherine and gripped her hands. 'Guess what?'

'What?'

Sally giggled, and grabbed her close and whispered in her ear, 'The Judge is asking for you.'

Frieda's sharp voice interrupted them. 'What are you two giggling about? You'll disturb the guests.'

'Nothing, Frieda,' Sally said. Sally was used to hiding things. 'The Judge wants more spring water,' she lied.

'More water? What's he need more water for?'

Saucily Sally said, 'I don't know, Frieda. Maybe he wants to take a bath in it,' and she snickered hysterically at her own joke.

Frieda shoved the bottle of water toward her. 'Take it up and stop that cackling.'

Sally handed it to Katherine. 'Please, you take it. My back's hurting from running up and down the stairs so much. My aunt's visiting, you know.'

Katherine blushed at Sally's brazen mention of her period.

Frieda disgustedly went back to the kitchen muttering to herself, 'Hare brain. That girl's lazy and hare-brained to boot.'

Katherine took the bottle of water up to William's room. He looked with surprise at the third bottle of spring water, then realized the blonde had a knack for conspiracy. He placed it next to the two unopened bottles on the night-stand and smiled at Katherine. 'I brought the book.' He held out the large picture book about stars to her.

Her brow knitted as she smoothed the glossy cover; she opened it and saw the simplistic drawings of the heavens, realizing it was a book for a child.

Instantly he, too, perceived his mistake. He had assumed her simple. Hurriedly, he explained, 'I'm afraid it's the only one the bookstore had. It's not bad for a beginner. Why, I often read children's books when I want

66

an overview of a subject. I'll keep a lookout for something more suitable.'

'Thank you. This one is just fine.'

It was the silly uniform, or something cold that stood between them now. The feeling of friendship was gone, or maybe he had imagined it in the first place. Somehow it was important for him to know her better.

'How's the garden?' he asked.

'Fine.'

'The rhododendron—'

'It's growing, it's good.'

'I'd like one for my greenhouse!'

She looked up; was he asking for hers?

'I mean, if you find another one . . .'

'For the greenhouse?' Deciding to be genuine she asked, 'What's a greenhouse?'

'Oh! It's a building all made of glass, small panes. It attracts the sun, keeps things warm and moist. You can grow anything in it, even out of season,' and he pictured the greenhouse now, knowing it was full of empty pots and withered stalks. The only things alive in it now was the Bonsai tree.

'In pots? They grow in pots in the greenhouse?'

'Yes. Why, I even have a tree.'

'A tree growing in a pot?' She couldn't imagine a tree in a pot. Sad enough that they stayed rooted forever in one spot on the earth, let alone in a pot.

They had the same love of things, she knew that, but his was bound in some way. Never mind, she thought, she could teach him. He could learn the freedom.

He felt words rushing within him; he had gotten past the starched apron and black uniform. Yet how could he invite her to sit down so they could talk? He was hungry to know her mind. He was certain it was not filled with organza curtains or mail-order kitchen gadgets, like Elizabeth's . . . nor with curlers or mascara or black filmy nightgowns like the whores at the Eagle's Nest.

He was hungry to know this lovely woman's mind. He felt a surge of happiness spring from an unknown source.
'Is that all, sir?'

They were maid and guest again. He turned away from her. 'Yes, that's all.' He did not tip her; he thought it unseemly now.

He heard the door click softly behind her. He poured a glass of whiskey, drank it neat, dressed and went to the Eagle's Nest to drown his unease. He selected the dark one, the girl by the jukebox. He insulted her, for he wanted to turn off the light and lose himself in animal passion. Once spent, he gagged at her cheap perfume, left her the money, and stumbled out into the cool night.

As he walked back to the hotel, he looked up. The sky full of stars blinked at him. He thought of her; he had been fooling himself. Yes, he wanted to know more of her – he wanted to know her thoughts, her mind. In their tentative friendship, he liked her, still it had not escaped him – and with surprise he realized this – her smooth skin, dark liquid eyes, the satin flow of her hair . . . They had registered somewhere within him, and he faced it fully now: *he desired her*. A painful throbbing want overcame him. He felt like a silly schoolboy with his first crush.

It was dangerous, this new feeling. She was too young, too naive, too trusting – one does not have casual affairs with a woman like this. He was certain she was a virgin. No good would come from getting involved. Wherever these stray, random thoughts came from, they must not be allowed to flourish.

He was a man of control, *in* control. He controlled many lives, he could control himself. He would never pass that boundary again. The invisible line would be re-drawn, putting her in her proper perspective. She was no different from the clean towel in the bathroom, the tray of spring water – all brought for his comfort. She would be placed among these inanimate objects. She was the hired help, he the paying guest.

That night he saw her, bathed in moonlight, her smooth brown body perfection, fragrant soft hair falling about his face, shielding out the world, the warm, moist touch of her lips, inflaming his. He heard the soft murmur of his name repeated as she whispered in his ear, her hot breath sweet.

It was not like anything he had known with any other woman, and in the dawn he awoke, appalled that he had had a wet dream.

In the morning, Frieda excused Katherine from duties, telling her gruffly, 'You help Sally pack. We have to get her on the train. Mr Taylor thought she was already gone – he's not much for giving free room and board.'

The girls enjoyed the day, ironing and folding Sally's fancy clothes. 'Don't know when I'll next be by an iron,' Sally said, although they both knew the carefully pressed garments would crease as Sally had only one large suitcase.

Although close in age, the girls were two very different people. Katherine's naivety sprang from a lifetime of growing up with no one. She had shared the road with her father, but they had been total strangers to one another and she could not think back on any of the pleasant memories without that last terrifying one entering her mind. She knew so little of men. They usually frightened and confused her as if they belonged to a different species, yet she trembled with love for the Judge, without even knowing what the love between a man and a woman should be. Sally ranted and raved, cursing the hotel, cursing Castlewood and Mr Taylor. She hadn't saved any money, and when it was time to go, it was the last weekend when Justin, the salesman, came this way and stopped here. Sally told of his generous tip. Now she could finally be on her way.

'Lookee here,' she said, holding up an embossed silver square. 'He gave me his card and told me to call him anytime.'

Katherine took the card and read it:
> *Justin Tique*
> *Nature's Way Products*
> *Laxatives Tonics Cosmetics*

'He loves me,' Sally proclaimed. 'He told me that he loves me.'

Handing back the card, Katherine said simply, 'That's wonderful.'

Carefully, Sally put the card in her purse. 'And effin he doesn't work out, I just might take me a train to California – Hollywood, that is. Justin said I look just like Carole Lombard.'

She studied herself in the mirror, fluffed her bleached hair and leaned forward to see if the dark roots were showing. 'Katherine, do you think I look like Carole Lombard?'

Not wanting to displease her, Katherine replied, 'I'm sure you must if he said it, but I've never seen her!'

'God, you are a hick, never seen her in the movies.' She realized she was being sharp with her so she changed the subject. 'You still liking the Judge?'

Katherine blushed; she had regretted a thousand times telling this to Sally, but today she would be gone and the teasing would stop. She didn't answer the question, for Frieda called up to them: 'Bruce is here to carry the bags.' They heard his slow, careful tread on the stairs.

'Wait, I have to leave you something,' Sally said. She re-opened the bag, dipping through it carelessly, leaving the carefully packed clothes a mess, and brought out a blue silk camisole. 'Here, take it.'

Katherine felt close to tears. They had nothing in common, yet she liked her. Sally was warm and generous.

'I couldn't take it . . . it's so lovely.'

'Sure you can. I'll get lots more in St Louis or maybe even in Hollywood.' She winked. 'Wear it for the Judge.'

Bruce came in and picked up the heavy suitcase. He

wore his normal blank smile; he was happy.

Sally looked around the room for the last time. 'Oh God, I forgot about the dummy ... I can't afford much.' Then, getting an idea, she took off her rhinestone earrings – a couple of stones were missing anyway. 'Here, Bruce.'

He took the earrings, and his smile widened as he saw the lights change in the glass. 'Ow – I'm going to give these to my mother. They're so pretty,' he said.

Katherine would have liked to go to the train station with them, but she followed them to the porch and stood waving vigorously every time Sally turned around. She knew she had to be in the kitchen soon to make the tea for Mr Taylor's arthritis.

# CHAPTER 8

Bruce came early in the week to find out how many brooms and brushes Frieda wanted. She sent Katherine to choose; she followed him to the shed. His sense of order in his occupation was totally opposite from the care he took of his person. Today he wore a wool cap pulled low on his head; his ears stuck out, growing red from the crisp north wind. The buttons on his jacket were long since gone, replaced by two large safety pins. His trousers were two inches too short for his long legs, and he walked slowly in the painful shoes that were too small. His face usually beamed his good nature and a smile remained minutes after the initial smile. Sally had teased him and claimed to be afraid of him . . . 'He's strange, real strange,' but Katherine felt no unease in his presence. It was as Frieda said: 'The child in him was frozen there. It's an eight-year-old child in that big body, never you mind. He wouldn't hurt a fly.'

The shed had a new-mown smell to it. Stacked in the corners, careful heaps of broomcorn were separated . . . some the golden wheat color, others red where Bruce had harvested the straw after it was completely ripe. In a barrel filled to the top were seeds where Bruce had combed the corn with a child's saw. The stacks of finished brooms leaned against the wall, divided by sizes and uses; it was the arrangement that Frieda could choose for the hotel what she needed, before Bruce took the rest of his handiwork from clubhouse to clubhouse to sell. Most owners prided themselves on buying at least one broom or brush out of sympathy to Mrs Wiley, Bruce's mother, but truth was he made the best brooms in the area, and not given to counting, Bruce often sold his handiwork on the donation basis . . . Whereas some cheated and others were generous, it evened out.

Katherine selected one hearth broom for the fireplaces; these were made of stalks without a handle. She tested the stalks and they held well. She picked a kitchen broom; she saw Bruce's disappointment that she had not chosen the red one, for Frieda said brooms made of overripe broomcorn were brittle and not so durable. She selected two more that would be left on the different floors in the house. She examined them carefully, and saw that each was sewn with cotton thread tied sturdy and even.

'These are good, Bruce – very good.'

He smiled a smile left over from his original greeting to her, and rocked back and forth nervously, his mouth working as if trying to tell her something. In the dim hut she began to feel a vague uneasiness and recalled Sally's words: *He's strange, real strange.'*

Taking the brooms she said nervously, 'I have to go, Frieda's needin' me in the kitchen.' Bruce remembered how angry Frieda could get when she'd curse and chase you.

'But Miss Katherine . . . wait.' And his hand came around from his back holding it out to her. 'For you.'

He held toward her a small, well-made corn-shuck doll. She took it and turned it over gingerly. The doll was about nine inches long, with dark corn silks for her hair, and she was holding a small bouquet of tiny dried flowers. 'She's beautiful! Bruce, thank you. Thank you very much!' He shifted from foot to foot, then picked up her brooms that she had selected and followed her out of the hut. She was ashamed of herself for feeling that moment of fear.

Frieda was pleased with the selection and invited Bruce to sit down. She put a big plate of blueberry cobbler before him. He gulped the dessert, dripping juice down his chin, which he didn't bother to wipe off.

# CHAPTER 9

Katherine felt it drawing nearer. It would be. She looked in the Valentine box and felt ashamed. Would he only come to her because of these things? She held a cuff-link in her palm, warming the metal. She felt his essence, knowing him to be different from the way the world saw him. She felt his loneliness; it matched hers. She wound a strand of sandy hair around her finger. One by one, she held the articles before putting them back into the box. It was not wrong. They belonged to each other. She knew him. Maybe it was like the story Me Maw had told, of how, when the world was new, humans were one entity until an angry god split them apart, so they must search through eternity for the other half that they had lost.

She had found him. He was her other half – and if these things, the bits and pieces, made it possible to bring him to her, then it was good. She closed the box, and went into the woods to hunt for the rhododendron. She could not find one, and she could not bear to give him hers – so cruel to pull it from the earth, imprison it in a clay pot.

# CHAPTER 10

With a sense of gloom William looked around the green-house. Row upon row of flowerpots, containing only brown stalks indicating past glory, were all that remained.

Even though he had ignored it, the Bonsai flourished. It was a particularly beautiful tree, almost twenty-five years since he had cropped the roots; the oak had all the symmetry of a grown tree. It seemed wrong to leave it here among the dead plants. He would give it to the girl, Kathy. He could envision it placed on that plain dresser in her modest room.

He must tell her that it should be put outdoors at times, for the Bonsai needed to feel the pulse of the changing seasons. He felt the happiness of a giver.

It was strange how often something reminded him of her.

'Are you going to work on the greenhouse again?'

Her question startled him; he turned to see Elizabeth picking her way carefully down the stone steps.

'Well, yes – maybe I will.'

'The strawberries were lovely, especially when we had them at Christmas,' she commented.

'Yes,' he agreed, remembering when he had all sorts of exotic plants, fruits and berries growing in there.

She looked down at the pot he was holding. 'That looks healthy.'

'It's fine,' he nodded. 'I thought I'd give it to a colleague, a young lawyer who's very keen on gardening.'

He turned away from her, feeling guilty about the lie. He could never explain his friendship with the girl.

'Do you want Tom to clean up the greenhouse if you're thinking of working it again?'

'Yes, Elizabeth, that might be a good idea.' In her sweeping glance at the building, he could see her ordering, calculating things she must buy.

'What sort of peat and pots and seeds do you want me to get in? Why, Tom could pick up everything you need Monday. I could get him a very specific list.'

'Please don't bother,' he protested. 'I'm not sure if I'll have time right now. Just have him clean it up. You know, throw out all the dead plants and just tidy up the place.'

She hesitated. 'It's no bother.'

'No, there's nothing I want right now,' he said sharply.

Disappointed, she turned and walked slowly back up the steps. He felt a wave of pity for her; she had so little in her life. He excused her for her extravagance and waste. It didn't matter. Perhaps if the children had lived she might have been different.

On Monday he took the Bonsai to his chambers; it sat patiently on his desk as a permanent reminder of her. Among the files and the sordid cases the tree was a reminder of things William felt were still good and pure.

On Friday he packed the plant carefully in a box, setting it on the floor of the car. At the hotel he glanced out of the window hoping to see her tending her garden, but being late fall, just a few things were still green, and he realized the garden now needed very little tending.

He felt foolish, he could hardly go down and knock on her door. It was possible she wouldn't even be in.

He had not noticed her at supper; the buffet was tended by the older woman. Now the gift seemed crazy, unexplainable. He didn't understand it himself, yet it had seemed so clear, so right, just a week ago standing in the ruined greenhouse.

On impulse he went down the stairs, to examine closer the garden. In the twilight a few patches of color still bloomed, her wildflowers almost gone to seed.

He noticed the light in her room.

Against the shade he saw her silhouette; gracefully he saw her lift an arm, as she washed from the basin, and he felt like an obscene Peeping Tom as he observed the motion of her body, the outline of her breast, her profile. She dipped forward and he watched as she washed her hair. He held his breath, ashamed that he still stood rooted to the spot, spying on her shadow.

The wind came up, and the rustling sound of leaves falling broke the spell. William turned quickly and ran up the steps.

Now the plant on the dresser seemed to mock him. 'Foolish man, foolish old man,' he told himself.

He ran a bath, and took out some casual clothes from his suitcase; he thought maybe a card game at the Eagle's Nest would be a good idea. He spent the evening playing poker. He couldn't concentrate and lost consistently. The whiskey tasted foul, so he drank very little.

He returned to the hotel early, paced the room and finally decided to go down and give her the plant and be done with it. Angrily he snatched the pot and went quickly down the stairs.

He realized his knock was too loud. She appeared in the door, surprise visible in her face.

'Here.' Rudely he thrust the plant toward her.

She blushed and muttered a quiet, 'Thank you.'

Still she didn't reach for it. So he continued, 'It's a tree, a Bonsai it's called. It's twenty-five years old, a pin oak.' He paused. 'I want you to have it.'

A tiny acorn fell and he stooped to retrieve it. As he did so, he brushed her toe and they both jumped. He straightened, moved past her and placed the plant on the barren dresser.

'It's a real tree?' she asked.

81

'Yes. Bonsai is an oriental art. I became interested in it — ' He stopped, for she was crying.

Leaving her post by the door, she sat heavily on one of the beds and he heard the sound of her soft sobbing.

Helplessly he stood there, and the open door moved noisily in the wind.

'I'm sorry – what's wrong?' She looked like a small unhappy child, huddled over, her thin shoulders heaving, the thick auburn hair covering her tear-stained face.

'It's just – it's just so sad,' she managed to say.

In a blinding flash he realized it. Of course she would think that, he now saw it to be so – the dignity of this magnificent tree bound, imprisoned in this tiny pot. He caught the sadness of his act.

'It's OK,' he said, and he laughed.

He grabbed the pot from the dresser.

'Trowel,' he commanded.

She rose, wiped her tears with the back of her hand, and followed him out the door.

With the trowel, he cracked the concrete top that held the tree in place, gently massaged the roots, and in the middle of her garden, he dug the hole. It was a funny little dwarf of a tree, but here he felt it would grow and stretch as God intended.

He looked up and saw her smiling; her eyes were red, her face flushed, but she was smiling.

A slice of light from her room was a barrier between them.

'Thank you,' she said softly.

'You're welcome,' and he rose and went up the stairs, and he could see the white of her dress as she still knelt in the garden admiring the tree in the silver moonlight.

He undressed and lay across the bed; he felt good, so good.

There was a rapport between them that he could not explain, but he knew now he could not compromise her. She was different – naive, yet bright. He was certain

82

she was untouched; he would not act on his feeling of physical attraction.

He was certain that she did not suspect the desire that she kindled in him; he had no appetite for ruining young women. He would content himself with this strange friendship. She made him feel good. She brought back the young William who had ideals, beliefs – all that had been in him that was pure.

He settled for sleep, content that he had made another human being happy. It had been a long time since he had done that.

Elizabeth's picture on the night-stand accused him. He lay it flat, face down. It was not his fault the babies had died; it was not his fault that she had no interests, no passions in life.

# CHAPTER 11

With winter coming on, the women were busy in the kitchen preparing tonics. They started with basswood bark tea. They boiled the bark that they had gathered on one of their outings, strained it, then added honey and a drop of lemon. 'It's for colds. Mr Taylor swears by it,' Frieda confided. They used a small funnel to pour it into bottles that were boiled and clean.

Katherine made one trip to Bailey's general store. She had Frieda's list; she broke her silver dollar to buy the notebook. She looked among the cosmetics, pricing things she would like to buy Frieda for Christmas. Seeing 'Gardenia' cologne on sale for fifty-nine cents, she bought it. It would be difficult to keep it until Christmas. She owed Frieda so much. She had come to love the woman and understood it was a close relationship that was still distant. Katherine kept busy. In the long evenings, she looked through her Valentine box and her treasures. The corn-husk doll was the same height as the headless man, the ginseng . . . It was comforting at night to see their twin shadows on the window-ledge, side by side.

William would be coming Friday. To herself she now called him 'William'. He arrived at his usual time, 3 p.m., leaving a message that he would not be present at dinner. This changed the plans for the kitchen. Usually when there were guests, dinner was served at 6.30 in the dining room, but off-season, this rarely happened. Mr and Mrs Taylor at those times ate in their private quarters, which

were on the west wing of the house. Katherine had rarely
seen Mrs Taylor. She was an obese woman who slept late,
read magazines and craved chocolates. The Judge's key
was not on the rack; he was in his room and he rang for
service. Today Katherine wore the uniform – a black dress
with a snowy-white apron, and a small pleated hat that
perched on her head. Two sets of uniform had been
bought at an auction house in St Louis because Mr Taylor
had thought them classy. No matter what size the present
maid, these two were the only available uniforms. After
Sally left, Katherine tried on hers, but they were both
too small. Each hiked three inches above her knee, but
otherwise the bodice fitted well on her slender frame. Her
hair was pinned up under the cap; its silky texture made
it difficult to restrain, and usually several silken strands
escaped.

Katherine answered the bell and went to Room 8. He
opened immediately, not looking at her, and ordered a
bottle of bourbon and spring water. When she returned
carrying the tray, he called for her to enter. The room was
dim; the shades pulled halfway down rustled as a draft
blew in through the windows. He sat relaxed in the armchair, his coat slung carelessly on the bed, his shirt a
crumpled heap on the floor, his tie and watch on the
bedside table next to the picture of the smiling blonde
woman. His undershirt was white and the marks of a
summer sunburn remained still visible on his arms; above
the curved neck of the shirt was a mass of chest hair. It
was an intimate moment and Katherine looked away as
she placed the tray on the table beside him. The glasses
clinked; he looked up. 'Why, Kathy, thank you,' and he
searched her face. 'Today you look like the one whose
head hurts, you're frowning so.'

She didn't answer, looking down at the toe of her shoes,
waiting for him to dismiss her. 'Here,' he offered, and
reached for her hands. He massaged her thumbs in the
same manner that she had done. She stood before him,
her chest tight for want of breath; when he looked up she

met his eyes. He leaned closer. Perhaps he was mistaken, but he saw the way in which her dark eyes misted and smoldered. He had known many women – it was unmistakable. Raw want lived there; he felt desire kindle within him, brilliant and blazing.

Still holding her thumbs, he gently drew her to him, leading her gently to his lap. She felt the roughness of his tweed trousers and the bristle of his chest hair as she hid her warm face against his shoulder.

'You're so lovely,' he murmured.

He lifted her hand and placed a kiss in her palm. His lips were warm and moist; they moved, covering her neck among her silken hair. She felt the moistness as he kissed her ears, and the shallow sound of his ragged breath thundered in her ears. Her whole body quivered with anticipation, and like a symphony it moved slowly, but seemed to mount. Her white cap fell to the floor, and a tinny shower of hairpins began to slide from her hair. For a very brief instant she felt a stab of fear, fear of the magic that had brought him to her. She was less afraid of his smooth hands that crept up her stockings until they touched her flesh. Settling deeply into the chair he arranged her to him; she felt the sharp contrast of his beard stubble and the warmth and softness of his lips.

He tasted of mint. As he coaxed her with his tongue, a separateness overcame her. Only the sensations of her body were real, yet unreal. A slow warmth enveloped her. Outside somewhere, a bird called and she felt a part of it. The world, it was not a window any more; he had opened the door for her.

Gently he lowered her to the floor; the oriental rug beneath them was enough. It took all of her concentration of feeling, his mouth now sucking gently at her breast, his hands gentle, searching under her skirts. The clock somewhere in the hall chimed seven. The windows rattled with a new wind; she welcomed the weight of him as he lowered his body above hers.

Feeling his face pressed into the hollow of her neck,

# A. N. Steinberg

with an instinct as old as time she joined him in the rhythm with total abandonment, for the first time feeling pleasure. This was love, it had nothing to do with the other.

The shade rattled and darkness descended as a clap of thunder resounded; the sound loosened the mirror on the dresser and it tilted forward. In the gloom, she could see the back of his head, his undershirt white as snow, her dark legs wound around him, holding him, their movement back and forth in the motion of ecstasy. Dreamlike, she stared into the mirror and knew.

After a time, he slumped upon her; she heard the rapid sound of his breath. Not knowing what had happened to her, she felt spent and drained, her limbs weak.

He rose on one arm and smoothed her hair back from her face and looked down at her. 'Who was it?' he demanded, his voice icy.

She searched his face, not understanding.

'I thought you were different, not like the others.'

Katherine felt confusion. It had been wonderful – his warmth, his touch, but now his eyes were cold as glass, demanding something of her.

'Justin? – Mr Taylor? – one of the traveling drummers? *Who loved you before me?*'

Her lips trembled; she knew no answer.

His fingers bit into her flesh, demanding. 'Who have you been with like this?' A strange, frantic jealousy filled him. She was so fresh, so beautiful. She was a mirage – yet no different from all the others.

'I've loved no one,' she whispered.

He smirked. 'This is not the first time, oh no, not by a long shot.'

'I've loved no one,' she pleaded.

He sat up, looking down at her. 'I'm not a fool,' he sneered. 'You have known other men. How many were there? Five, ten – how many?'

'Oh.' She realized what he meant. She struggled to sit

88

up, looked down at her hands. 'It was not like this – it was not the same. It was ugly, painful. I never wanted it – it was my father. I had to . . .' She began crying, her shoulders quivering with her sobs.

'Your father? The son of a bitch!' He rose and began pacing the room. 'Your father, the bastard, he should be in jail. Where is he, this bastard?'

'He's gone,' she whispered.

A wave of tenderness rose within him. He came to her, lifted her gently, placed her on the bed. He bent toward her, murmuring, 'It's OK. I promise you, it'll be OK.'

He undressed her like a child, with care, removing her stockings. Gently, he tugged at the uniform, pulling the slip over her head. She lay before him now, her eyes closed. He admired the beauty of her young body, and he felt unreasonably touched as he saw her eyelids flutter and from her thick, dark lashes, one single tear hesitated before it rolled down her cheek. He bent toward her again, murmuring, 'I promise you, it'll be OK.'

His lips were gentle as he kissed her closed eyelids. He put her under the covers, turned out the light, dressed himself in the dark and told her to stay, to rest, to sleep. He went down and rang for Mr Taylor. He could always count on the hotel and its discretion; he paid well for it. When he returned, he pulled up the shade. The storm had passed, and bright moonlight flooded the room. He lifted the coverlet and crept in beside her. His body cupped to hers, he clasped her to him and he felt the steady rhythm of her heartbeat. They slept. During the night, they shifted; as she turned he saw the profile of her lovely face. He reached forward and soft as a butterfly wing he kissed her parted lips, until she awoke. Drowsy, she clung to him and experienced the fires of a deep consuming passion. He felt in her something very different. She was not like one of the maids whom he had taken in the past, nor was his feeling for her anything remotely like the sleazy lust he experienced in the arms of the scarlet women who laughed drunkenly in the dark. With those, once his lust was spent he couldn't bear their touch or even their presence. This was not the same. It was not only her fresh loveliness, but something protective, tender, beautiful that had arisen in him. He felt breathless, and there was a deep hollow in his chest. 'Kathy . . . Kathy.' He whispered her name knowing it was not a message or anything he wished to tell her, but a reassurance to himself that she was real and in that moment he was upon her, in her, a part of her, and he felt strange and foolish for he could only compare it to the words in the Bible. In the Biblical sense they were one . . . one being. His passion was so strong, stronger than anything he had ever known before. He said her name over and over, like a schoolboy with his first love. 'Kathy . . . Kathy . . . I think I'm in love with you.'

Roughly, he grabbed her heart-shaped chin and held it firm, his eyes shimmering with excitement. 'Say it! I know you feel it. Say it!' he commanded.

She licked her lips, feeling mute; she did not remember ever saying it to anyone. Perhaps she had murmured it as a child, she couldn't be sure. Her lips moved inaudibly.

He gripped her tighter and demanded, 'Say it!'

Finally, in a strangled whisper, she did. '*I love you.*'

He released her. Later she heard him crying him softly. The sound of his sobs made her bold and she reached out and stroked his hair tenderly like one would quiet a child. He stilled, and they slept till morning.

When he awoke, she was gone. Before he left, he visited the kitchen, where Frieda brusquely told him that Katherine was out. She had sent her to Bailey's for items that she needed for tonight's supper. He handed her a small envelope and asked her to give it to Kathy. He checked with the desk and arranged with Mr Taylor to have Katherine off on Fridays. He paid his bill, leaving an exorbitant tip, then started the twenty-mile drive up the dirt road to his house. When he arrived at Hilltop,

Elizabeth opened the door, pale and wan, dressed elegantly in a gray woolen dress. He kissed her cheek. As she chattered on about new drapes for the study, he was certain he had never loved her.

Katherine returned from the errand carrying the bags of supplies, puzzled, for Frieda had ordered items that were already in the cupboard. Silently, they put the food away. She glanced towards the key-board; the older woman did not miss her glance. 'He's gone,' she said. 'His key's up there.'

'Oh,' Katherine answered, and went on unloading the bags, her disappointment visible in her slumped shoulders.

Frieda fingered the crisp envelope in her pocket; she felt a well of protectiveness rising. She longed with all her heart to take the note and rip it to shreds, saving the girl the eventual heartbreak. She knew about men like the Judge. She had been young once – she remembered how selfish they were in taking their pleasure, and how soon it was forgotten. She reached up and touched the cameo earrings: they were all she had left.

Gathering her nerve, hope like a live flame in her eyes, Katherine finally asked, 'Did he leave anything for me?'

Frieda retorted, crisp and angry, 'What'd you expect – a ten-dollar bill?'

'Oh no,' Katherine protested. 'It wasn't like that.'

Wearily, Frieda knew it was pointless; she would love and hope like every young girl before her. Reaching in her pocket, she handed her the note that he had left.

Katherine grabbed the envelope and hugged it to her chest. 'Oh, thank you.'

Frieda's face turned red and angry. 'If you insist on going to his bed like a cat in heat, at least protect yourself, or you'll be putting a brat in the orphanage in St Louis, like I did!'

'What?' Katherine asked in a shocked voice. 'What did you say?'

Frieda ignored the girl's question. She went to the kitchen drawer, pulled out a sponge and with the poultry shears cut out a square. 'Now mind you, girl, put this up there, as far as you can reach when you're with him, and don't take it out till he's gone.'

Katherine shrunk from her and her gift. 'What did you say?'

Frieda began weeping; she let herself down heavily in a kitchen chair, covered her face with her apron and began sobbing for Anna. She had killed the myth; she could never find comfort in the stories again. Tears flowed as she called her daughter's name, over and over, as if someone was there who would answer. She seemed to hear the baby's high-pitched cries when she had taken her in the vegetable basket and laid her on the orphanage steps. The pain now was as real and fresh as it had been that day.

Katherine forgot her rough words in the horror of the revelation; timidly, she patted Frieda's shoulder. It was the first time the woman had allowed herself to be touched.

Between sobs she tried to justify her sin. 'Women alone like us, there ain't no way we can raise a bastard child . . . no way.'

Katherine felt afraid; she looked at the white envelope with terror. Perhaps it did contain a ten-dollar bill, or goodbye. Frieda's words had created anguish in her heart. She could not open the note now; she would read it later. She put it on the dresser, promising herself she would read it tonight. But the letter lying there appeared ominous. She delayed. She would read it in the morning. It stayed there unread for days. In her daydreams, her dreams at night, her imagination composed terrible messages of degradation and dismissal. The letter lay there unread for six whole days. When Friday arrived, Mr Taylor told her that hereafter this was to be her day off. That knowledge gave her courage and she ripped the

92

envelope open. It contained only three words. *'See you Friday.'* It was signed *'W'*.

On Friday she bathed and bathed; by three o'clock Mr Taylor complained that something was wrong with the water-heater. He sent for a repair man from St Louis, as hot water was needed for the guests. She did not share with them the information that she had taken six baths.

She had starched the white dress she had worn when she first came to Castlewood. From the heart-box she found a length of orchid ribbon and tied it around her waist. With trembling hands she fastened the imitation pearls around her throat, and combed her hair loose; it billowed around her face like a complimentary frame. Three o'clock found her dressed and sitting stiffly on her bed, waiting. Her heart beat wildly. Though the room was cool, she felt beads of perspiration forming on her forehead.

The Judge arrived at his usual time. He was ill at ease. He had had time to think things over; he couldn't understand his rash behaviour. Perhaps it had been something to do with his recent birthday. The half-century mark had sent him into the depths of despair. He felt foolish and old and he had the insidious feeling that he had missed something important in his life. He had respect, wealth, a lovely wife, he was the Judge . . . could any man want more? And if so, what?

He couldn't decide. Should he send a note, with a check, or should he give it to her in person? He must resolve this somehow, or his visits hereafter would be awkward, yet he felt reluctant to face her. He rang for the bourbon, certain that she would not bring it, for he in a silly moment had arranged for her to be off on Fridays.

The older woman brought it; he saw scorn in her face. He sat sullenly in the room drinking, yet the place reminded him of her. He should choose another room. Like a man craving more, he postponed sending for her.

He faced the fear; he was afraid of finding out that those moments that had seemed so sublime were merely illusion. The emptiness that stayed with him always, began to grow! He felt incredibly tired after a week of decisions. Deciding how lives would change for others was a terrible burden, and he cursed his father for putting this burden upon him. It was his father who had urged, cajoled . . . no, *insisted*, that he make the law his life's work. A radiator in the room hissed; mentally he went over all the regrets in his life, and there were many.

When the clock struck nine, Katherine rose from her bed. Her limbs were stiff from sitting so long. She climbed the stairs, knocked softly several times. When he did not answer, she opened the door. She only meant to see his room, touch his things. She did not expect to find him sleeping in the chair.

Like a cautious cat, she crept in and sat on the floor before him. His face was slack with sleep, yet he looked dear to her. She noticed minute things about him that she could not study while he was awake: the steady pulse that throbbed in his throat, the network of veins in his hands, the well-manicured nails. Then the unbelievable happened. He murmured her name in his sleep.

She drew close and kissed his hand. He smiled, thinking that this, too, was a part of his dream . . . She could say it now, clear and without any embarrassment. 'William, I love you. I love you.' He heard it, coming out of his dream. He opened his eyes to see her drawing near. She laid her head against his knee. He stroked her silken hair and her presence drove the emptiness away.

He came every weekend. He loved her with a passion that he had never felt for any woman. She had found within him, and reawakened, his child's heart. Their passion was colored with a desperation so fierce, that she held him in a grip so tight that he felt faint, and in their lovemaking she tore him with her nails and bit his shoulders and his cheeks until he grew a beard to cover the bruises. There were dark times when he questioned her, and badgered her about her faithfulness until she cried in exhaustion . . . then, too, came the joy of making up. He told her of his fears, of men who would come – younger than he, more vigorous, more desirable. She tried to quell his fears, but in the joy of having found her, he discovered within himself an alien emotion . . . he felt at times a raging jealousy. She never told him of the things that happened now – the sneers from other men, even Mr Taylor – boldly looking her over and wondering aloud if she smelled.

Things Sally had told her about now occurred regularly – bold, unwanted attentions such as a subtle touch, furtive winks. She ignored them as best she could. The community gossiped about the lovers – and she was called 'the Judge's whore'.

One weekend in December when it turned unseasonably warm, the locals talked of hurricanes and looked warily at the sky, which was a peculiar grayish-green.

William came with presents and watched as Kathy unwrapped them, sitting on his bed. He brought dresses and jewelry which she could only wear for him. Unwrapping it, she shrank from the box she had just opened. 'You don't like it?' he asked, crestfallen. 'It's rabbit. I wanted you to be warm,' and he held up the white coat!

She smoothed the furs, feeling all the life that had once been. Not wishing to displease him, she put it against her cheek and was reminded of the day in New Mexico when she had heard it speak. He paced the room, restless, opened the window and felt the unusual thaw. He ordered her to dress warmly, then left to make the arrangements for a surprise. She wore the fur coat to please him and as they left the hotel, the men rushed to the window to watch them leave – 'her', as she was called, prancing like a queen, wrapped in white fur, and 'him', as he was referred to, carrying a picnic basket he had gotten from the kitchen. They watched them drive off. 'Damn,' Mrs Taylor said to herself as she peered at them. 'It's as if she has bewitched him. A picnic in December!' In the barroom they laughed and commented, 'There's no fool like an old fool.'

He rented a john-boat and seated her in it. From the trunk of his car he brought two red satin pillows, and she leaned back against them as he rowed down the silent brown river. Watching the curious greenish sky, she found one fluffy white cloud. 'Look, William, it's like a lamb skipping.' They slid past stark, dark trees that rustled in the wind; only the pin oaks clung to their brown leaves, reluctant to let them go until spring.

Overhead in a 'V', mallards honked, changing lakes. He felt an incredible sense of peace, happiness and awe with her beside him. It was not only that he had found in her a rare beauty both inside and out, but as he viewed her, wrapped in the softness of the furs, her full head of hair spread out on the pillow, her face turned up to the sky watching the ducks in their flight, he felt a catch in his throat. He had released her from the silent, brooding girl to a woman fulfilled, who chattered easily, smiled often and hummed without realizing that she was creating music. Her total happiness had left behind the silent Katherine; she had been replaced by this radiant Kathy. It was this in itself that spurred his jealousy on.

On the bank, they picnicked. He spread a blanket among the crackling leaves; they were but a spot of color and life among the bleak landscape. They ate the cold chicken, drank strawberry wine, and as he rested, finding pictures and memories in the clouds, she foraged among the brush and discovered some holly. In jest she wove a crown and placed it on his head. 'I'm so happy,' she told him.

'I'm glad,' was his reply, and the crown reminded him that he had brought her some more books – some Shakespeare and more Greek mythology. She now read avidly.

Often they talked of literature since he had opened this new door for her.

They spent the day outdoors and returned happy and rested, their cheeks red. He checked his watch; it was hours later than he usually left. In the room, he packed and unpacked; he walked to the lobby rehearsing what he would tell Elizabeth. When finally he picked up the receiver he was told that because of high winds, the phone wires were down. He could not make the call.

In the lobby he saw Bruce sweeping out the hearth. He offered him a sum of money that was inconceivable to the young man, to take a message to Hilltop. 'I'll rent a horse from the stable,' he suggested. 'You could make it there and back before dark.'

'No, no,' Bruce said and backed away from him, pure terror in his eyes as he ran home to tell his mother.

William told Kathy of his unsuccessful attempt to send a message to Hilltop and the peculiar response from Bruce. 'His injuries,' Kathy reminded him. 'He's afraid. He was kicked by a horse when he was little.'

Fifteen minutes later, Bruce knocked on their door. 'My mother,' he blurted out, 'she said I am very strong. I'm not afraid of the dark. I run very fast,' and he held out his hand for the money. Quickly, William scribbled a note and handed it to him with the large banknote.

Bruce had just bought them a stolen Sunday. They awoke early and took a drive among the hills. They stopped to eat in a restaurant on the outskirts of St Louis and later visited the riverfront. Kathy looked at the giant width of the Mississippi River and said, 'This was our destination. My father heard of work on the river, but from sheer exhaustion, we stopped at Castlewood.'

Like a man possessed, William's face flushed with the knowledge of his near miss. 'Oh Kathy, thank God for providence – or whatever makes these twists of fate happen. I might never have found you.' A vague thought in his mind blossomed forth. 'We'll buy a cottage, with

97

acreage. This spring, we'll find it, whatever you want. It will be our house – would you like that?' He caught her unspoken questions. 'I can't leave her. She is fragile, she has nothing. Even the babies . . . in her womb they withered and died.' He wondered now if it would have made a difference if their two sons had lived. He thought not.

'She has nothing,' he repeated, 'and we have so much.' He held her, forcing her to look into his eyes. 'Kathy, I swear to you, you are more my wife than she is. In God's eyes, in my heart, you are my wife.'

She clung to him. 'If only that were true!'

'It's true, I swear it. I pity her and love her as one would love a sister. She's a spoiled child. I do not love her as a woman or a wife.'

Kathy hated herself for saying it but it stole out. 'But you go home to her.'

He patted her, comforting her. 'We'll have a home . . . our home, yours and mine.' He felt the excitement of the idea as his mind whirled on. 'I can retire – God knows I have enough money. We can buy time. We'll find this cottage, I promise you.'

Pictures of their home danced in her head. 'Can we have chickens and cows?' she asked, catching his excitement.

'Yes, yes,' he promised, 'whatever you want . . . and it's curious that that's all I ever wanted. I wanted to be happy, to be with the land. I never wanted to be a judge!'

He knew he had an obligation to spend some time at Hilltop, but this idea was a real possibility. He would *make* it happen!

When William was in the city, Katherine hummed, did her work, and never tired of telling Frieda about the cottage. 'Oh Frieda, you can come and stay. It'll be so nice, having our own cottage. We'll have chickens and fresh eggs . . .' She talked on and on; the cottage seemed real and within reach. Even the older woman, who prided herself on knowing just how the world worked, softened, began to hope that maybe this would turn out different.

A telephone call came from Sally; they were shocked to hear her voice, a pathetic whine, asking if Justin were there. The tone of desperation stilled Frieda and she asked no questions. She sent Katherine to the young man's room to see if he were still in; his key was not on the hook.

She knocked on his door. He called, 'Come in.'

She left the door ajar, for she didn't like the way Justin looked at her now, his smooth lips curling, his eyes sharp. Sally had thought him handsome – and to most he might have seemed so, but there was about him an aura that Katherine mistrusted.

'Telephone, sir.'

His eyes flicked over her and stopped, resting on her legs and the short skirt. He came close, too close. 'Who is it?'

His presence unnerved her. She wanted to say, 'I don't know,' instead, she blurted out, 'Sally.'

'Tell her I'm not in, but sweetie – I'd be in for you.' His hand brushed her breast. She left, but his cruel words followed her: 'Don't act so high and mighty with me. When you're through being the old man's whore, you can be mine.'

Rage made her want to turn around and smack his arrogant face, but she couldn't afford to do that. She could tell the Judge, but in the past when she had merely hinted at some sort of insult, he grew livid with rage, questioning her again and again. Was she certain that she had not flirted with the offending party? No, she could do neither thing; she must wait. It wouldn't be too long ... the cottage was so close.

Sally was told that Justin was not in. She called twice more, but Justin had left instructions to tell her he had checked out.

Pushing aside this unpleasantness, Katherine felt good, keeping busy making the apple pies for dinner. Both women had their sleeves rolled up, their arms powdered with flour, cutting the dough. The kitchen was fragrant with the pleasant aroma of spices and cinnamon. Suddenly the world went dark.

'Jesus, Mary and Joseph,' Frieda whispered, crossing herself. The kitchen bulb burned weakly, yet outside the window, the sunlight was gone. It was dark as the darkest night, yet it was noon. They heard shouts of alarm and the sound of running feet coming from other rooms in the hotel. Both women stood frozen like statues for what seemed an eternity, but was only minutes. Like an unseen hand turning on a light, sunshine again flooded the room.

Then they heard it, the scream – an awful, hoarse sound that went on and on. It issued from somewhere outside at the back of the house, a scream so full of terror that it fluctuated in pitch until it became one ongoing agonized roar. The women clutched each other in fright. Mr Taylor came running through the kitchen and flung open the back door. They followed him timidly into the yard where they could see the bushes by the shed trembling violently.

Mr Taylor grabbed a stick from the woodpile and advanced toward the bush. 'Come out,' he commanded, and the sound of his voice seemed to have a calming effect, for the shrubbery still waved, but less violently. He parted a bramble bush, cursed and sucked his finger where he had been stabbed. Cautiously again, he parted the branch; behind him they peered, trying to see.

The sight froze them to the spot. They could see him clearly now, thrashing, tearing at the shrubbery . . . then he stopped momentarily as if a new idea had crossed his mind in his madness; they watched in horror as Bruce lifted his hands up and tore out large clumps of his hair. His face was a frozen gray mask of terror – his eyes bulging white and rolling wildly in his head, his lips frothed with bloodstained saliva that oozed slowly down his chin.

'Bruce . . . Bruce,' Mr Taylor called, but he was beyond hearing.

The hotel owner turned to the people gathered behind him, and as if they couldn't see for themselves he said, 'It's Bruce having some sort of fit. Send for the doctor.'

Others appeared, watching helplessly as Bruce thrashed about the bushes with the tortured screams still issuing from his throat. They all knew he was slow, yet no one had ever seen him in a fit. From the firehouse they came and subdued him with a net, took him off struggling wildly against his captors.

Later, they were told it was the eclipse. He, not knowing, had stared up at the sun unblinking, watching nature's phenomenon. Now, in addition to his other afflictions, Bruce was totally blind! Katherine shivered. Me Maw had told her of this . . . beings who were born under a bad star. She had always believed before William that she was one of those unfortunates, but now . . .

Katherine had trouble sleeping that night. She was remembering all sorts of legends, myths and spells that she had been told about when she was a child. *The Golden Bough*, which William had brought her, talked of legends too . . . of omens good and bad, and she was sure that an eclipse was a very bad omen. The smell in her newly papered room added to her discomfort; she barely slept, just dozing a bit to find frightening things waiting for her in her dreams. She knew others in the hotel were uncomfortable with the odors of fresh paper and paint, but this was when redecorating always occurred, in the off-season . . . it was late April. She went to open the window slightly for fresh air. A nagging thought she couldn't quite place followed her back to bed. Try as she would, it was something about the room. Something was different, something had changed!

Next morning, she dressed slowly. That's when she noticed it – it was gone! It had always sat on the window-ledge. She looked under the beds, tore every drawer apart, flung the silk dresses William had bought her on the floor, then ran out to the ash pit and sorted feverishly through the rubbish that was there. It had barely a foot of trash . . .

it must have been cleaned and hauled away recently.

When she looked up at the gray sky, there was someone on the balcony. 'Lost something, honey? Want me to help you find it?' She became aware that her slip strap had broken; she was standing there in her madness with her breasts exposed. She ran back to her room, hearing Justin's laughter on the porch above her.

It wasn't there! It wasn't anywhere, the heart-shaped box. She went over the contents in her mind: a cigarette butt, a cuff-link of William's, the imitation pearls, three strands of William's hair, a pair of red garters and the prize manroot, the corn-husk doll. It did look like so much trash. The workmen must have thrown it away . . . A chill went through her; she shivered. She felt in an inexplicable way that the magic of the box had brought William to her . . . now it was gone and she felt winter in her heart. There were two bad omens in one day. She fell into bed and burrowed under the covers and cried until she could cry no more. Frieda came looking for her, pronounced her ill, told her to stay in bed. She did so for three days; she would not eat, only now and then taking a sip of water. From the den she stole a bottle of whiskey. Her mother, Papa, William and all the others – they searched for answers in the amber liquid. It made her sick and crazy. She wanted to tear the heart out of the world. William came on Friday and was told by Frieda that Katherine was out of her head. He could not believe what he found. She had torn all the silken gowns to shreds, breaking all her nails in the process. Her fingertips bled. He carried her to his room, filled the tub with soapy water and washed her, telling her, 'It'll be all right,' but he didn't believe it himself, for the unaccustomed smell of whiskey on her breath made him think of blowsy women and lonely nights. He had trouble retrieving her unscathed in his memory; jealousy boiled like a frantic thing within him. He wanted to know with whom she had drunk the whiskey. He spoke, asking his questions gently, holding the beast of jealousy at bay. His anger grew as she neither answered him or even tried. He took her silence as guilt.

Gently he washed the bruises where her body was injured from bashing herself into the furniture. Lovingly, he dried her, then wrapping her in his dressing gown, he carried her to his bed. He ordered food and tried when it came to coax her to eat. He held the glass of buttermilk to her lips, but she would not swallow. He was annoyed at the raucous laughter from below, where a poker game was in progress. She seemed not to notice. From his pockets he took the scraps of paper, the newspaper ads, and he read them to her. He read on and on of acreage and cottages, and forest land . . . anxiously watching her face to see if she had heard.

'It's too late,' she wearily answered. 'The magic has worn itself out. The eclipse . . . it's a bad omen, and the April moon,' she said, her voice rusty with disuse.

'No, darling, it's nothing but one of nature's wonders,' he assured her.

She babbled about boxes and the manroot; he suspected that she was still drunk.

Sitting on the bed beside her, he smoothed her forehead. 'Kathy, what is it?' he pleaded.

Her voice was an angry screech. 'I told you . . . it's too late. The magic has worn itself out.'

He regretted bringing her the books of myths; he promised himself he would bring her no more. He asked the question that burned like a fire in his brain. 'Do you love me?'

She ignored the question. 'The eclipse – it's a bad omen.'

'I know about the eclipse and I heard about Bruce. Maybe I can give him and his mother some sort of work at Hilltop.'

She seemed to be as one talking to herself. 'It's too late; the painters have thrown it away.'

Nothing he did or said got through to her; he would try what had bonded them in the beginning. Undoing

103

her dressing gown, he very lightly touched her breast. Reaching down with his tongue, he traced the circumference of her nipples; he traced her stomach, her hips, with a touch that usually inflamed her. She lay before him cold as stone. He felt as though his love had become abuse. He stopped, pulled the cloth together, retied the sash. He felt the deep humiliation of her indifference. She rose and went to the porch and walked out and breathed deeply as if she had been deprived of air. The night sounds surrounded them; there was the pleasant smell of early honeysuckle. He put his arm about her shoulder. She shook as if with revulsion. Quickly, he dropped his arm from around her. Anger flared, high and bitter. He did not know her; she was not the Kathy he had left – she was someone strange and different who was keeping terrible secrets from him. Controlling himself, he asked, 'Do you wish to go?'

She nodded a silent yes and started for the steps.

He slammed the door, bolted it, went into the bathroom to draw a bath. He turned on the tap, the water gurgled, running noisily into the tub. And his frame shook with fear.

The moon came from behind a cloud for just a moment before hiding again. It was not silver or even orange; it was blood red. That was when she knew: it had come, the omen that foretold evil. It was here on the steps with her. It cleared her head; she felt the soul of the hare beating within her. *She was hunted.* A slim hope turned her, intending to rattle his door, but it was too late, just as she knew it was . . . the magic had worn itself out. In the dark night she could not know where it lurked, yet she felt its presence. She knew it was there.

Halfway between two points, she could not decide; it was as far to run down as it was to run up. She sensed it above her, somewhere in the dark. In terror, she started down the wooden steps, but before she reached the lower porch she heard the rustle of dry leaves and the trellis

104

shook. He leaped from it, and upon her, like an avenging angel – landing on her back, sending her crashing forward onto the wooden slats. Splinters tore into her palms; her breath was expelled from her lungs by the force of his body. Vicious fingers grasped her throat, cheating her of air. The point of the knife stung her neck.

'I want what the Judge gets,' he hissed. She struggled beneath him, trying to regain her knees; the knife pressed deeper into her throat. He tore at the loose dressing gown, gaining easy access to her bare buttocks. Light filtered across the slats, as the moon once again emerged from the night clouds. The sight of their shadows thrown forward across the boards paralyzed her; it seemed like a giant insect squirming across the slats. She thought of the praying mantis and began reciting the Lord's Prayer in her head. Fiercely, she struggled under him, but fingers like steel pried her legs apart. He entered her cruelly, blind with lust. She chose not to feel anything of this evil attached to her like a parasite, thrusting, thrusting. It went on for an eternity; her breath stilled, held down, stuffed in her throat, her nostrils flared seeking air, she tried to bite the hand that held her so tightly. Her teeth finally worked until they achieved their goal. She sunk them into his flesh . . . and for just a moment he loosened his hold. A scream, a sigh, a moan so high, so inhuman, escaped her . . . that he wasn't sure it emitted from the form he rode so viciously. Lights went on, flooding the porch. They were framed as if in a still photo, in their pose of degradation.

Doors banged, voices shouted, created momentary relief. He was out of her, she heard the knife clatter through the slats of the porch. With limbs like jelly she tried to right herself. She could only manage to regain balance on her hands and knees. Trembling, she looked upward and saw his face looking down. William's face was ashen, his eyes gleamed with fury as he saw her on all fours, her buttocks gleaming in the moonlight.

Someone yelled, 'Well, I'll be damned!'

Justin struggled with his pants, looking up at the Judge. 'I'm sorry, Judge, if this was private stock. I couldn't help it. She's been after me to meet her out here ... she likes doing it like this. Whoah, just like an animal she is. Sorry, Judge.'

The Judge surveyed the scene, his mind a mass of confusion and fury, fast turning to disgust.

'Cover yourself, you bitch,' he spat down at her, then he slammed the door, turned out the porch light and ran to the bathroom, where he retched for half an hour.

As the door slammed, she fell over on the slats, thankful for the dark. The robe was torn, no longer covering her. She gasped in quick shallow breaths. Everything swam before her; lack of oxygen made her faint. She lay as if in shock, too stunned to sob. That was when she became aware of the stealthy noises, shadows creeping nearer – and again he grabbed her, stilling her words, 'Oh God, please, no!' as out of the darkness they came. Her fists beat at them like a moth against the flame. The first one lowered himself on her. She could not cry out, as he pulled roughly at her breast. They formed a circle and watched; the whiskey made them bold. It was a silent struggle. She felt another lower himself above her face. They rolled her this way and that, pinching and clawing at her; three of them took their pleasure of her at once.

The scent of them made her gag – the whiskey, the musk of them. There was no way, nowhere to escape ... there was only one place she could go. In her mind she retreated under her bed in Gallup, where she often hid as a child. Away now, she saw the dust gather in the corners, the specks flying in the sunlight. 'I must hide,' she told herself, and she stayed there – a tiny ball, where nothing touched her, even though they violated her in every way possible. It didn't touch her, for she was far away, crying silently for the soul that died.

Frieda found her in the early dawn just as the rooster

crowed – spread-eagled on the slats, dried blood on her legs, their issue caked in her hair and over her body, her eyes wide open, staring, without seeing the dawn.

'My God! Oh my God, what has he done to you, that no-good bastard – and him a judge! Who will judge him?' Frieda half-carried and half-dragged her into the kitchen. Propping her on a chair, she washed her. The cold water made her stir. Her eyes unset, and she began blinking rapidly. Frieda held smelling salts under her nose; she shook her head from side to side, becoming aware.

'Stay here,' Frieda commanded, and ran to Katherine's room, but she could find no clothing there that was not torn to shreds, except for the gray cape. She brought fresh clothing of her own, all far too big. She put on a cotton slip; the panties would not stay up. Over Katherine's head she threw a long gray housedress of her own and wrapped the cape around the trembling girl.

'Wait, Katherine, do not move. Stay still – I'll get the doctor.' She ran quickly to the lobby to telephone, but returned some minutes later to find Katherine gone. 'Katherine!' she called, her voice loud and frantic in the beautiful April morning. She called until she was hoarse.

Blindly, Katherine stumbled through the woods. She ran and ran until she could run no further, then, collapsing into a heap of pampas-grass, she slept for a whole day. She awoke as a hare crept close to her, staring; she caught his essence, felt the terror of his days. Her eyes fluttered, and he scampered away. She heard the call of the jay, alarmed at her presence. And she heard Justin's words, meant to wound: *She's just like an animal . . . just like an animal.'* They echoed in her mind. An animal, she thought. What a noble thing to be. They were not dishonest or deceitful. They did not misunderstand—. A pain high in her abdomen gnawed at her; she mistook it for hunger. Sitting up, she found berries ripe and juicy, and ate. Stretching, she reached for it . . . the forgotten talent. Straining with all her might she brought it to her. She heard them, the creatures in the woods . . . they spoke to one another, and she knew of what they spoke.

By noon Frieda had prepared a bundle of necessary things. She called at the edge of the woods. In the pack she had included some pots, a tin of kitchen matches, utensils and two notebooks full of recipes. Frieda knew she had taught the girl well; she could survive. Frightened that with each day she would be farther and farther away, she went and got Bruce, who was terrified, now that his world had shrunk further. Taking Bruce and leading him to the edge of the wood, she implored him to call, 'Katherine.' He was frightened, but she urged and begged and he didn't understand any of it, but he did as she asked.

His voice bellowing and calling to 'Katherine!' made Katherine pause and wonder. Bruce so recently injured – what did he want? What was it she could do for him? There was nothing she could do for herself. Yet quietly she crept closer; she could see through the veil of trees, Frieda leading him and between them they carried a knapsack. She could not go to them; she felt now she could not go to anyone. She heard Bruce's voice grow hoarse with calling. She saw them place the sack on a rock then turn away, walking back toward the hotel. Frieda led him by one arm; his other arm flailed the air, searching for obstacles, his new world of darkness, his new cross to bear.

She went forward and saw her two notebooks lying atop the bundle. She knew these things were meant for her. Regaining her strength, she wandered though the woods, following the sound of the water. She thought she was following the bend of the Meramac, but she was mistaken. She was following Kiefer Creek.

The warm months went by in a succession of forgotten days. Food was plentiful and sometimes, when she found a small cave, she dared to cook. Often around the caves or water she saw the print of the bobcat. It lived here, too. She felt no fear of them, the animals that lived with her; she felt closer to them, much more so than to the humans she had left behind. At night she looked up at the heavens and wondered, how did one ever escape from the curse of being born under an unfortunate star? It seemed tragic to her that any of them, the stars that glittered there, could be unfortunate. She did not mourn for her lost love, nor even feel the degradation that had sent her here. That part of her had died. Like the squirrel, the musk-rat, the possum, the gentle fawns . . . even the bobcat . . . she spent her days as they did, searching for food, drinking from the clear creek, seeking out a warm place to rest and sleep. She did not think of the child. She had not told him, for then she had not been sure. Now she ignored her pain, pretending it did not exist, for if it did, it, too, was as helpless as she was, and in her womb they had tainted her and the fetus. The pain came often; it was a gnawing pain that tore at her insides. She pushed it away and escaped under her bed in Gallup . . . creeping under the small bed, feeling the soft dust in the corners, and watching the motes of it floating in the sun. It could not find her there, when she hid so carefully.

Around the creek she found the wild peppermint plant, which grew in wet places, its purple flowers and dark green foliage easily visible. Chewing it, she knew it was a remedy, and it made her want to sleep. She also found yarrow, which grew alongside the road. She could spot its tall heads with their white flowers and its finely cut gray-green foliage. When she was sure that no one else was about, she would creep to the roadside and pick some, not wishing to be seen.

She placed the leaves from the yarrow in her shoes, for she knew it to relieve blisters. She used it to bind up her scratches and wounds as well. The wood and land were abundant; gathering dill and swamp rose for food, soon she felt the cold of autumn. The fetus grew. She must stop, for the time was drawing near; yet still it twisted and turned within. Holding on to a willow tree, she felt its restless soul within. 'Tell me, spirit, what should I do?'

She implored the sun god, god of the wind . . . all things in nature that she knew to be divine, yet none answered, or gave direction. Never, but never, would she call on the God of her father. She felt the spirit of creation around her, yet none could be reached. In the late autumn she saw the gold of the manroot, its five-fingered plant growing low in the dark, damp places. She filled her sack, digging only the old ones, careful to plant the berries just under the leaves, scattering some as the birds would in nature. Chewing the manroot gave her renewed strength. She found no roots in the man-shape; those she dug were large and old – she knew this by the number of knobs on the stem. And they were straight. She didn't expect to find one so special again. Frieda had told her . . . they were prime and very, very special. An early frost warned her she must find shelter, for the thing that grew was near its time. Two days ago, she had passed a fine house on a hill. Near it lay an abandoned cabin. She must try – she could pay. Frieda had told her of the manroot's value, and by now she had gathered an entire sackful.

Doubling back, she tried to remember certain trees, rocks, streams. When she was dizzy and exhausted, the hares whispered to her; she turned and found her direction. A morning's walk, and the house lay before her. Going to the back door, she knocked, hoping whoever answered it would be kind.

The door swung open. A rotund woman in a flowered housedress answered, then started to close the door in her face. 'We don't want any gypsy around here.'

'Please, ma'am, I'm not a gypsy,' Katherine whispered, swaying, threatening to faint.

Hannah peered out to see who might be lurking behind her. Seeing only the girl, her face painfully gaunt, wrapped in a tattered cape, she softened. 'I can give you some food. Wait here.' And the door slammed with a finality.

'Please,' she whispered to the god who resided in the giant oak behind her. 'Please,' she implored a cloud which passed overhead.

When Hannah reopened the door, she practically fell in.

'You can't be sleeping here,' Hannah told her. With her foot she began moving her along, trying to hand her a bundle of food.

'What is it, Hannah?' Her mistress' voice came behind her.

'Some gypsy, I think. I was givin' her some leftovers. I would have given them to the dog anyway.'

Elizabeth joined her on the doorstep, her face troubled at the sight of the pathetic girl. 'Can you stand?'

Katherine nodded. 'Yes.'

Between them, they led her inside, to the table.

'Hannah, I think hot tea.'

A steaming mug was placed before her. She cupped her hands around it and drank noisily.

'Who are you, and what do you want?' Elizabeth asked.

'I'm Katherine Sheahan. My father and I were going to St Louis; he got ill and died. I'm alone,' she lied.

'Should we call the sheriff?' Hannah asked.

'No, please,' Katherine begged. 'I just need someplace to rest. I saw the cabin . . . in a day or so I'll be fine . . . I can pay.' Weakly she tried to hold up the sack to prove it.

Both women looked puzzled at the bedraggled burlap sack.

'It's ginseng. I can sell it at Castlewood and I can pay for the use of the cabin.'

'I don't know,' Elizabeth began, sorry that this problem had landed on her doorstep, and tired of it already. While deciding, they heard the sound of the car. She looked at the cook for assistance. 'It's the Judge.' They stood there feeling helpless with their problem.

'Where is everybody?' he called, and he strode through the kitchen door.

111

They felt foolish. 'It's a young girl . . . her father's dead, and she's wanting to rent the cabin.' The words rushed out of Elizabeth in a flurry.

'Yes.' Hannah spoke up, feeling responsible for the problem. She was the one who had opened the door. 'She can pay . . . she has a sackful of ginseng.'

He stepped further into the room; drew back as if he'd been slapped when he saw her, how wretched she looked, her eyes hollows of pain, eyes grown large in a wan face.

Gruffly he said, 'All right, all right, have Tom clean it out,' and he pretended anger to cover his feelings. 'Is this why dinner's late?'

He backed out of the room, feeling as though he had been hit in the stomach. In the library, he stared into the fire. What had been between them had been another time, dreamlike. Now in his life he felt nothing – numbness an integral part of him.

Sipping the scotch, he told himself it was some lack within him that had made her into something she was not. He tried to dismiss her as just another servant girl who liked men and presents. Then the horror that was etched in his mind flicked like pictures in the nickelodeon and for the first time he saw it as it really was.

How could he have been so stupid, he that sat on the bench judging? The meaning of his whole life's work was in jeopardy now, for he had failed to see. The beast of jealousy had clouded his view and he had blamed her, unfairly. He had doubted and condemned her when in truth she had been the victim. They had raped her and he the Judge had just stood by and let it happen.

He knew she was as he had first thought – 'genuine'. Too late, everything in life comes too late. This was a different girl, a different time. He had let love slip through his fingers like water through a sieve. There was no recalling it. Love, pure and honest, did exist. He knew it now.

This one – she who stood in his kitchen – was not her. He was as responsible as those who had defiled her, for his lack of faith. As sure as blue and red make purple, that day was the last time he felt any emotion.

Sorrow – regret – had passed him by. He felt old and tired; he knew that other birthdays would not bother him now. Life was just a series – another day, another problem.

Here was another day, another problem. After hearing about Bruce's accident he had made a commitment, telling the sheriff at the autopsy that he would sign papers to be legal guardian for Bruce now that his mother was gone. Maybe he'd put it off till tomorrow. He knew how Elizabeth hated afflictions. He knew how she would abhor a blind man stumbling about the house. He had planned on Bruce being housed in the cabin.

# CHAPTER 12

It was Allison who had noticed them. She was sitting in the window in her peignoir, painting her nails, listless now that it was September; business was bad. She cursed fate and wondered if St Louis would be any livelier. Now that the stories had circulated about the Judge's woman being public property, Allison had tried over the summer to interest him. She had seen him playing cards at the Eagle's Nest ... she lounged on the jukebox, winked at him when he looked up from the cards, the smoke making a halo over his head, but he had stared right through her. Times were tough; with winter coming, they wouldn't be getting any better. She watched now as the old woman led Bruce down the road to the river. It was a pathetic sight. She held one of his hands in her gnarled paw that was bent and twisted with arthritis – some said people got it from living by the water. Hell, she wouldn't be here long enough to get that old. Bruce's other hand clawed at the air in constant motion. She looked at them with distaste yet knew, as winter came, even a blind man with two bucks would be welcome ... even a dummy. Hell, she laughed, he was both!

Watching their slow progress up the hill, she wondered where they could be going. After what seemed an eternity, they reached the bridge. They couldn't be fishing; they had no poles. And it was far too cold for bathing. Watching them made her feel superior. She was only thirty – no afflictions, still had good trade, all her own teeth.

'Jeez, ain't they a pair?' she said with contempt.

'Who?' asked Marcella, coming over to the window.

They both laughed. 'Ain't they something?' Allison said, distaste again curling her lips.

They watched, struck dumb, when they realized what the woman intended. Lifting one leg over the rail, they saw the motion of her head talking rapidly to Bruce. Now the other leg was painfully lifted over the rail, both hands pulling him through, coaxing.

'For Christ sakes,' they said together. 'Look what she's making him do!'

Both women ran screaming from the house; their screams were heard. People started looking out of windows and both ladies ran to the bridge, their high-heeled house slippers making clunking sounds in the road. She had succeeded.

They were both in the water, the greenish water covering her gray head. She didn't struggle against it; she was pulling him down, down with her. The dummy now knew, and he fought, trying to tear the claw from his arm that held on like fingers of steel.

Bruce's head bobbed up and under, blind eyes open wide. His mouth yawned, hoping to scream, yet when he had his wind, that hand kept pulling him under. His long stringy hair was plastered wetly across his face, the unseeing eyes peering through.

Without thinking, Allison tore off her robe, leaned far out over the railing and dangled it before him. He touched the rayon – and his hand clutched and tore trying to climb the mysterious ladder that had been offered to him. It was a struggle. With one hand he held onto the lifeline, and with the other his mother held him fast. An eddy caught them, and in slow motion they began to rotate, the cloth twisting, growing shorter with each rotation.

A voice beside her said: 'Allison, you're brilliant. You're a real smart girl; the dummy can't swim.' And he was thrown the lasso by the sheriff. It stuck under one armpit and it took several men to haul him up. Down in the water they could see the strands of gray hair floating, now whirling, faster and faster, until the whirlpool sucked her under. Allison was elated. They bought drinks, and she felt full of good will. The Judge came, and the drinks were free. Allison felt important, like maybe somebody would suggest giving her a medal or something. It was after a time when heads spun, the men got awfully drunk, and she smacked Marcella right in front of everybody. It was Marcella who said it: 'Jeez . . . that was stupid. Why'd you have to save him, a blind dummy? He'd have been better off down there with his mama; those two never been apart.'

Allison began crying in her beer.

# CHAPTER 13

The shock of seeing William forced Katherine's head down to stare at the floor. Already his wife had lost interest in her, and had followed him out of the kitchen, indicating that the whole affair of what to do with the stranger was up to Hannah. William had okayed it, telling Tom to run down and clean the cabin. Hannah plopped a big bowl of stew in front of her, looked her in the eye, and with an unbelievable fierceness said, 'Don't you cause any trouble, you hear?'

'No, ma'am,' Katherine agreed, gulping the stew, burning her tongue in the process.

The housekeeper bustled about the steamy pots and the gleaming gas stove. 'Supper's late on account of you. Judge's home and supper's late.' She tended the pots and oven intermittently, packing a box, putting in several cups with broken handles, the oldest fry pan, two towels that were worn through, a couple of sheets. She left the room, coming back with several garments over her arm. 'These are the Missus'. You can have 'em – she was giving them to the church rummage sale anyway.'

Katherine looked around the sleek kitchen. It was very different from the one at the hotel. Every modern convenience that existed was here – the large gas stove, a gleaming electric refrigerator, counters abounding with appliances, blenders, toasters, mixers. There was no frugality practiced here.

Tom returned, and Hannah asked him to carry the

119

boxes up to the cabin for her. She dismissed Katherine with a second warning. 'Now you go on. Cabin ain't much, but it's out of the cold. Don't you make the Missus sorry that she let you stay.'

Nodding, Katherine mumbled her thank yous and started after Tom, through the woods that had grown dark.

The back door reopened, and a shaft of light cut through the path. 'Wait, wait up!' Katherine went back, and Hannah pushed a bag into her hands. 'I almost forgot – cabin's got no electricity. There's matches and candles . . . What did you say your name was again?'

'Katherine – Katherine Sheahan.'

Thorns cut through her thin-soled shoes as she followed Tom to the cabin. She was too tired to even think. It felt odd to know he lived here, a different life than the one he had in Room 8 at the hotel. This slim blonde woman was the same he had told her of. 'She has nothing,' he had said. She looked back at the magnificent house – she knew he probably sat beside the fireplace with her . . . and this was the woman he had described as having nothing. She didn't understand them – men, women. She understood the toad skittering at her foot much, much better.

She followed Tom into the cabin, where he lit a candle, and putting it in the holder, placed it on the sturdy table for her. He mumbled a goodnight under his breath . . . he didn't like it, not one bit, taking in strangers. His wife and the Missus were fools for anyone with a good story. Maybe barren women were like this – always lookin' for strays. Well, he wasn't taken in. There was more to this than met the eyes. He would watch her carefully.

Alone now, Katherine looked around the cabin. It had a cold, unused feeling, a faint smell of must. Still, it was secure and well-built, and it kept out the wind rattling around the windows. She noticed a small black wood-stove. It would do fine. A faint warmth emitted from it; she was grateful that he had laid a fire. The double bed had a thick feather quilt covering it, both blanket and spread. Feeling weariness overcome her, she lifted the covers and crawled into bed. The down reflected the warmth. She curled into a fetal position, turning away from the silver moonlight coming through the curtainless window . . . remembering what Me Maw always said: it was dangerous to sleep with the moon on your face, for its rays crept beneath the lids and filled the sleeper with madness.

Keeping her face to the wall, she found that secret place, 'away' . . . No longer lying in the bed with the fetus turning and tossing within her, she was 'away', sitting by the fireplace with William at her knee.

He stoked the fire; for some inexplicable reason he sat on the floor, his hands grasping his knees staring into the leaping flames, barely aware that Elizabeth had left the room. He felt that presence next to him, her gentle hand smoothing his hair. He knew he had been mistaken: she was as he first thought, and more. He dozed and they were together.

# CHAPTER 14

Morning arrived. Patterns of moonlight were replaced by weak sunlight; shadows of leaves danced across the pine floor. Katherine awoke slowly, forgetting where she was. It was difficult coming back. She looked about the small-ish room: in the dark she did not know it. The room began with the smooth plank floors, a colorful rag rug, its oval shape covering a portion of the floor, dominating the room. The cabin contained only the bare necessities – a sturdy table with two chairs, well-made but plain. The wood-stove had a logbox next to it; it was full. Under the solitary window stood a pine dresser with drawers for storage. There were two copper buckets for fetching water. An enamel basin of white with blue edging, chipped in several places, allowing rust to show through, hung by a nail. On a shelf next to it were several bars of strong naphtha soap. Against one wall was a pine rocker and a blanket-chest of cedar. The only disorder in the room came from the boxes waiting to be unpacked. She was grateful to see on top of her assortment of mismatched dishes a loaf of bread and a brick of cheese. She went out with the buckets to get water; Kiefer Creek ran close by the side of the cabin. The morning air was crisp and cold. The cabin was huddled into the hillside. On the ridge above it was a stand of trees, like erect sentries guarding all they overlooked. She noticed that some of the trees were mature walnut. The water in the creek ran icy and transparent and on the bottom you could see large black

123

rocks, where huge fish played hide and seek. The creek seemed to sing, as it rushed over the rocks on its way down to meet the river. Filling the buckets, she carried them slowly back up to the cabin; their weight made her side ache. She set them on the solitary step, and made her way to the abandoned outhouse some yards behind the cabin.

Returning, she gathered small twigs, putting them into the stove. They crackled and caught and the banked fire flared up, warming the cabin. After a breakfast of coffee, bread and cheese, she heated water in the buckets, stripped off her filthy clothes, threw them in the stove, filled the pan with hot water, and with a rough cloth and the naphtha soap, began washing herself. The soap was strong and pungent, with a medicinal tang. At the hotel they had used it for laundry. It stung her skin, yet seemed to wash away the months of misery, as well as the dirt. Shivering naked in front of the stove, she was now aware of how swollen and taut her stomach had become. During the time spent in loose-fitting garments, she had pretended – but now, looking down at her engorged breasts and stomach, she realized she could not see the floor. Her time was near, and as if to make this truth, her stomach rippled as the child turned.

From the box she selected the largest dress . . . a plain affair in gray. It was too small. She slit the seams, and putting a loose sweater over it, found it covered her. It would do. She had not burned the cape – she needed it to hide her secret. She took it outside in the sun and hung it over a bush to air. She dried her hair by the stove, fluffing and rubbing it with a towel. Looking into the cloudy mirror that was near the dresser, she felt no fear of it. Now she braided her hair, winding it around her head and securing it with a bit of string. She would never wear it down around her face again. Satisfied, she stared into the strange face. It was older now. Thinness made her cheekbones stand out and her eyes seemed enormous.

Her heritage blended and added a different dimension; from the eyes you could see her Spanish grandfather, the dusty rose of her skin revealed her Navajo grandmother, and her father's Irish blood formed her nose and generous mouth; they all blended curiously in her face. At first glance, unless you looked hard, you missed the exotic beauty that she was. The casual, the hurried, would only think her plain.

The flutter in her stomach was an intermittent reminder, but she would not think about the child. She knew it was his; superstition made her shiver when she thought of those pigs... They had tarnished, contaminated, what grew inside her. They had touched his seed.

Concerned that the manroot did not grow damp, she undid the sack; only those at the very bottom had a mold and were no longer good, but the majority of the root was fine. Making a clothes-line of sorts, careful not to string any too near the stove, she tied the root inches apart. It mustn't dry too fast. She knew that she must take it to town once it was ready; it would be difficult, but she needed to pay for the cabin, having no money, only the manroot. She would think about that when the time came.

Satisfied that the roots were placed properly for drying, she heard something scratching at the door. Opening it, she was greeted by a large, reddish dog; in his mouth he carried one end of her tattered cape. He panted and wagged his tail in friendship. He had smelled the scent of his master on her cape. 'Here.' She stooped, retrieving the cloth from his mouth. The dog stood with his front paws on the step, peering inside, but would come no farther. 'Come on,' she coaxed. 'Come on.' But the creature wagged his tail furiously, and would not budge.

'All right,' she said, and swung the cape around her shoulders, took the burlap bag and started out toward the dense trees. Frieda had taught her well... She searched the sky for birds and heard the chattering of song sparrows and headed in that direction. Sometimes the dog led, sometimes he followed, as they picked their way through the woods going away from the cabin. Vegetation grew profusely here; bushes and trees fell over each other seeking the rays of the sun. Katherine sat to rest on a stump; close by she heard the singing of the song sparrows. The activity of the birds shook the foliage. She knew she had found a clump of bushes heavy with mulberries. The branches hung with an abundance of fruit. Some was over-ripe, some had already dried out, but many were still good, and her bag grew fatter as she picked and ate the berries. Now and then, the dog chased a squirrel or other small creature, and she heard the sound of twigs cracking and leaves scattering as he enjoyed his chase, a soft yipping in his throat from the excitement. Birds called warnings to each other about the intruders in their woods. The sack grew full; it began to ooze. She started back to the cabin. Now the dog ran between her and the creek, stopping every so often to lap up the cool water. He followed her into the cabin and lay in front of the stove, his head on his paws, dozing as she prepared the berries. Carefully washing them, picking off the stems and leaves, she placed the best ones in a large wooden bowl. Having finished, she gathered her cloak, and the animal reluctantly gave up his space of warmth and followed her to the house. Intending to leave the bowl on the back step, the dog gave her away with his whine. Opening the door, Hannah caught her bending over, midway in her intention to place the abundant bowl on the step.

Hannah's face broke into a pleased smile. At Hilltop, hers was lonely work; no neighbors were nearby and one couldn't talk on equal terms with the Missus. This was a chance to chat with someone. She took the bowl from Katherine. 'You can't leave them there – the squirrels will have them picked clean.' Standing aside, she said, 'Come in.' She put the bowl on the sideboard and gushed over the berries. 'Oh, these are lovely. I thought they were all gone by now. You must have picked them in the west woods – no one ever goes there.'

'I guess so. It was past the cabin, by the stand of willows where the bushes get very thick.'

'That's it, the west woods. It's pert near wild up there. The berries look so good, it's an excuse to make cobbler. Well, sit. I'll make us some coffee.' Katherine sat awkwardly on the edge of the chair, holding the cape fast around her.

Hannah served the coffee in an elegant china coffee service, the delicate cups edged in gold, the design beautiful with tiny rosebuds. She noticed how timidly the girl handled the cups. 'These aren't the good ones.' She nodded. 'The Judge's wife has the best of everything. Why, in the hallway she had the marble floors sent all the way from It-lee. Come here.' She motioned Katherine to look through the swinging door. 'See there, that floor? It's real Venetian marble.' They both admired the rose-colored floor that shone brilliantly in the hall.

Wiping her hands on her apron, the gesture reminded Katherine of Frieda. Sitting at the table sipping their coffee, it was obvious the housekeeper wanted to talk.

Hannah studied the quiet girl. Today she looked older than she had originally thought. With her hair long and tangled about her face, it had given her the appearance of an unkempt child. Now, with it pulled severely back and braided – the turquoise earrings the only bit of color on her person – she appeared older, much older.

'You said true when you said you weren't gypsy?' she inquired.

Katherine nodded. 'My mother was Indian and my father wasn't.'

They sipped their coffee in silence, Hannah already on her second cup. Rabelay's tail made a steady sound, pat ... pat ... in a slow rhythm as he wagged it up and down on the waxed linoleum, drawing their attention to him.

'I see you met Rabelay.'

'Oh yes, ma'am, he's a nice dog. I love animals.'

'He's the Judge's dog. He's quite fond of him. Mostly he don't take to strangers. He's at loose ends all week when the Judge is in town – can't wait till the weekend, when he comes home. Makes a bit of a pest of himself till then.'

'I don't mind really.'

Katherine looked down to reassure herself that the cape covered well enough, twisting her fingers nervously, wanting to say something about payment for the cabin. She was not sure that it was proper to talk of payments to this woman. She finished her coffee, then decided to go ahead anyway. 'I'm drying the ginseng,' she began. 'It will be dry enough in a day or so for me to take it to town and sell it, to pay for the cabin. Should I talk to the Missus about it?'

'No, it's not a good time. She's laying down now, she's not a well woman. She's fragile. I wouldn't want to wake her . . . but I'll tell her. She's not worrying about payment – she's not that kind. They're wealthy enough, God knows!'

Now that the subject had been brought up it was easier for Katherine to continue. 'I'm not sure just how much they'll pay for the manroot, but I know I was told the price at the hotel. The cook always sold hers to Bailey's and at a good price.' Her voice trailed off, knowing she had said too much.

Leaning forward intently, Hannah, who never missed much, noticed the girl's slip. 'Did you work at the hotel?'

'Yes, ma'am, for a short while.'

'Seems like a pretty good job, working down at the hotel?' Hannah said, carefully watching the girl.

'Oh, it was, but they don't need anyone now. It's the off-season.'

Hannah's curiosity and suspicions were now raised. 'Going back in the summer?'

'I don't know. I guess so,' Katherine lied, feeling her face flush.

The housekeeper looked at Katherine closely. She had heard about the loose women that hung around Castlewood, but this one didn't seem the type. She was too plain, with her face scrubbed clean, no make-up. No, she didn't smile enough – she wasn't gay enough to be a paid woman!

Uncomfortable under the woman's scrutiny, Katherine redirected the conversation back to payment. 'I'll be going to sell the ginseng for certain in the next couple of days.'

'How you gonna get there? It's twenty miles to Castlewood. You can't walk twenty miles dragging that sack.'

'Yes, ma'am, I can walk,' Katherine assured her.

'Nonsense! Tom goes every Monday for supplies – he can take you.'

'I couldn't ask him.'

'You don't have to – I will. He's my husband . . . He goes anyway every Monday, so you're not putting him out.'

'Well, thank you. I best be going,' and Katherine rose from her chair.

'Oh, the cabin doesn't have a calendar. Here's one from the bank.' She saw Katherine's hesitation. 'Today's October the seventh, in case you weren't sure. Tom's going Monday the eleventh.' Walking her to the door, Hannah moaned, 'Oooh, darn knee of mine!'

'What's wrong?' Katherine asked.

'Nothing, child. It's just the rheumatism.'

Shutting the door after them, she was glad that the dog was following the girl; she didn't need him lying around underfoot in her clean kitchen.

Katherine walked slowly back along the path someone had used years ago. It was full of brambles, overgrown from neglect. The dog burst in front of her, his rapid ascent flattening the bush. She knew that soon, with the various trips back and forth, the path would become well-trodden again.

She lit the lantern, put the calendar on the wall and looked at the date – 7 October 1941. In the town, progress and new things the world embraced. She didn't belong here; it was as if she were misplaced from another time. She cleaned the cabin in an effort not to think. Now that she had found a place to stop and shelter, she could not rest too long. To pay she must sell the ginseng, and Castlewood was the only place to sell it. There she would encounter the men who gathered in the feed-store to sit around and exchange talk about the war in Europe, or local gossip. Her own shame must have filled many hours of idle conversation. A core of dread grew larger; the child tossed and tumbled violently, and she felt needle-like pain as if something feasted on her entrails. She opened the door and relieved her stomach of the coffee and blueberries. Trembling with weakness, she sat in the rocker; the dog came over and licked her hand in sympathy, and whined softly as she rocked.

She found her notebook and carefully ripped out a page. She couldn't make the remedy for Hannah as she did not have the ingredients, yet she knew its properties. In a careful hand she wrote: *Grate 3 tablespoons of sharp horseradish, stir into this a half cup of boiled milk, soak a cheesecloth in the mixture for five minutes, then lay the cheese-cloth, properly wrung out, over the painful part for relief from the rheumatism.*

She would leave it for her in the morning, in the mailbox.

# CHAPTER 15

Early Monday she packed the manroot; it was lighter now that it was dry. She carried it over one shoulder as it still weighed a lot. She waited at the back door of the house for several minutes before Tom came out. Hannah was there, looking over his shoulder and smiling. She shared the information, 'It worked! The potion worked. My knee is much better – I can bend a lot easier.'

Katherine smiled a genuine smile; it made her feel good to repay a kindness. Tom studied a list in one hand; he had slung her sack over his shoulder. 'I'll carry it,' he offered.

He threw the sack into the back of the pickup, helping her as she stepped up on the running board. She reached the leather seat and sat back, trying to relax. Tom was like his wife, open and friendly. It was the first time he had gotten a good look at her.

His question was direct. 'You Indian?'

'My mother was. She died when I was a little girl,' Katherine answered. She had never said that before – was it the truth? She didn't know. It was a vague, dreamlike memory, the screaming woman. That's when she would go and hide under her bed, among the dust in the corners with the sunshine a shaft of light across the floor pretending to catch those flying bits as she lay under the bed, hardly breathing . . . silent with fear. She didn't know if her mother was dead. Papa and she never talked about her. She started from her reverie. 'I'm sorry, what did you say?'

'I said, you're not from around here?'

'No, I'm from New Mexico – Gallup. After my mother died, my father and I traveled some, looking for work.' Her answer was true enough.

He nodded, slowed down as the road ahead had deeper ruts, but not losing his train of thought, he continued: 'My wife said you'd worked at the hotel.'

'For a short time.' Her answer was barely audible.

A doe darted in front of the truck. 'Damn.' He swerved to keep from hitting her. The truck slid sideways, gently bumping into a tree. He got out to see if there was any damage.

He got back in. 'She's OK. No damage,' and he began whistling, paying closer attention to the road. Katherine looked out the window at the passing woods. The dread was like a rash over her entire body. When he came to The Crossroads he said, 'Looks like we're here.'

She nodded agreement. He stopped in front of Bailey's general stores. She took the bag from him, and they entered together, but no one assumed that they were together. Tugging awkwardly at the heavy sack, she headed for the back of the shop where the scales were kept. The men seated around the stove smoking, ceased all conversation. Interested, they began watching her awkward path to the back. No one offered to help. A contagious smile of recognition broke out among them. They strained forward to hear her words to the clerk. 'I'd like to sell my ginseng,' she stated.

The clerk caught the smiles and snickers of the men. He recognized her; he wasn't there that night, but he had heard about it in detail. Deciding to prolong the fun, he opened the sack, rustled his hand through the full bag of roots. 'Where'd you get it?'

Panic was a live thing within her, but she fought it down. 'I picked it,' she answered softly.

The clerk smirked, enjoying himself. 'Speak up, I can't hear you! Where'd you say you got it?'

'I picked it,' she repeated louder.

He looked in the sack, picked out a root or two. He knew it was prime.

'You picked it?' he said loudly. 'Damn, I can see that. Maybe you did and maybe you didn't . . . but on whose land?'

'It's honest,' she protested. 'I found it in different places in the woods. No place had signs saying No Trespassing. It's honest.'

'I didn't say you weren't honest, ma'am.' He stressed the word *ma'am* with an edge of sarcasm.

The owner came out from the back; he had noticed the hush and his clerk's loud voice. He came up to them, looking from one to the other. 'What's going on? Something wrong?'

The clerk, flushed with his own importance, hitched up his trousers and trying to impress his boss said, 'Everything's OK, Mr Bailey. This here half-breed is trying to sell ginseng.' He took a handful out of the sack and winked. 'It looks OK. I was about of offer her a couple bucks.'

Mr Bailey's eyes took in the bulging sack. 'I guess we could do that, Stanley.'

'A couple bucks?' Katherine gasped.

With that, Tom, who had finished his purchases at the other end of the store, came over, aware of the tension. He looked from Katherine to Bailey and back to Stanley. 'Is something wrong?'

Recognizing Tom as the Judge's handyman, he said, 'Naw, Tom don't concern yourself. Seems like this half-breed is selling ginseng!'

Tom looked at Katherine. 'Did you come to an agreement?'

She knew that Tom was the only friendly being here; soon he, too, would have that taunting look about his eyes, once he knew.

'He offered me a couple bucks. It's gotta be worth more than that! I was told—' She stopped and stared around helplessly.

Tom looked back and forth at the men: he knew their

game. In a threatening voice, he said loudly enough so that the men eavesdropping by the stove could hear without straining, 'It's the Judge's ginseng – it's prime wild and mature. I believe the going rate's about four dollars a pound. The Judge sent her; he was sure you'd want to buy it!'

'Of course, of course,' the clerk muttered. 'Why didn't she say so?' He heaved the sack on the scales. 'Looks like forty pounds we got here.'

'Yep,' Mr Bailey agreed. 'I gotta go in the back. I don't keep that much cash in front . . . I'll get her money.'

He returned, and seeing that Tom kept his hands in his pockets, reluctantly counted out 160 dollars into Katherine's hand.

'Didn't know the Judge sharecropped,' Bailey said to no one in particular. Looking directly at Tom he said, 'Give the Judge my best.'

'I'll do that,' Tom assured him.

They left together and the men rushed to the window to watch her climb awkwardly in the truck.

'I'll be damned,' they mumbled among themselves. 'He brought her out to his place. Never thought he'd do that to the Missus – especially after he found out about her . . . seen it with his own eyes. Well I'll be damned'. They knew they'd talk, but only among themselves. After all, Judge William Reardon was the richest man in the country, and no one, absolutely no one, would take a chance on offending him. They smirked and wondered about Justin; he was the only one who'd ever gone against the Judge – and the story was never clear. Some believed one side, some believed the other . . . but it still took a heap of nerve either way. Whether it was her choice or whether it was rape, she was still the Judge's whore, and Justin was the only one ever dared to get a piece of the Judge's pie. Most men respected Justin for it . . . yes, it took a whole heap of nerve. As for his accomplices, no one could really be sure who else had joined in that night.

134

To hear tell, most everyone male at the hotel that night did!

Outside in the sharp air, Katherine's head cleared a bit.

'I'm going to the grocer's – you need supplies too?' Tom said.

She counted out forty dollars and put it in her pocket, then she shoved the rest of the crumpled bills toward him. 'You give it to the Missus or the Judge or whoever should get it.'

He nodded and put the bills into his pocket and buttoned it, knowing he might be 120 dollars richer. He knew the Missus would never ask, and he felt sure the Judge didn't even know there was to be a payment arrangement. 'Hell,' he justified it in his mind. 'I've worked for them for ten years. They don't need it.'

In the grocer's, they went their separate ways. Katherine picked basic things that would last, like coffee, flour, sugar, salt. Her supplies mounted; she mentally went over what she needed to fix food. She was frugal, for she knew the land abounded in plenty. She could still hear Frieda's words: 'Plenty of food around here . . . free for the picking.'

They put their bundles in the truck and Tom said gruffly, 'You best wait here. I'm going to the hotel to wet my whistle. I won't be but an hour or so.'

She knew when he returned he would despise her like the others. She sat on the running board, but feeling cramped and restless, walked over to the bridge. She looked down at the swirling brown-green water. It was an ugly river – she remembered thinking that the first time she had seen it. She looked into its depths and wondered if her father was down there, caught on a branch. Instead of sadness at this end, if it were his, she could only know peace – for his search for the golden liquid that had made his life bearable would be over.

Staring at the water, she saw a leaf flutter down. It began to whirl slowly in an eddy that reached up to take it – the river seemed a greedy thing. She watched hypnotically as the eddy picked up momentum; the leaf spun and spun at a dizzying pace, then fingers seemed to reach up and pluck the leaf under to a secret place. Flashes of light reflected up from the water. Like a procession, another leaf fell to join the dance, then another. It seemed so simple to be swirled away into nothingness. She thought fearfully of the Oh mu; still the swirling water called her. She put one leg over the rail, then the other. She was inside the railing straining toward the water, her hands behind her twisted at a funny angle, still clinging to the iron rails. She looked down into the yawning depths; above her, a hawk shrieked in the gray autumn sky. She was as two. Her body yearned to throw itself into the hypnotic whirlpool; swaying outward, still her hands, as if they were welded, clung. It was her hands, against her will, that held on tightly. Then she knew that to do this she must incorporate the two wills within her. In order to kill herself and the child, she must be murderer and victim. She had been a victim all her life; she was comfortable with this. It was the murderer within her that she could not arouse to act. The victim within her was already down there, swirling away in the water . . . but that portion of her which must commit murder could not, and still she clung to the rail.

'Wait, wait! Stop!' he called, his voice carried by the wind, as he ran toward the bridge, breathless.

Tom reached for her. 'May God forgive you,' he hissed as he pulled her through the rail and marched her back to the truck. His face was flushed with anger. They rode in silence up the narrow road, where night was coming quickly.

Tom had heard the story from the men in the hotel. It was a lurid tale. He knew now that she had been the Judge's woman. He had felt uneasy at her coming; deep down, he knew she would change things. Even in the beginning he had had a bad feeling. God, how he wished the Judge would give Hannah and him their parcel of land. He had promised as much; the Judge was a man of his word, but the promise had been vague and long-standing. And he had believed it. But now he wished that he had the land; for he'd sell it and go to St Louis.

He said no words to Katherine on the long ride home, and when they arrived, he left her to carry the heavy sacks up to the cabin herself. He had not even acknowledged her thank you! Tom knew he wouldn't tell Hannah . . . the story was too grisly. Hannah never knew women like her even existed. He'd watch her, he'd keep a close eye on her. What else could he do?

Katherine's side pained by the time she reached the cabin. Rabelay joined her and took his usual spot by the stove, which was almost cold. She put logs in the fire, then crept into bed and fell asleep and dreamed of New Mexico and of playing child's games in the soft purple dusk at twilight at Me Maw's house.

The days, that fall, slipped by in an easy rhythm. William never contacted her, but from time to time she found books left on the doorstep. He often stood watching her from the window of the green room as she gathered nuts in the now-barren woods. She visited Hannah in the kitchen and once she had been summoned to cure the Missus' headache. On that occasion, remedy after remedy failed, until a vinegar-soaked rag was tied to Elizabeth's forehead and she lay quietly listening to symphony records. Elizabeth swore by the healing; thereafter it was never mentioned when Katherine would be leaving – it was taken for granted that she would stay. William, after receiving a queer visitation, decided to move into the green room on the north side of the house. He wondered about his own sanity, for the vision – dream – whatever it was, brought him joy, then agony. She came to him in the night, touching a cool hand to his forehead, laughing softly. He felt her hair brush his face and the warmth of her body . . . so real the pleasure of their lovemaking, her limbs smooth and warm around him. And afterwards, her fresh breath blew gently against his neck as they slept intertwined. More than once, he lurched from the bed and turned on the light; only yesterday he found one strand of hair, dark brown with a hint of auburn, on his pillow.

He watched her, by the stream, in the woods, on the path walking with his dog beside her. It was not this solemn woman who came to him in the night. No, it was the other – the Kathy whom he had known in Castlewood.

One cold morning in November, a stray cat came to the cabin. It was thin to the point of obscenity. Katherine picked it up and brought it in. It found the spot by the stove that had been Rabelay's. She noticed the bulging stomach on the otherwise emaciated animal. Before the week, it had had a litter of four kittens in the partially-filled woodbox. One did not last the day, and she buried it under the pines. The others were also tiny and malnourished, but they fought valiantly to live. Even the dog that came to visit did not disturb the mother, who groomed constantly their plain gray fur. Katherine asked the house-keeper for some canned milk, for now she no longer accompanied Tom to town for shopping; he merely took her list. Hannah thought this exceedingly kind of her husband – she didn't know the real reason. Hannah now accepted Katherine kindly in the month that she had been here. She had advised on different matters – her remedies succeeded. She was called when the canary did not sing, or when the hens would not lay. She had controlled Hannah's rheumatism, and the Missus swore by the headache cure. Hannah pronounced Katherine as someone God blessed with the healings. She swore by her.

Katherine kept busy; suddenly there was an unexpected frost, so she did not go to the house for several days, as the path had a glaze of ice. The trees glittered with coated frost. She grew large and clumsy and a pain in her back persisted. She worked over the stove, cooking tonics. She knew her time was near. There was a strange south wind that blew that day, and far into the night, bringing a smell of salt from the pool at Castlewood some twenty miles away – the pool that in winter was filled with barrels to bob and float and keep the concrete from cracking. It had been a curious day; birds had gathered, chattered nervously in the barren branches, and it was not a natural time. The cat had rolled over and smothered one of her kittens, and in a panic over the death smell she ran away and abandoned the other two. Katherine, awkward and heavy, knelt over the box with bread crusts, soaked in canned milk, and dripped droplets of milk into their demanding mouths. They bawled piteously, and moved constantly, looking for the security of their mother.

It was on this night that she took to her bed, knowing that the time was now. She put the dog outside and when his whining ceased, hoped he had gone home. She lay timing the pains; they began slowly and mounted to an excruciating pitch. Hours ticked by on the noisy clock. At the proper moment, she slid out of the bed with an inborn instinct, and squatted, holding fast to the bedpost, crouched over the clean towel that she had laid down. One enormous push and he came forth, in a rush, the afterbirth minutes behind. He lay motionless on the towel, a tiny child. She was tempted to cover him and leave him in silence. Without thought, she clutched his heels and held him upside down and smacked him one hard, stinging slap. He cried lustily. With her strong teeth, she severed the cord, and with a cloth, she wiped him clean.

Putting him on the bed, she crawled in beside him. He cried angrily. She was weak and dizzy . . . her stomach heaved, she felt tightness, then a hard cramp gripped her. To ease the pain she pushed, then realized. Again, she pushed and panted. It was minutes before he came onto the soiled towel, and she shrank back from it . . . in the dim light, she could not be sure. It glistened there on

the floor before her. It was another child, encased in a
glistening sack; he was born in a caul. She did nothing . . .
tiny fists tore through his veil and he cried on his own.
Finally she reached for him, and the sack fell from him
in a quivering, iridescent heap, gleaming wetly in the
candlelight. Exhausted, she slid back into bed, her breath
a harsh sound in the cabin. The sucking noises as the
babies nuzzled the cover looking for food seemed loud
as thunder. She rolled over on her back, drew one child
up to her breast; it nuzzled her and began sucking hungrily. She drew the second child up to her other breast; it
too searched through the warm flesh seeking her nipple,
and found it. At once a searing pain shot through her.
She tore the child away from her bosom, and saw the
blood on its lips. She looked down at her breast; the
nipple bled.

Putting him down, his scream a thin wail as she brought
the candle near, she wiped his mouth. She looked closer;
with a finger she separated his lips. What she saw there,
she could not believe! Her second son had a row of per-
fectly-formed teeth.

When the first child was satiated, she coaxed with her
finger milk into a clean glass. It nauseated her, as she
dripped droplets much in the same way that she had fed
the kittens. She could not bear to look at the yawning
pink mouth, gagging and grasping at the unfamiliar drops
of milk falling into its mouth; with a gurgling sound,
it swallowed. The babies slept; with its mouth closed, it
looked like the other one, but she had the distinct feeling
that they were one . . . *one*, not two separate beings. Their
skin was red, not olive; the down on their head was light
– they were William's sons. They seemed identical. It was
a vague thing that crept through her thoughts. She could
not place it. It belonged with her grandmother's forebod-
ings – of mirrors, of photographs, of things that looked
alike – the old Indians' fear of stolen souls. She lay there
and wished herself away. She came to him, lay by his side

in the cloistered bed in the green room, and tried to draw strength from him.

He must tell her what to do, yet he slept, turned and whispered her name, and she was still . . . for the gods would decide for her. Before daylight, she returned; she saw its yawning mouth and the obscenity of those wicked teeth. She rolled upon them and felt their death struggle beneath her – tiny fists pushing and squirming . . . much like the motion they had created while still within her body. It was the same, now they were outside her body. Then she rolled off and they gasped for air, and began pitiful screaming.

She fed them as before. She could not keep them . . . yet she could not abandon them on the orphanage steps. The gods would decide! The day slid by . . . they ate, they slept. She was in terror that someone would hear their cries. Looking at them as they slept, she knew feelings of love for her sons so strong, that she could not bear what she must do, yet still it stayed with her, *this eerie feeling, these strange thoughts and fears; what did it all mean?* It was like the iridescent sack – a transparency, as if one of them could be laid over the other, to make one whole. It was a crazy thought that came to her: perhaps Providence had planned it for the one who could eat – *perhaps his destiny was to devour the other?*

She looked into their faces and felt that love well up again, strong and flowing. Images seemed to swim before her, she was tired, so tired. She needed to sleep.

Afraid now that she would roll onto them, she looked around the room – safe – she must place them somewhere safe.

The clothes basket, of course! She emptied it, lined it with a pillow and placed the babies there. She covered them with her flannel gown and moved the basket closer to the stove. She saw their arms entwine as they slept peacefully. They were safe, she could rest.

Hours later their cries of hunger awakened her. She sat

up weakly and it came to her in a flash – the babies, the basket. She imagined bulrushes springing up, cushioning the basket – it was the answer, the only answer.

She took the first child to her breast and he drank greedily while the other wailed. To quiet him she offered him her finger and he sucked, he chewed – the pain was excruciating.

Satisfied at last, her first son slept; gently, she laid him on the bed.

Again she coaxed the milk from her breast and fed the second baby as she had done before, dripping the droplets of milk into his gaping mouth as he choked and swallowed. At last he too was satisfied, and she laid him alongside the other.

She made a strong tea, laced it with ginseng and sat at the table staring into the cup, thinking of the bulrushes. Could she do it? For their sake she had to. But in this short time the love, the well of protection that she felt for them was already endless. She had never felt a love like this, flesh of her flesh. In their creation she had seen once again one of God's many miracles.

Hearing a soft whine at the door, she got up and let Rabelay in. The dog sensed the excitement and went straight to the bed, where he nuzzled the blankets and washed the babies with a tender tongue. They stirred.

'No – here, boy' she coaxed, and reluctantly he left the infants and came to her. She patted his head absently, thinking of the babies, the bulrushes . . . she must make him understand.

The dog's brown eyes sought hers. She stared down into their depths, and knew he would help her. He did understand; from the first moment there had been a communion.

She did not allow herself to think as she made the preparations. She found a hollow log, gathered moss and fern and soft green willows – she could not chance cloth, it might be recognized. She would lay them in the log, cover them as best she could, and Rabelay would help her. He would watch over them and deliver them safely.

She sat on the floor, searched the animal's eyes and spoke to him in that silent language. Then she took the blanket that had covered the babies and held their scent out to him; he sniffed.

They sat mute for over an hour. Her concentration, her message – they were so important! Her nose bled and huge splashes fell into her lap but still she held his gaze and he absorbed her command. Then, satisfied that he was ready, she resumed her preparations. She unwound the rags in which she had swaddled her babies, and the coolness of the leaves made them cry out. She settled them in the hollow of the log, covering them with the greenery she had gathered and began her journey to the creek. Rabelay followed, running back and forth between her and the water. The importance of his task rendered him impatient.

She stopped at the edge of the lapping waters and held the babies' garments out to him. He inhaled their scent again, then she offered him the corner of her cape. 'William. They are William's,' she told the dog. 'Protect them. Save them. They are William's.' She grabbed the scruff of the animal's neck and stared deeply into his eyes again, sending her message, her command one last time.

She waded into the freezing river to test the log. It floated perfectly; the current was already tugging at it, drawing it away. She could not look at her sons' sleeping faces, already so dear to her. She stood there poised, clinging, resisting the water's flow until somehow she found the strength to let go.

Rabelay ran along the bank barking urgently; he plunged in and out of the water nudging the log, steering its progress. Katherine ran breathless through the trees, prepared to jump in if there was a mishap. Her heart almost stopped with fear when Rabelay veered from the creek and went on ahead, to bark and scratch at Hilltop's back door.

She was about to dive in and retrieve her sons when a

light came on in the house, and the back door opened. She crouched down, peering out through the leaves and saw Rabelay again in the water guiding the log as Tom hauled it in with a long-handled net.

*They were safe!* The beat of her heart seemed to sing the phrase. They were safe-safe-safe . . . her babies were safe!

Still hiding in the woods, Katherine saw more lights go on in the house, one by one. Later, a car drove up the long driveway, and from her view through the trees, she saw them leave – the doctor, the Judge and his wife, and they took with them two bundles wrapped in blankets.

In the big house alone, Tom cursed his wife. 'You fool, look what you've done! Now they have two sons.'

Katherine didn't know how long she sat there, but Hilltop was quiet again now and dark, as if nothing special had happened that night. Somewhere an owl called and she suddenly realised how cold she was. Wearily she went back to the cabin, an ache of emptiness within her. She took comfort in only one thing, her gift to William. These were the sons he had yearned for – sons with golden tomorrows full of promise, and she hoped with all of her heart that she could stay here and watch them grow and flourish like two strong trees. She would do whatever she could to remain; just to be near them had to be enough.

Katherine stayed in her cabin, tending the kittens, holding their tiny gray bodies close to her, as if they could replace what she had given away. She walked the small space of the floor, ate and slept in an erratic pattern. Three days had passed when Rabelay came whining and scratching at her door. Opening it, she saw he held a wad of paper in his slobbering jaws. She took it from him, unrolled the lined notepaper and read the brief note.

*Dear Katherine,*

*I know the path is icy, but please come to the house. I have important news.*

*Hannah*

She dressed in the hand-me-downs from Elizabeth and the dress fitted her loosely now, the hem high, as Elizabeth was a much shorter woman.

Rabelay sniffed the kittens, and pushed them about with his nose. They took no fright of the large animal. Shutting the cabin door tightly against the wind, carefully she started down the icy path. On reaching the kitchen at the big house, Hannah opened the door. She was animated and excited. 'Sit down. Oh Katherine, something wonderful has happened!'

She served a hot lemon tea with fresh cinnamon rolls. She stirred her tea, ate a bun, yet still did not speak. Finally, she held forth a square cardboard note.

'It's the Missus' birth announcements. She had twin boys!' Her face glowed with euphoria.

Katherine took the card, drew in a sharp breath, then carefully read the announcement: twin boys named Ryan and Kyle Reardon. With relief she said, 'I didn't know the Missus was expecting.'

Hannah looked down, not wanting to meet her eyes. 'Most didn't. She wanted to keep it a secret, after the other times when her two sons died – or I guess I should say, they never lived. Both were stillborn.'

'Oh, I see.'

Hannah continued: 'Tom's in town buying drinks for everyone. It's the Judge's treat. I thought you had such a nice hand, maybe you could help me address the cards.'

'Oh yes, ma'am, I'd be glad to.'

'There's no use in calling me ma'am, so formal-like. Just Hannah will be fine.'

They finished their tea, and Hannah prepared a place in the library. It was the first time Katherine had seen the other rooms in the house. She knew – but did not know how she knew – the green room upstairs. If pressed, she could describe every stick of furniture and everything in the room.

They sat by the large marble fireplace, each with their

list. Hannah felt better now that someone was in the house with her. It had been a strange time – the day the birds had gathered and chattered, and those two babies had been found floating down the creek like Moses. Something out of the ordinary was happening. Tom had warned her not to be a silly gossiping woman; he had put the money in the bank, and said that the Judge and the Missus deserved their loyalty. There was more talk of which acreage they would be getting.

'Where are they now?' Katherine asked. She realized she had unconsciously been listening for the cry of babies.

'Oh, they're still in the hospital in St Louis. They have to stay another week. It seems that one boy needed minor surgery, but it was nothing serious.'

The Judge and his Missus had a wide circle of acquaintances. The women wrote the names plain, and put stamps on the announcements. Tom would be going back to town to mail them in the morning.

'Workmen are coming tomorrow, to fix and paper the rooms,' Hannah confided. 'Each boy is havin' his own room. Seems the Missus got upset, for the Judge wouldn't give up the green room. Kinda silly, as that room's not special, but he wouldn't hear of it. I can't wait to see what fancy fittens she bought. The decorators from Scruggs, Vandervoots and Barney in St Louis will be out, too. The Missus, she wants the best of everything for her sons. Seems a nurse will be coming back with 'em, to care of 'em. Good thing, really. Tom said they can't be expectin' nursemaid care, too. I'm only the housekeeper.'

They addressed the cards and talked, and the dog walked back and forth from the kitchen, as if expecting someone.

Hannah held up a card. 'This here Mrs Brookshire, she's the Missus' sister living way up in Cincinnati. Sad, she's a widow with a new baby – little girl named April.'

While the housekeeper was busy chattering small talk, the secret in her fluttered and wished to be said out loud, but she remembered Tom's words and the Reardons' summoning them to the library for Tom and she to lay their hands on the Bible and swear that the secret would remain locked in their breast, and from that day on she made herself believe the lie . . . 'What a miracle, after all this time and two stillborn sons lying in the churchyard, our Mrs Reardon has been blessed with two healthy sons.'

Hannah looked for every reason to ask Katherine up to the house. Truth was, she didn't like being there alone. The owl that had been by the kitchen window came back each night, and she didn't like it, not one bit. She was a sensible, sane woman without much imagination, but an uneasiness clung to her; she felt better with people in the house. She loved the workmen running up the stairs, stopping in the kitchen for mugs of hot coffee. She even liked the effeminate man with the paisley scarf who put on airs and ran around with sketches under his arm – he brought his own tea, a special blend from China. He used her water and with all the excitement, she didn't have much time to think.

Katherine became acquainted with the large, twelve-room house. She saw Elizabeth's vanity in all the fine possessions; she worried that the babies would join the ranks of things Elizabeth owned, but it was far better than to wonder your life through, and make up stories of gypsies and stolen children. She knew now and forever her son . . . *why did she always think of him as one?* Her sons were Reardons: the small, expensive announcements said they were.

The work was finished in a week, and on Friday, 5 December 1941, the twins came home to Hilltop accompanied by a nanny who would not let anyone near them.

# CHAPTER 16

Two days later, the air around Castlewood and the surrounding county came alive with the shriek of sirens, and church bells rang – each bell blending with another over the Missouri foothills. They rang incessantly and did not quit. Their frantic sound sent Katherine running down the hill to the house.

Hannah, crying, answered the door. 'It's the war. Listen, we're at war,' and she scooped Katherine in and they sat by the radio. 'It's President Roosevelt. We're at war. Japan has attacked American troops at Pearl Harbor.'

It was two weeks after that horrendous day that Frieda came. She had hired a cab all the way to Castlewood . . . she even made it wait! First, she stopped at the big house, but Hannah sent her up the hill to the cabin. Katherine answered the door to her. She grabbed her and hugged her, and the older woman allowed this. 'Katherine . . . I can't stay. I've a cab waitin'.'

'A cab?'

'Yes. I had to bring you this letter that came for you, and ask if you want to go with me to St Louis. They're hiring men, women and boys to work in the war plants. Why, Ama Tarp in St Louis have already hired me. They make torpedoes – pay good money. It's a chance to be a person . . . no one's servant no more.' She reached up and touched her barren ears, where the cameos no longer glittered. 'I left 'em behind. Women, we sell ourselves too cheap. We shouldn't have had to sell ourselves at all, but times were hard.'

Katherine knew what she was saying, but she heard a different drummer. She heard the beat of her sons' hearts and knew she couldn't leave them. Someday they would need her, and so would William. She had not sold herself to William. She belonged to him . . . and he to her. 'I can't go. I really don't want to go,' she told the older woman.

Frieda knew the girl was different from most. She looked around the cabin. It belonged to a different time – but then so did Katherine. She looked down at the letter that the young woman now held. 'Aren't you gonna open it?'

Katherine saw her father's scrawled handwriting and felt relieved that he wasn't down there, caught on a branch in the river. Nevertheless she lifted the grating on the stove and fed the letter to the fire, which licked hungrily at the edges and soon devoured the paper.

She didn't need to know; her destiny was here, she knew that now.

The war and talk of the war made Tom restless. He heard of lucrative work in town, in the factories, yet because of the promise of the land that would someday be his, he stayed at Hilltop. Resentment boiled a cauldron within him and he began stealing fifty dollars a week out of the grocery money. It was too much; babies and a nanny and now Bruce the dummy had been released from the hospital. Because of the Judge's generosity to others, a blind man would soon be stumbling around Hilltop, and because of the woman in the cabin, the blind man would be in the house! It was too much. He dreamed of blackmailing the Judge. He knew he wouldn't do it, but he felt so angry. All this fuss – decorators, announcements, lies and more lies – because of two bastard brats, floating in the creek. If Hannah hadn't seen them, and if that damned dog hadn't kicked up such a row, he would have let them float. He enjoyed the thought . . . one more mile on the river and they would have been at the mercy of the current, sucked in and down. It wasn't fair! Hannah and he had been faithful servants . . . and now two bastards had moved in and taken over. When he laid the fire in the Judge's study, he saw all the legal papers that lied. Someday if he got mad enough, or drunk enough, he'd tell. The hell with it. They had everything, and Hannah and he were relegated to the kitchen.

It wasn't four months later that the nanny quit and Elizabeth Reardon frantically called the agencies, only to be told there wasn't anyone who wanted domestic work. The women were all in the war-plants making fabulous money.

That was the day she sent for Katherine!

# CHAPTER 17

After degrading lessons in hygiene and much fuss over the fitting of uniforms, Elizabeth gave up. The black uniform looked like a French maid's – in it even the plain girl looked seductive – and the white one was too much like a nurse's uniform. She didn't want anyone to think her sons frail! The pastel ones resembled those worn by waitresses in the fast-food restaurants that were springing up everywhere. No, none of these would do.

Instead, Tom took them into town, and in St Louis Elizabeth selected Katherine's wardrobe of plain dresses, skirts and blouses. She had to look decent. When they went anywhere with the children, their nanny had to look ordinary and not stand out. Satisfied at last, they returned to Hilltop. It was five months since Katherine had seen her sons.

The boys had adjacent nurseries with interconnecting doors. Each room contained a maple canopy crib, one with blue fabric, the other with green. Each room had a rocker, bassinet and chest of drawers; already a year too soon the rooms were fitted with elaborate hobby horses, toyboxes brimming with plush teddy bears and wind-up toys of every description.

Elizabeth chattered incessantly as they climbed the curved staircase to the nurseries. Katherine followed on legs that felt like rubber. So many times during those early months, she had sat with Hannah in the kitchen and heard their cries somewhere in the house: it had taken all of her strength to resist them, to block them out. She had wanted to run to them then, as she wanted to now. She had pictured them so often in her mind, their dear little faces, yet she did not really know what to expect. She had parted with two tiny newborns, but what would they look like at five months old?

Elizabeth showed her to a small room that was alongside the nurseries – this would be hers. It was only when she heard the final click of the door closing, leaving her alone, that Katherine found the courage to tiptoe to the crib.

Her heart leapt to her throat with happiness. The child lay on his side, one plump thumb still caught in his rosebud lips. He stirred and his pink cheeks moved with the motion of sucking, only to stop after a moment, deep in sweet sleep once more. She had to hold him, it had been so long.

She reached for the precious bundle. He squirmed slightly until he settled into her and she felt the faint, quiet rhythm of his heart beating against hers. She caressed the firmness of her baby's body and thrilled as she ran her cupped hand over the yellow down of his perfect head; it felt like a peach not yet ripe. Holding her cherished child she tiptoed to the next room.

Shifting awkwardly, she lifted the second sleeping baby. Alike, they were so alike! Even their closed lashes were blond against their fair cheeks. William lived in these miniature faces, the stamp of the nose, the curve of the mouth, the high broad forehead. Oh, they were beautiful, her babies. God, how she had missed them.

Lowering herself into the rocker, she rocked slowly and hummed quietly to the sleeping babies. The emotion was exquisite. She was filled to the brim with love and happiness and she gathered their warmth closer, reminding herself not to hold them too tightly.

It was either their touch or her deep emotion which created it, for later she noticed the stain on her dress. Her milk had dried up months ago but now it was as if her breasts yearned to feed them. Her milk flowed but she knew she must not feed them that way, it would be too dangerous. She would bind herself, hide the tell-tale stains, for no one must know.

When the babies awoke she undressed them, for she needed to see the perfection of their limbs and reassure herself that her sons were perfect. Gratefully she saw that they were.

Over and over she caressed the velvet of their skins, cooing softly to them and only when she rang Hannah to bring up their warm bottles did she remember.

She offered the bottle to the first baby, and saw that he had two tiny teeth just breaking through his bottom gum. Then the second child anxiously took his bottle and he had only one small tooth. Both of their upper gums were smooth, no sign of any teeth.

The Judge had hired the most skillful surgeon money could buy. Neither child had a noticeable scar where the teeth had been removed. She would never know which one. She tried to imagine that it had never been! They took to her, and she nursed them through colic and other childhood discomforts; she loved them both with a fierce, protective love. She was happy and these were the times when she could forget her grandmother's warnings that some were born under an unlucky star.

The Judge doted on the infants, but his work kept him away a great deal of the time. He bought the swim club at Castlewood, as the owner joined the army. He now owned land and fields for almost twenty miles square. He knew she was their mother, and sometimes in the quiet nursery as she rocked them, he thanked her with his eyes. Yet she was strange to him. Their love had been another place, another time, and he could scarce imagine that he had lain with her and loved her so. It was the other that became more real; he no longer worried or wondered about it. It came like a dream, and if that is

what it was, so be it ... Time stood still in that place
and she laughed and loved and chattered in his ear and
sometimes when he awoke he could still hear her singing
in a voice that he had only heard in the boat on the
river with the mallards flying overhead in a V. It was a
hallucination or illusion; whatever it was, it was more
real to him at times than his waking life. And in truth, he
aged, but there in that place, he did not.

# CHAPTER 18

The pool at Castlewood, like everything the Judge
touched, made money! Soldiers came, handsome and
young, with girls clinging to them, their eyes starry. It
was a frantic time, with lovers leaving, and the club grew
crowded with men in uniforms who stayed late on the
summer nights to dance under the lanterns.

The pool closed on Mondays. That's when Elizabeth
took Katherine and the year-old babies to enjoy the solitude of the place. After all, they owned it. Those summer
days, Tom loaded up the car and drove the two women
and children to Castlewood. He stayed in town and
played cards and drank at the hotel and only occasionally
was it ever mentioned, the curiosity of the two women
being together. The war, the excitement of the times –
they were far more interesting topics than the two-year-
old rape of the Judge's whore.

Elizabeth's health was still pronounced delicate by the
doctors, who heartily approved of the salt-water bathing.
It would improve her constitution – they were sure of it.

The boys grew tan and sturdy and their light hair was
bleached almost white by the sun. Their blue-gray smiling
eyes, just like their father's, looked deep into Katherine's
and she was glad that nothing of her showed in their
shining faces to link them with her. They had already
taken to murmuring words; they pronounced Dada and
Mama clearly, but when coaxed to say her name, they
could not. One day, she was not sure which, proudly on

157

small babies' tongues, stumbling over the word Katherine, it came out 'Kack', and she was called that ever after. Curious, her mother's nickname repeating itself, one thousand miles away, and separated by seventeen years. Soon they both took to calling her in a sing-song manner, Kack . . . Kack . . . Kack . . . pleased with themselves and pleased with the word.

The summer came round when the twins were three years old. Elizabeth's widowed sister Jenny arrived on the train from Cincinnati to spend the summer with them, bringing her daughter, who was almost the same age as the twins. April was a pretty child with fair skin, brown hair that curled, and clear blue eyes that leaned to violet. Elizabeth, the perfect hostess, had their room painted lilac and saw that they spent a happy summer. It became a ritual. Jenny came with the girl every summer. Elizabeth told the Judge that the girl's presence would help the boys get some manners; she was unused to roughness and when they became too active, she looked for Kack to take them away and somehow settle them down.

Those summers the sisters played with their children, Elizabeth never told Jenny of the boys' unusual circumstances of birth. At times they even talked of their pregnancies, and Elizabeth could almost imagine their births. They compared term, and how easy or difficult, and Elizabeth spoke of her real pregnancies which, to her, had always culminated in the birth of these two boys.

She had shrunk from the Biblical names that William had originally suggested, for they would have always reminded her . . . She purged the bulrushes from her mind and felt glad that her sons had been given modern names. Ryan and Kyle seemed to go with the times.

As the twins grew older, Kack moved back to her cabin. She found time once more to gather herbs, to mix potions – and every fall she hunted the manroot. This life suited her. The woods turned up animals – hurt, sick, or abandoned, and she made cages of rush for them. Most times a creature was an occupant of one of the cages to be let go when it had healed or mended. Bradley was the boys' friend who wished more than anything to be a doctor when he grew up. Often he even came alone to the cabin carrying some wounded creature, and implored Kack: 'Make it well.' He watched as she brewed potions and applied compresses and left the patient in the rush cage, covered, explaining, 'They feel safer when it's dark.' But of her sons she knew them to be very different. Kyle had a touch for machinery; he got a camera for his eighth birthday. As he was left-handed, William had a custom-made camera sent all the way from the Orient. Elizabeth scolded the Judge, for she felt Kyle too young, yet he showed remarkable talent. He climbed the trees and took aerial pictures, and was often to be found in his darkroom in the cellar. Kyle was like the Judge; he had a presence. Everyone liked him, for he knew what to say, and he charmed with an aplomb far beyond his age. He was a sharp bargainer, too; he often sold or traded with Tom for things, and always got the best end of the bargain by far.

Ryan was more solemn, more at home with himself. One time in the woods Katherine saw him, perched on one bended knee . . . while a foot away stood a doe frozen in motion. She knew the child was in communion with the beast. The doe's large liquid eyes were caught in his spell, yet the animal did not tremble with fear; she knew him, and he, her. He had the magic.

Later, he had shown the picture he'd painted in water colors of the doe, so life-like, the picture near breathed. Seeing his talent, Elizabeth sent for an art tutor. The man stayed for several weeks and accepted the exorbitant fee he was given, yet he knew that he had taught the boy nothing. Ryan already knew line, form and color, and shading, and of all media he preferred painting the creatures and catching their likeness, in a moment of time suspended. He made them live!

The summer Ryan was twelve he grew annoyed at his mother's bragging and would not pick up pencil or brush; he said he was no longer interested in drawing. Yet Kack saw him in the forest, lying on the branches of the oak above the river, some creature caught in his gaze . . . his eyes taking him within, to understand, to breathe, to be . . .

The locusts had come in a swarm that summer, as they did once every seventeen years, but aside from this event it was a typically leisurely June and in a day or so the holiday visitors would arrive. The twenty-mile ride back from the train station at Castlewood was awkward and strained for the children. Elizabeth had reminded the boys at least a dozen times to mind their manners and had insisted they wear ties; now they squirmed in their seats in the car, shooting April dirty looks as if it were somehow her fault. The women chatted easily about clothes, child-rearing and even recipes, which Elizabeth knew nothing about. The children were all twelve that summer; there was talk of a combined birthday party. The Judge drove in silence, and outside the car, the persistent 'zzz' of the cicadas in the woods filled the soft dusk.

At the last turn, the house appeared as it always did, sitting atop the hill, majestic among the trees. Jenny and the girl were given the same room; already the vacation was spreading itself, smoothing out the perpetual crease of worry on Jenny's forehead. She had been ill of late; raising a child alone in the city was not easy. The war had been over for some time. It was impossible getting work that she could do, now that she had frequent asthma attacks. She felt grateful to her sister and the Judge for their generosity at Christmas and at Easter when they sent substantial checks which helped her raise the girl. To Jenny, it seemed as if Elizabeth had grown stronger, and that it was she who was delicate now. She survived on social security money and her late husband's small pension. Although she knew that Castlewood with all its vegetation could bring on her asthma, she couldn't deprive April. Here she could run and play in the sunshine with her cousins and have a wonderful vacation.

On arrival they were served a cold supper in their rooms as the long train ride had been exhausting.

They rose early the next day, and Jenny dressed April in blue jeans and a plaid cotton blouse. She was a beautiful child. Her dark hair curled about her peach-soft face, her blue, almost violet eyes, were very bright and alert, and usually smiling.

'Mama, I wish we could stay here always,' she said as she flung herself into her mother's arms.

Jenny held her daughter tightly. 'I know, I know, but don't go spoiling the summer wishing for things you cannot have. Child, be grateful we have three months . . . ninety glorious days!'

'Oh Mama, I have so much fun here.'

'That's good, honey!'

Elizabeth knocked softly, then came in. 'What a beautiful sight, Jenny – you're so lucky. Boys won't let you hold them or hug them.' They laughed, knowing it was true, and absent-mindedly Elizabeth picked up a silver hairbrush and began grooming April's hair, twirling the curls around her little finger. 'I do so wish I had a precious little girl to fuss over,' she said, almost to herself. 'Of course, I'm so lucky to have the boys.'

Then she gave April a kiss and hugged her hard. 'Run along, honey, the boys are in the kitchen waiting for you. Hannah's made pancakes with blueberries.' It was difficult to tell the twins apart, as they were identical. Their hair had darkened since they were tow-headed babies. Now close-cropped, it was a very light brown. They had strong, square jaws, with deep blue eyes that seemed to change at times to gray; each boy had a sprinkling of freckles over his cheeks. They were handsome lads. At the table they gulped their milk and swirled the pancakes

161

around in the syrup, paying no attention to Hannah's running dialogue. They ignored April, angry that their mother said she must tag along. After finishing breakfast, Ryan said sullenly, 'Let's go,' to her. Trying to act agreeable, April asked, 'Where are we going?'

'Fishing. We're going to the river.'

'OK,' she answered, and skipped and hurried along after them, breathless. The pole they handed her caught in the bushes, and every so often she had to stop to untangle the line, again running quickly to catch up with them. The river seemed sluggish today; the murky water had a scum atop it and occasionally you could see a small eddy.

Kyle looked at his cousin and said, 'Don't be going so slow. If you're tired already, we're not stopping. Ryan always picks the spot. He always knows where it's good.'

April was patient with them; she knew it took a day or so until the boys stopped acting so smart-alecky and would accept her. It happened every year . . . and then they would become fast friends, and at the end of the summer it was hard for them to part.

She trailed behind them to a narrow bend. Ryan stopped by a sycamore tree whose soil had eroded. The tree tipped over at a crazy angle and grew horizontally above the water, its leaves touching the surface.

'This is good,' Ryan stated. 'Catfish almost always hang around here.' Taking the fresh night-crawlers that Tom had dug for them, they baited their hooks. Each child picked a spot and cast into the river, careful not to tangle lines with each other.

The sun beat down warmly on their backs; a bee buzzed in the air near them, and birds calling in the bush made it a typical summer day. Within fifteen minutes Ryan shouted. He swung the pole behind him and a large catfish flopped on the bank.

'It's really a big one,' April said with admiration.

'Watch it . . . don't get too close. They can stick you real bad with their whiskers,' he warned.

Expertly he retrieved the hook and put the fish on his line. He allowed the catfish to slip back into the water, tethered. After a time, Kyle grew restless. He moved his spot twice and began whistling.

'Shut up! You can't whistle when you're fishing, it scares 'em away,' Ryan cautioned.

As he baited his hook and resumed his statue-like posture, squatting patiently on the bank, April imitated his rigid style, staring at her hook, which seemed to move, but it was only the motion of the waves. An unproductive half hour passed. A persistent horsefly hovered around them, landing first on one then another. They swatted at it, but it kept on returning.

Ryan pulled in his second fish – another cat slightly smaller than the first.

Suddenly Kyle yelled at April, 'Watch it, dummy, you got a bite!' Too late, she jerked the pole up; her hook was bare and she felt embarrassed.

'You didn't catch anything either,' was her retort to Kyle, who was growing bored and jealous of his brother's catch.

'Who cares?' Kyle answered.

Kyle didn't really like fishing very much. His brother always knew the best spots and always caught the most fish. Kyle hated losing, and whenever they finished, he felt he always lost, although Ryan never made it a contest. It seemed like one to his brother. Twice, Ryan asked him to stop moving so much or talking so much, and finished by saying, 'Why don't you pick another spot?' Kyle moved away from them, but they could still hear the noise of him rustling through the bushes.

In a few minutes, they heard him holler. They looked around but didn't see him. The annoying sounds continued. Finally Ryan spotted him. Kyle had crawled out along the trunk of the sycamore, and was way out in the flimsy branches which would have been the top of the tree if it had been upright. The branches dipped and swayed dangerously over the water.

'Kyle, come back, darn you. Come back! You know about the river.'

'I'm not scared of the river,' he taunted, glad now that he was the center of attention. And as he shouted, the branches bent lower toward the water.

'Stop it! Come back right now.'

'You can't make me,' was Kyle's answer.

With the distraction, Ryan had been holding his pole lightly. In that moment of inattention, something snapped at his bait, jerking the pole right out of his hand. He watched as it slid into the water, bobbing up and down, and then disappeared quickly into the stream.

'Now you did it! See what you made me do? I lost my pole,' Ryan screamed furiously, and without thinking he began scaling the sycamore trunk, crawling out toward his brother, all the while threatening, 'Now you're gonna get it.'

Kyle catcalled, 'Well, I guess you're not scared like April.' He jeered now that he had his brother mad, and he tried teasing her.

Ryan crawled on the precarious tree toward his brother. Now that he had started for him, he couldn't imagine just what he would do, out on that swaying tree.

'I'm not scared neither,' April said, and to prove it she laid her pole down, secured it with a rock, and she, too, started climbing on the leaning trunk.

From the steep bank where the tree grew, it did not seem high up, but over the water it felt very high. The bark was peeling in many places and the smooth white trunk made her feet slip as she crept along. She looked down and told herself she wasn't scared of the river neither. But April, like the boys, had always been told to never, never wade or swim in the river. She had promised never to and so had they . . . but they weren't, they were only climbing above it. As the trunk tapered and slimmed down, she, crawling on all fours, didn't look ahead. See couldn't look behind, either. She could only look down, and that's when she felt it – the first raindrop. Everything darkened as the sudden summer shower began. Now the tree shook violently as Ryan reached his brother, and with one hand they slapped out at one another. As her cousins fought, April felt her feet slipping. Her leather shoes would not stay on the wet trunk. She tried to hold on, but her hands, too, were wet. Then she lost her grip and she was falling down, down about twenty feet, and she landed on her back, which knocked the wind out of her. Swiftly she sank into the water. Her eyes opened. She could only see the darkness of the water; she could not swim. Fear was in complete possession of her. When she bobbed up she clutched futilely at the air, only to sink again and have her mouth filled with the murky water. Above her head she heard their frightened voices. She sank again, deeper; she saw a floating log drift nearby. If she could only reach it. Her arms flayed frantically as she tried to swim toward it. Miraculously she reached the log, and with both hands grasped it. It rolled over, sending her head down again under the water. Then she saw them – a mass of wriggling snakes, water moccasins . . . lazily at first swimming away, then slowly turning around, reluctant to leave their log home. Fear was now a wild thing. For a second she thought someone had reached her, as she felt something clutching at her ankles, sucking, pulling violently. It was the undercurrent. Like a strong wet wind it tugged, taking her under, the fingers of the current urgent and cruel. Her head bumped on a log and it took her down further to the bottom. Her lungs filled with water. She heard the long, slow peal of a church bell tolling in her head. *Bong . . . bong . . . bong . . .* slowly it rang with a measured beat. She was so tired now that her arms and legs, leaden, could not fight anymore against the current's incredible strength. So her journey continued. It tugged, pulled, tossed her. She heard the continuous toll of the bells and was so tired now and at peace. She was a leaf, a bit of debris that created no resistance. Miraculously, the current rushed her to the bend, where the river tossed her out. She lay spent on the rocks, then rolled over and vomited. Her body was racked with choking as she turned her head, gasping at the precious air. In the distance she heard them calling her, but she couldn't answer. She could not tell how long till they came upon her. She heard Kyle crying and making promises to God as he knelt by her while Ryan ran the mile back to get help.

# CHAPTER 19

The near-tragedy sent Elizabeth to bed with migraine and nerves. Her tiny frame was bolstered up in bed with mounds of pillows, three under her head and one at each side where her pale, freckled arms lay supported in an unnatural position. She insisted that this made her feel better.

The wooden ceiling fan droned insistently and a gentle breeze stirred in the room. Ringing the bell for Hannah, she alternated her requests between iced tea, coffee, lemonade, ice water. She worried that the Judge would blame her for the incident. Nothing would soothe her. Finally she requested that Hannah send for Kack to bring a tonic.

Hannah knew that this was one of those times when the Missus either wouldn't or couldn't cope. She was glad for Kack's calm presence in the house. Kack brewed a mixture of herbs and ginseng in a tea, and before taking it up, Hannah laced the pot with a generous dash of brandy. Sleeping, Elizabeth would be less trouble. God knows she wasn't any help awake.

Katherine inquired after April. Hannah told her that the doctor said she was out of danger. He had prescribed sedatives, saying the child needed to rest. She mentioned that Jenny was still by her bedside and had been there all night, watchful and praying, thanking God that her daughter was safe.

Together, they went to the room. Exhaustion was in every line on Jenny's face. Between them, Katherine and

Hannah convinced her that she, too, needed to rest. Katherine offered to continue the vigil. Finally, Jenny consented and went to her room, where she fell into a troubled sleep.

It was noon before April stirred. Katherine reached over and tenderly smoothed back the tangled curls from her damp forehead. 'You're safe now,' she assured her.

Puzzled, but remembering the horror, April struggled weakly to sit up, looking around the room as if seeing it for the first time.

'Your mother sat here all night watching you. She was very tired, so she went to sleep now. If you want her, I can get her,' Katherine said.

Usually an obedient child, April remembered that they had disobeyed in a very serious matter. 'Is she mad – real mad?' she questioned.

'She's happy that you're safe,' Kack told her.

The child began to cry – soft, gulping sounds. 'We didn't mean it. We didn't mean to be bad, honest we didn't.'

'I know. Hush now, it's up to you to rest and feel better.'

'What's gonna happen?' the child persisted.

'I said hush. Don't you worry about that. Doctor said you should rest. The boys have been sent to the attic until the Judge comes home.'

Between sobs, April continued, 'It was Kyle – it was his fault, all his fault. The Judge should whip him good. But my mama never spanks me. I bet she will this time. I know it,' and she continued wailing.

Her voice firm now, Kack began, 'Doctor said—'

'I'm tired of resting,' April sobbed. 'Can I get up now?'

'If you feel strong enough.'

April swung her feet over the side of the bed; her head swam with a short spasm of dizziness. When it passed, she stood up. Her legs felt like rubber. Kack steadied her and helped her to the bathroom. She left her there, telling her to wash her face and brush her hair.

As Kack was laying out fresh clothing, she heard Hannah banging on the doors. 'Come quick – it's Kyle! He's in one of those spells.'

Both women bolted down the hall. Elizabeth stood in the doorway, swaying unsteadily, wringing her hands. 'Oh, why isn't the Judge here? He'd know what to do.'

Hannah calmed her. 'I've already called the doctor. Kack's here, she knows what to do. She's seen it before.' She patted Elizabeth's hand, leading her mistress back to her bedroom. She would only be in the way.

Ryan stood by the bed, a look of pure terror on his face as he fanned his brother, who lay there as if dead. Kyle's face was bloodless. His cheekbones stretched out prominently, shimmering, and there was a strange gray glow to his skin. His waxen lips, like some Hallowe'en novelty, were drawn back over his teeth.

Katherine was struck by the contrast. Ryan, his cheeks rosy, the nervous jitter as he juggled one foot up and down, arms strong and brown as he fanned his brother.

Taking the fan, she gently pushed him down into the bedside chair. 'He'll be fine,' she promised the terrified boy.

Leaning over Kyle, she spoke softly. 'It's OK, you'll be fine.' She stroked his forehead, massaged his temples. 'Close your eyes,' she said. They stared up, glazed and unfocused. With cool fingers, she lowered the lids on the unseeing eyes. 'Breathe deeply,' she commanded. Then, pressing on his chest, as if resuscitating him, she continued the motion. 'Calm, Kyle. You're calm. You're breathing deeply.' She leaned over and blew into his mouth, straightening up over him.

Her voice droned on, chant-like. Within her own breast she kept the panic at bay.

Now massaging his hands, she continued, 'Calm . . . breathe deep and slow. You're calm . . . you're fine.' She stared at the boy, her eyes fierce, willing it to be so, when beneath her was but a fragile shell. Life, movement,

A. N. Steinberg

childhood, had deserted him and left behind a form – a head, two arms, a wooden-like torso and two legs rigid as stone. The only spark of life seemed to be in the waxen eyelids that fluttered like a dying butterfly. Behind her she heard the jiggle of Ryan's foot agitatedly tapping the floor, and the harsh sound of Hannah's nervous cough.

She willed her own panic to still. She had seen it before, in Ryan, in Kyle; each of them had endured it.

This 'draining' of the twins was inexplicable. Dr Martin could find no cause, no explanation, but Katherine knew – she knew. Still, she chanted and willed him to come back to be. The organdy curtains blew in a welcome breeze, a clock ticked like a steady heartbeat, and within the hour the metamorphosis took place. Kyle's cheeks refilled with color, perspiration beaded on his forehead, heat replaced the coolness, the limbs fell into relaxation. Whatever had gripped him had fled.

He opened his eyes and looked around. 'I'm sick of being in bed. Can I get up now?' he asked.

With a surge of relief, she nodded her consent. She felt weak, spent. Once more it hadn't happened and Katherine was grateful for Hannah, who took charge again.

'You stay right in this room, young man. Dr Martin's on his way.' As if to prove her point, the doorbell rang at that very moment.

'Rats – I'm not sick! I hate that old geezer, poking sticks down my throat and junk. Hannah, do I have to?'

'Yes, you do.'

'Him, too.' Kyle gloated and pointed to Ryan. 'If he's here to look at me, he's gonna check you, too.'

'I'll let him in,' Katherine offered. As she passed Elizabeth's room, she heard her muttering.

'Nasty boys – always in trouble. Probably play-acting just to scare me. Wait till the Judge gets home, then they'll see.' She brushed her hair and put on some lipstick so she'd be presentable for the doctor.

Katherine paused on the porch to get her breath. The

170

fear, the rush down the steps to let the doctor in, had her
heart racing. She leaned against the banister, looking out
onto her beloved woods. It was a beautiful summer day.
The sound of songbirds filled the air, sunlight shone
brightly. It seemed impossible that death had stalked the
children for the past two days.

Her eyes scanned the bushes, the trees, as if half-expecting
to see someone standing there – the Grim Reaper.

April and Bradley, who sat in the porch swing
unobserved, watched her. The fierce expression on her
face postponed the favor Bradley wanted to ask.

'I'm afraid – you ask her,' he whispered to April.

'It's your stupid sick bird. You ask her.'

They watched her straighten up, take a deep breath and
go down the steps toward the path to her cabin.

The soft peeping from the shoebox gave him courage.
Bradley jumped up now after shouting, 'Miss Katherine
– Miss Katherine! Please . . .'

They went to the cabin with her. When she saw the
tiny, almost bald robin in the box, her eyes lit up and she
made a sound, a soft clucking sound, as she talked to
the bird.

Fascinated, they watched as she mixed a potion, and
patiently with a toothpick, urged the tiny bird to eat.
After trial and error, the infant stretched his neck and the
gaping, hungry mouth was filled again and again.

'Good bird, good baby,' Kack crooned. 'Enough now.'
She reached for the tiny bird. He hopped from corner to
corner to avoid her hand. Finally she grasped the
struggling baby loosely and put him into a wicker cage,
covering it with a dark cloth, telling the children, 'Animals
that are hurt or sick like the dark. It makes them feel safe.'

'Why?' Bradley asked. 'I'm afraid of the dark, especially
when I'm sick.'

'I don't know why, Bradley, I just know.'

'He ate a lot. He was a hungry bird,' April observed.

'Yes, that was a good sign,' Katherine agreed. 'I can't

promise that I can make him well, though. Birds are very difficult – they scare so easy. Sometimes they die of fright just being so close to people.'

Both children looked solemn. Katherine tried to cheer them up. The last two days had been bad enough. Brightly, she said, 'As long as you two are here, you can do some work and keep out of trouble.' She set them to work shelling peas.

Both children liked visiting the cabin. It smelled of roots and spices and always in the corner of one of the cages there was a creature mending.

Dr Martin had prescribed castor oil and sunshine, so the boys could not be sent back to the attic for punishment, as originally planned. They were banished from outdoor pleasures, however, and only allowed to go as far as the porch. The Judge would be home Friday; then he would decide what to do about their disobedience. Jealously, they watched April and Bradley set out for the cabin each day.

Some of the freshly harvested manroot was strung about the cabin to dry.

'Is it over, the sang-hunt?' April asked.

'No, child. There's plenty more out there. It's hot days and cold nights that make the time right to pick it.'

'Can Bradley and I go with you?'

'Sure, if you promise to mind the rules.'

'We will.' In the cabin, on the string above April's head, a small, headless man dangled. 'Is it magic?' she whispered.

'Not exactly, but it is very special. It's good for lots of things. When you were sick, we put ginseng in the tea. It made you well.'

The week went by very slowly. The boys were prisoners of the house, the boundary being the porch. They wished their father would return to decide their punishment and be done with it.

When he returned on Friday night, he was told of the mishap. He listened to every detail. He said nothing. The next morning, Hannah told them that the Judge had said they were free to leave the house, but they were not to go to the river.

They whooped and hollered and ran about the lawns like wild Indians. Even the sight of Bruce coming from the woods laden down with wheat-stalks did not distract them. Usually they couldn't resist the urge to tease him in some way, but today they ran over to help him carry the stalks to his room by the kitchen.

Each boy prided himself on how good he was. They played summer games with Bradley and April, they built a fort in the woods, put canteens and blankets in their hideout and imagined themselves rough woodsmen.

It was two weeks after the mishap when on an early Sunday, the house was awakened by the ringing of the bells. The firehouse, schoolhouse, and every church in the valley rang their bells, and the sound echoed ominously throughout the Meramec Valley.

The Judge came down and found the children seated at the table ready to eat. 'Get dressed,' he ordered. 'April, too.'

'Wh-where are we going?' Kyle asked. The smile died on his face as he saw his father's fierce expression.

'Get dressed! White shirts, blue trousers, and your Sunday shoes.' He turned to April. 'Your mother will tell you what to wear.'

The three children looked at one another, puzzled.

As they went up the stairs, they heard Elizabeth pleading with him. 'Please, William, it's too harsh. Please, not April. Don't make her go.'

'No, it's decided. I have Jenny's permission for her to go.'

William climbed into the front seat of the Lincoln with Tom, who was driving.

April sat between the twins in the back seat. They dared not say a word.

The men talked companionably about baseball and cars.

The Judge asked Tom to take the car in next week as he'd heard several rattles that he hadn't noticed before.

They arrived at The Crossroads. Small groups of men were huddled at the corners, solemn-faced and grave.

Tom stopped the car in front of the sheriff's office.

When they alighted, the Judge was greeted again and again; 'Mornin', Judge.' The salutation came from many different lips.

The children's eyes were big as saucers. Had they broken some law? Was he taking them to jail?

The sheriff came out and shook hands with the Judge, ignoring the three silent children standing before him. 'Come in,' he said, and he stood aside the door.

Tom left them to join the groups of men that stood outside the jail.

The sheriff's small, dingy office was piled high with papers and the walls were decorated with Wanted posters.

The boys stared at the harsh faces on the posters. Kyle almost whispered to his brother that he was sure he had seen that guy, the one with the beard, in Bailey's store. Gee whiz, there was a reward and everything.

The Judge offered the sheriff a cigar. He sniffed it appreciatively before he lit it. The room soon grew stuffy with cigar smoke.

'In there,' the sheriff indicated, nodding.

'Let's do it,' the Judge said.

The sheriff walked to the glass door marked *Private*.

'Go in,' the Judge said to the children. They walked into the room single file; the cigar smoke could not cover the odor in that room.

April gagged. The room reeked of antiseptic which did not disguise the stronger stench of decay. On the porcelain table they saw something mounted up, covered completely with a pristine white sheet.

The sheriff stepped forward. Like a careful housewife, bit by bit he carefully folded back the sheet.

They stared, fascinated and fearful. It lay there like

174

some horrible matted thing, gray-blue, swollen to twice its normal size. The thing's stringy hair was plastered close around its face, with mud and sticks a part of the grisly cap. The hands – huge gray shiny things, with fingers thick as sausages, were spread wide, forever frozen in the pose of grasping.

The eyes of the creature bulged and glistened white. Whatever color they had been was gone.

'How many days?' William asked.

'Found him this morning. I reckon he's been in about three days.'

Silence again – only the clock ticking loudly.

They stared as the Judge's voice boomed: 'Walk around him. Look good – no, children, open your eyes! Walk around him, I said.'

They obeyed like robots. Eyes watering, gulping, they walked slowly around the table. Suddenly the corpse's mouth drooped open; a trickle of stagnant water leaked out. Hypnotically they watched as something bubbled to the surface. It was round and an unpleasant green. They watched in horror as it unwound, paused on the man's lower lip. The head turned, the small antenna moved. Then the worm crawled carefully down the corpse's chin.

April bolted first. She ran outside to be joined in the bushes by her cousins, where they gagged for a time. There was nothing to bring up; they hadn't eaten their breakfast.

Tom offered his handkerchief and searched his pockets. Usually Hannah put two somewhere on his person.

They rode silently back to the house. When the car stopped, the Judge turned around and looked at their faces, studying the effect, then he said, 'Don't ever tell me you're not afraid of the river. Only a damn fool would say that.'

# CHAPTER 20

For weeks afterward they all had nightmares, seeing in their dreams the bloated corpse. In the daylight hours the boys talked about the body with a false bravado. When Bradley came to play, they went over and over the description of the body, and in the telling a few details were added. As well as the slimy worm, they had spiders and scorpions crawling out of the dead man's eyes and ears. April hushed them and tried to interest her cousins in the homeless fledgelings or tiny rabbits that Bradley invariably seemed to find. This always instigated a trip to the cabin to see Kack, who could usually find another cage for the new charge.

The boys were quiet and helpful around the Judge; they helped him in the greenhouse. The sweet, cloying scent of the flowers was unpleasant to them, but the treat of snitching an almost-ripe strawberry from his section of edible plants made the work bearable.

The Judge assigned them to help Tom, who was building an add-on to the porch where Bruce would be housed.

They fetched nails and hammers and held the ladder for Tom. Both boys made fun of Bruce when no one was looking, following behind him, arms flaying and parodying the blind man's walk.

Elizabeth watched the blind man with distaste. 'William, is this really necessary? I thought you were checking into places that would be more suitable for him?'

'Now Elizabeth, you know how I've tried over the years

but there's absolutely nothing available, given his limitations. There are long waiting lists and with his mental capacity he doesn't qualify for most of those institutions anyway.'

'He's not really our responsibility,' she said peevishly.

'Elizabeth, please. He's never bothered anyone. Hannah and Tom give him chores, he helps in the greenhouse and he seems so happy just making those brooms. I thought you'd be pleased. The room addition will have its own entrance and moving him out of the kitchen room gives Hannah more pantry space.'

'I don't want him in other parts of the house.'

'You know he never ventures beyond his own room or the kitchen.'

She didn't answer for she knew this was true but she hated anything ugly or unpleasant and just the sight of Bruce, stumbling along, made her head throb. She turned away from William abruptly and went up to her room to lie down.

The twins grew bored with their good behavior. They missed going fishing. They built a treehouse, played Indians and were delighted when Kack announced that it was time for the sang-hunt.

August found the woods splendid with color, and they each grabbed a burlap sack. Bradley went home, for he knew that he always got poison ivy or poison oak when he had gone deep into the west woods with them before.

They walked single file following Kack, until she would stop and point at the plant of vivid yellow.

'There, Ryan – and remember to plant the berries.'

They had a game of who would find the prize manroot. The boys argued with each other – 'I've got the most' – and then each sat down to rummage in the sack to settle the argument.

The favorite taunt when mad at each other was, 'I hope you fall in the river and drown,' and each time one of them said it, they shivered with fear and took it back.

They stopped for lunch and Kack spread a cloth and

set out the peanut butter and jelly sandwiches; from the thermos she poured them each a cup of Kool Aid. For dessert, there were wild Chickasaw plums.

Before they had finished, they looked up, and through the maze of trees they saw a doe, silent as a statue.

'Now Ryan,' Katherine whispered, 'as I taught you.'

The boy leaned forward. His eyes glittered brightly; he caught the doe's eyes. Sweat beaded on his forehead, and he drew in his breath and paced with the animal.

A beam, a tie of energy – something – held them motionless, the boy and the animal. Nothing stirred but the wind.

Time stood still for Ryan. He was in communion with the beast.

'This game is dumb,' sputtered Kyle.

Released by the sound, the creature whirled and sped away, leaving the bushes trembling.

Kyle and April were jealous of the game that Kack and Ryan knew. Kack said they were antsy and they didn't sit still. They didn't concentrate, so they could never learn.

In the next hollow, Kyle found the prize root – six inches long – a headless man. It was the first and only one to be found that day.

The children grew bored with the hunt. At first it had seemed like a treasure hunt, and the competition of who found the prize manroot was exciting, but now it was only hard work, dragging the sacks through the dense woods.

Eventually they came to a dead tree, which Ryan skillfully scaled to the top. He came down instantly, his face flushed with excitement. 'I saw them, a whole bunch of them!'

'Who?' Kyle urged.

'Gypsies! It's their camp, just down the ridge.'

'Gypsies?' April said with awe, feeling important.

Ryan went on, 'They look like terrible people.' His imagination took over. 'I think they have big sacks probably full of gold.'

'Really? Gold?' Kyle repeated with awe.

'Let's get closer,' Ryan said. 'I wish we had our spyglass.'

They abandoned Kack, left their burlap sacks of ginseng where they lay, forgotten, and marched single file through the brush, the sound of cracking twigs audible in the woods.

Ryan led the way, for he knew which direction the camp lay.

After ten minutes, they stopped, picked a tree, and decided to climb it to see if they were any closer to the camp. Ryan went first. He scaled the fir tree, noticing the smoke from the fires, and saw a wagon very near. Excitedly, he came down.

'They're real close,' he whispered.

'Let me see,' Kyle begged, and he began climbing the tree.

'Me, too,' April pleaded, and Ryan cupped his hands so she could stand in them and be able to reach the first branch.

Before April was halfway up the small tree, a loud voice startled them: 'What are you doing? What do you want here?'

An old gypsy woman parted the bushes and stepped forward. Her many skirts swished, her armful of bracelets rang musically. Her face was very round; patches of rouge stood out harshly on her cheeks, and wisps of grizzled gray-black hair peeked out of the purple scarf around her head. Huge gold earrings tinkled along with the bracelets. Her black eyes took in all of them in a second, appraising.

Her appearance so startled April that she let go of the branch and felt herself sliding roughly down the tree to land hard on a stone at its base.

To April's dismay, it was the woman who leaned forward, grabbed her by both arms, and pulled her to her feet. April's behind hurt terribly from the fall. She would have cried if she weren't so frightened.

Ryan looked at his birthday watch. 'We have to go.'

The gypsy's eyes followed his movement and rested on his arm. Her voice, now smooth as honey, coaxed, 'Not yet. Come, I will show you something wonderful.'

She still held fast to April's arms. Then she let go, took the small hand within hers, and started leading their cousin away.

The boys looked helplessly at each other. They could not leave her. They would be punished. They followed, their hearts hammering loudly with fear. Kack was too far away: she could not help them. They walked through the brambles and came to the clearing.

A dark man shoeing a horse looked up, smiled, and went back to his job, his hammer ringing.

She led them to a bench alongside a wagon; two dusky children paused in their game of hide and seek to stare at them. 'Shoo-shooo,' the woman hissed at them.

They ran off.

From the wagon, she fetched a large black sack. Her arm disappeared inside it, and she brought forth a round object.

'This is a crystal ball. In it I can see tomorrow – and many tomorrows.'

'You can?' April said in amazement.

'Now child, take off your locket.'

April had forgotten she was wearing it. 'Why?'

'Because I need to touch things that belong to you, so I can tell your future.'

April struggled to find the catch; twisting the locket around, the chain broke and she started to cry.

'It's all right. I will make two,' the gypsy crooned. She took April's hand, turned it upward, smoothed her palm, and peered intently into the small, dirty hand. 'Oh, yes. You will marry well — ' She looked up at the boys' faces, mirror images of each other. 'You will marry him.' She pointed to Kyle.

Then she frowned, confused. 'No, no. You will marry *him*.' She pointed to Ryan.

181

'It doesn't matter. You will marry well, live in a big house, and have many lockets,' she promised.

'What about my locket now?' April asked, looking toward the pocket it had slipped into.

'Never mind, child. Tonight I will bury it by the full moon, and tomorrow look under your pillow. There will be two.'

'There will?' she said, delighted.

'Now you,' she drew Ryan forward, 'give me your watch.' Seeing his hesitation, she coaxed, 'Come now, I need to touch it.'

Reluctantly he unstrapped the watch. She held it in her palm, closed her eyes and murmured softly to herself. 'Now let's see.' She pulled his hand forward and appeared to study it carefully. 'Ah yes – you will be famous.' Ryan smiled. 'Very, very famous. Many people in the world will know your name. You will — ' She stopped – halted – a shadow fell over her face. 'That's enough, you're lucky enough. Not everyone can be famous.'

'Me, me. What about me?' Kyle urged, shoving his hand under her face. She searched his person for valuables and saw none. Disgusted, she looked down into his palm. Her eyes widened. She looked at one boy, then at the other. Her head swiveled back and forth swiftly. Looking again into his palm, she shrieked – an unearthly scream: '*Junto, Junto!*' and clearing her throat, she spat into his palm.

Like one person of one mind, the three children turned and ran stumbling through the woods, running until their lungs were fit to burst. They only stopped when they had reached the east lawn by the house. There they fell into the manicured grass, panting.

'What about my locket? Do you think I really will have two?' April wondered.

Ryan looked at her. 'No, stupid. She tricked you out of your locket and she stole my watch.'

Kyle rubbed his fouled hand on the grass. 'She told you both nice things because you had something to give her.'

Ryan remembered and began laughing hysterically. 'She spit in your hand! That dirty gypsy spit in your hand. I bet you'll have a wart.'

With that, they began fighting, chasing each other around the yard, falling and wrestling viciously in the grass until Hannah called them in for supper.

As they walked to the kitchen, April mused, 'Which one of you will I marry? I wonder.'

They snickered. 'Don't be dumb. You're our cousin.'

'Oh,' she answered, not knowing why that made a difference.

The next day, they accompanied Kack back to the woods to locate the half-filled sacks that they had abandoned. The cold snap had turned the trees, and vivid reds and yellows were a beautiful sight. Activity was high, the animals sensing that winter was near.

Kyle and April lagged behind. 'My brother's crazy. Did you see him yesterday with that doe? He's definitely crazy,' Kyle whispered.

'No, he's not.' April defended him in an angry voice. 'You're just jealous because you can't do it.'

'Yes, he is crazy. I know, the mirror told me.'

'How can the mirror tell you?' April reasoned. 'It's only you in the mirror telling you.'

He ignored her rationale and asked, 'How would you like it if someone stole your face?'

'Is that what being a twin means?' she asked. 'I hope I never am one.'

'Stupid. Stupid April,' Kyle shouted, and ran ahead, leaving her lagging behind.

Kyle spotted the tip of the dead tree. 'There, Kack! It's over there. That looks like the tree Ryan climbed.'

They found the three half-full abandoned sacks. The boys decided to combine them into two and they would carry them. As they sat dividing and arguing – 'You've got less than I do,' Ryan accused: 'My sack's the heaviest.'

'No it isn't. Look, let's measure them,' Kyle suggested,

and as the argument raged, it came . . . a soft, anguished wail.

Kack froze; her face blanched white. 'Hurry, children, we must hurry,' she urged.

The sound rose. Its pitch was urgent, bouncing off the trees, the rocks – changing directions. It was a banshee scream, the total terror of it full now at its peak of urgency.

Kack studied their faces. She could see that they heard nothing. She felt it was near, coming closer – *it seeks!*

She gauged the distance. The house was too far. She knew a cave that was closer.

'Hurry, children, hurry. Run!' They couldn't ignore her urgent voice, still they did not understand. A strong wind had come up, whirling the leaves about.

'Hurry – run!' she shouted, herding them before her.

When they reached the small cave she said, 'Go in. On your hands and knees go in.'

They crawled into the small, dank opening. A lizard ran over April's fingers and disappeared into the recesses of the cave.

Kack entered last. She sat up, and with her back to the opening, created a shield to protect them.

'What is it?' Ryan asked. 'Storm's coming?'

'Never mind,' she said, turning her head. Her ear cocked; she traced its path. It skipped among the rocks, dying gently, losing strength, then rising to a frantic, erratic pitch, its scream one of abject terror, for it knew . . . *it knew what it was*.

'Cover your ears,' she ordered. It was a superfluous precaution, for she knew they did not hear its eerie voice. It was a privilege or a curse that she heard it so clearly.

They put their fingers in their ears and squinted their eyes closed.

She began humming. She needed a closer sound so she could not hear it so clearly.

April leaned back against the smooth coolness of the wall. She closed her eyes.

'No, no.' Kack shook her. 'Do not sleep. It is the Oh mu.'

Too late – she had said it. Now she must distract them. 'Oh, I'm a silly old woman,' she lied. 'I thought for a minute it was one of those awful summer storms – the Indians call them Oh mu. Let's play riddles,' she said brightly.

'Me first, me first,' Kyle insisted. 'I know a good one from Daddy. What's black and white and read all over?'

'I know, a skunk,' April said, certain that she was right.

'No,' Kyle said. 'Guess again.' And they each sat there thinking.

# CHAPTER 21

Three nights in a row they found April sleepwalking. When she awoke, she would sob, 'The river – the river. I'm scared of the river. Kyle shouldn't have — ' She stopped in mid-sentence. She was afraid to even tell her mother about what she had dreamed.

The women kept silent, never sharing with each other the thought that the Judge was to blame. It had been too harsh a lesson. After all, the children were only twelve years old.

Only Hannah had a real inkling of what they had seen. Tom had described to her vividly what drowned men really looked like.

Jenny couldn't blame the Judge entirely. She *had* given her permission. However, she felt that she should cut the visit short. If they left now, it would only be ten days earlier than they had originally planned, but she put it off, not wanting to hurt the Judge or her sister's feelings. What happened the next night forced her decision. Their feelings were less important than April's safety.

It was after midnight when Tom left the house to set out the mole traps. The creatures had taken to favoring the west grounds, and their persistent tunneling there was creating havoc with the raspberry bushes. It had killed off a few already.

He moved off across the lawn. The bright moonlight cast his shadow looming before him. Plainly in the silver light he saw the upraised furrows of their tunnels. He knelt, and digging with a trowel, he opened the furrow, placed the trap inside the tunnel, then patted the loose dirt back over it.

He surveyed his handiwork, pleased, although he knew it was going to take many nights and many traps to clear them out completely. The Missus had told him to take any moles that he caught and turn them loose in the west woods. Sure he would, he said, and he laughed to himself. Women and their foolish ideas!

Starting on the next tunnel, he wasn't sure what made him stop to listen – something in the night, a misplaced sound. His neck prickled. The moon danced behind a cloud and he listened, then out of the corner of his eye he saw a flash of white.

He straightened, clutching the heavy trap in one hand. Never been any problems around here, he thought. He rose and walked slowly over the lawn in the direction where he thought he had seen something.

He wasn't mistaken. Before him now at the edge of the woods, something white really was there. He was a sensible man, so he dismissed the nonsense of ghosts and such. Something was there. He could see it moving, changing direction, making for the river.

He took the short cut. When the moon reappeared, he saw her clearly: her eyes wide open, hands at her side, moving like a zombie, tears streaming down her cheeks.

He didn't know what to do. She walked past him, not seeing him or anything that was real. Whatever her tear-filled eyes were seeing, it wasn't the dark woods.

Jeez, he thought. Why did he have to find her? He remembered some sort of old wives' tale that said you shouldn't wake a sleepwalker or they'll die. It wasn't his kid or his responsibility. He saw she was too close to the river. He didn't have time to go back and get the Judge. He'd have to do this himself.

He came abreast of her, reached tentatively for her small hand. 'April! April, honey. Let's go this way,' and with his other hand he reached across her back, touched her shoulder and eased her around.

There was no resistance. She walked where he led her. She tripped a time or two. Her face changed; her eyes widened. He was afraid, so he went slowly now, walking in short steps that matched hers.

Slowly, they got there. He released her hand and opened the door.

Up the steps they went. He wasn't sure – should he get the Judge, or her mother? Then the decision was out of his hands, for she tripped on a step and fell sprawling on the landing, which awakened her and she began crying loudly.

Lights came on one by one. The Judge appeared in his bathrobe, then Jenny, and Hannah; only Elizabeth didn't awaken as she had taken a sleeping powder.

'My God, Tom, what are you doing?' the Judge demanded.

'I found her walking in her sleep, headed for the river.'

Jenny rushed forward, crushing April to her. 'Baby, oh baby.'

Between sobs, April gasped, 'Kyle shouldn't have—' Again she stopped herself. The recurring nightmare was so vivid, so real to her, that she had become afraid of falling asleep. She saw her cousin Ryan, or was it Kyle? – she saw him lying drowned, on the table, so blue, so cold, with only a green worm slithering down his bloated chin . . .

It was understandable that they needed to leave early. April's own bed at home, her own room – familiar, every-day things from her real life and not the summer visit, seemed the answer to Jenny.

April needed to be away from Castlewood, from her cousins and the river.

The dream was slow in leaving, and many a night Jenny rose to comfort her sobbing daughter, so it was easy to turn down the invitation the next summer.

A. N. Steinberg

The summer following that, the boys were going to Boy Scout camp; the summer after, the Judge took his family to Europe. Thus the tradition of the summer visits was broken.

Letters and holiday phone calls kept Jenny in touch. Over ten summers later, the Judge and Elizabeth went to Ohio for Jenny's funeral. The boys were backpacking in Europe and couldn't be reached in time.

It was the day after her mother's funeral, when her aunt and uncle had returned to Missouri, that April had it. She hadn't endured it for years – the dream.

It was as real and vivid as ever. Shaking herself awake, she wondered was it Ryan or Kyle in the dreams? She still wasn't sure. She remembered her small cousins; she hadn't seen them since they were twelve.

She arose, made some hot tea. With fondness she recalled the ginseng. Many people put it in their tea these days: Kack had been ahead of her time.

She cupped the warm mug, looked into the amber liquid and sipped slowly, knowing she'd be awake now till morning. The dream would pass: it had before. A word tumbled over and over in her mind.

*Precognition.*

# CHAPTER 22

A week after the Judge's seventy-fifth birthday, he knew he couldn't wait any longer, so he scheduled the appointment with the doctor in St Louis. It took an incredible effort to pretend in front of Kyle and Ryan that all was well. They had been in town for the birthday celebration, but were now safely off to pursue their lives. Kyle was in the state capital of Jefferson City, and Ryan had returned to Africa.

After preliminary tests, the doctor persuaded him to remain at Barnes Hospital. Tom had taken Elizabeth off in tears, the Judge reassuring her that he was fine, yet knowing deep down that he was not.

She returned the next morning, Tom following in her wake laden down with the photograph albums and scrapbooks. Some vague, peculiar thought was in her mind that if he viewed the record of their life and happiness, he couldn't possibly leave her.

In the long hours of waiting, he was restless; he wasn't used to inactivity. Even after his retirement, he donated the swimming pool and grounds to an organization for handicapped children; he sat on the board, made sure they had everything they needed to create a working, viable camp that would enrich the children's lives. He kept busy with the greenhouse, he saw that Katherine was supplied with books, he looked after Bruce. He was not an idle man. So, to sit in the stark hospital room, interrupted only by nurses and interns sticking him with needles, made him impatient.

He did open the books in which Elizabeth had so faithfully recorded their lives. He took no interest in the photos of him and her, young and smiling. It was when the babies appeared that his heart fluttered. Such a gift, such a marvelous gift. It was she who had given his life meaning.

Those two handsome faces staring up at him: Kyle in his photographer's phase, Ryan the young artist – the record of happy summers. Two barefoot boys with their fishing poles; two brown Indians swimming in the pool.

She had given him this incredible gift, and Katherine had taught them well; their love of the land and the creatures came from her.

Still, he had been a good father to them. He had controlled Elizabeth. He had not let her inflict the sameness on them; he'd refused to allow her to dress them alike, he had insisted upon their individuality. Even now, their paths were diverse from each other – Kyle with his law degree, Ryan in Africa with the art commission. He remembered how they had searched for their real selves, and how he had remained silent. He did not advise or prod; he did not make his father's mistake. They had chosen their own paths.

His sons, they had brought him a lifetime of happiness. He loved them both as he loved nothing else in his life, except . . .

In a matter of days he was told that it was cancer and inoperable.

# CHAPTER 23

The Judge insisted on being released from the hospital.

The talk of a hospice, and nurses calling her, only upset Elizabeth, and she took to having Hannah say she wasn't in.

Elizabeth was exhausted from the traveling back and forth to St Louis, and Tom, who drove her, was frantic until he heard every day that indeed the Judge was still alive.

Tom fumed and fretted to his wife, going from anger to anguish: 'We don't have any papers about the acreage he promised,' and, 'He's already given away Castlewood.'

'The Judge has always been a man of his word,' Hannah commented quietly.

'I know, but what good is that if he's dead? Can't give his word then – and she,' he nodded upstairs, 'what does she know about anything except buying things?'

It disturbed Hannah that after all the years they had worked for the Reardons, Tom should have grown so bitter toward them – more so when he drank! Personally she loved them all. They were her family.

Bringing the Judge home was encouraging to Tom. Now he could look for the right moment to introduce the subject of the promise. It was tactless, he knew, but Hannah and he had spent their whole life at Hilltop and it wouldn't be right. A man's word is his bond.

The Judge came home a different man – thin to the point of gauntness, his hair a shock of white, his firm step still there, but no one knew the effort it took to pretend. He was exhausted after the short trip from the car to the house.

Elizabeth had moved his things into the east bedroom, and when he heard of it, he sat wearily in the hall while he ordered Hannah to move it all back to the green room which he had occupied for the last twenty or so years.

Elizabeth was upset, and with tears shimmering in her eyes, she tried to explain. 'But dear, I thought the morning sun would be nice, and the balcony – and you can see the river from that room.'

'There, there, Elizabeth, it's all right. No harm done. Hannah will soon have it all put back.' He comforted her as one would a small child.

He was glad for the delay. It gave him time to sit in the high-back chair to catch his breath and summon his strength so he could manage the long flight of stairs without help.

Elizabeth fussed with his overnight bags and felt angry that he preferred the dark green room which faced the woods and the cabin. Nothing to see from the windows, she thought. It was the one room in the house in which she felt uncomfortable. It kept quiet gray gloom even with the fireplace lit; the room had a strange cool quality and she felt a presence of something there that she did not understand.

He refused the cold supper and called Tom to light a fire. As he knelt working with the chips of wood, Tom cleared his throat, not knowing how to begin. Each time he started to say something, the Judge was overcome with a spasm of coughing and eventually Tom left the room, the fire roaring cheerfully. He cursed himself under his breath for not having spoken out about the acreage.

'How could you ask?' Hannah sympathized. 'At a time like this – why, he would think we're burying him today!'

'Well, maybe we are – who knows? He looks bad enough.' Sullenly, Tom went to bed, certain that it was their fate to be gypped out of what should rightfully be theirs.

The Judge went to the window; he found her slight figure bending over, planting or watering at the side of the cabin.

In the twilight he watched her strong motions as she bent and stretched, working in the soil.

His eyes fastened on her, feeding on her strength.

Then her hand arrested in mid-air. She rose and turned to face the house, one arm up shielding her eyes from the last rays of the sun. She looked and saw him standing in the window.

Satisfied, he lay down and she came to him.

# CHAPTER 24

It was Hannah who hinted, then remarked, then blatantly said to the Missus, 'Why not let Kack come and see to the Judge? Her potions and remedies can't hurt none. Why, the medicine from the doctors don't seem to do no good, and I know he's hurtin'.'

Elizabeth cringed; she didn't like to hear unpleasant things. Still, she was unsure. The doctors had said he was 'terminal' – that was a harsh and terrible word, she thought, and took to her bed to rest and watch soap operas.

She gave into Hannah's request to send for Kack. She knew Katherine would come bearing leeches, herbal infusions, vinegar-soaked rags ... what difference did it make? Her husband was dying.

Katherine came with nothing. She was led up to the green room. It was just as she knew it to be, though she had never been inside it. Every piece of furniture, the paintings, the glowing embers in the fireplace, the huge rosewood bed ... and William. She did not see him as he was now.

She bolted the door, dropped the loose dress to the floor, undid her braided hair, and slid into the crevice where she had lain on many nights before.

She fitted herself to him and his cold flesh warmed.

'I love you, Kathy.' His voice was a hoarse, tired whisper.

'I know.' She pressed her fingers to his lips to still him, and they slept.

197

She was allowed every day, and she came and really tried, with compresses, salves and tonics... and they heard the lock slide and no one dared disturb them.

Hannah saw the visible signs of fatigue in Katherine when she left after hours of ministering to the dying man.

It was the sight of him that changed – like looking at him through waves of water, distorted, altering. Katherine felt the strain of this. Sometimes he was very clear – a thin husk of a man, breathing harshly, his thin veined eyelids fluttering like a moth against a screen. Then her vision would change and he was smiling, unchanged, himself – like the other times when she had been here in this room, in this bed with him.

It was while she held him, willing her strength to flow into his body, that she dreamed of it – the Oh mu, and for days she struggled with the thoughts and the idea that the dream had produced...

Eventually, she decided that the dream was a sign, and when she came bearing the tiny sleeping rabbit, wrapped in her cloak, Elizabeth commented, 'This is too much! It's unsanitary. It's, it's—' she struggled for a word.

And Hannah, when bringing his tray each day, the tray that was left untouched, knew he was very near the end. She said gently to the mistress, 'It doesn't matter now,' and she patted the hand of the childish woman.

'Oh,' Elizabeth expelled the word in surprise. She never wanted to face facts. Then, biting a nail nervously, she asked, 'Do you suppose we should send for the children?'

'Yes, ma'am, I think that would be a good idea.' Hannah knew how they must hate being referred to as children. Why, they were in their twenties now.

Like an afterthought, Elizabeth looked up into Hannah's broad open face and asked, 'Is the owl still there?'

'No, ma'am. He flew away this morning.'

'Thank God,' she exclaimed, and got up and bustled to her room. Maybe now without its annoying hoot, she

198

could concentrate on a new book that had arrived today from the book club.

The shades in the green room were pulled halfway down; the day being overcast kept the room in shadow.

Katherine put one log on the embers; the fire flared up, then died down, filling the room with a warm, soft glow. She took the slumbering rabbit over to the bed. The two-week-old animal was soft and pliant; unbuttoning his pajama top, she lay the creature on his chest. In a matter of minutes they synchronized and seemed to inhale and exhale together.

She watched them as tears ran down her cheeks.

'How long,' she whispered. 'How long has he been given?' In a moment would it stop – in a week? Or would the shallow breathing continue? How could she know?

Gently she lifted the rabbit off and placed it on the chair next to the bed, then she climbed in beside him.

He stirred and reached for her, fighting to emerge from the tranquilizer. She smoothed his hair back from his damp forehead, ran her fingers gently over his hollowed cheeks. She touched him as one would comfort a sick child.

He turned toward her, not able to press her close enough, and she realized that in this moment, she had created out of the mere shell of him desire.

Gently she rolled him back and climbed atop him, aware of the fragile shell beneath her.

Leading him, it was slow and gentle, and neither of them saw reality as it was. It was love, it was lust, it was everything between a man and a woman. He smiled the briefest smile. She turned aside and could not bear the struggle within herself.

What should she do? The dream – it led, it warned.

She heard the rustle on the chair nearby and saw the newness of the rabbit; its freshness so heady. She looked at William, who seemed no longer there, but a shell, a husk. Crying hysterically, she took the pillows, flung herself across him and felt the stirring beneath her.

Closing her eyes, she wished herself away and lay catching sunbeams under the bed in Gallup, as he struggled feebly beneath her and was finally still. She heard the wail of the Oh mu and knew this was a sin, but she loved the Judge so she had saved him – to touch, to hold, to love in a small bundle of fur.

She left him, picked up the rabbit into her lap and stroked it gently. She could hear the shallow breathing in the room so loud; it was her own breath, coming ragged and edged with fear and surprise at what she had done.

In an hour, she called them. They came, Elizabeth hovering in the doorway. She looked at Katherine, who now held the bucking rabbit. 'I hope the animal hasn't soiled anything.'

Elizabeth then commented that it was good they had sent for the boys. Her mind reached, turning and tossing. Who else, who else should she send for? There must be someone who could help her. It wouldn't be right asking all the servants what to do.

# CHAPTER 25

The plane approached the airport; swirling clouds rushed past the windows.

The captain had informed them that they would have to circle as the fog had created a wait for the runways.

A tenseness hovered among the passengers; it would only dissolve when they sensed the bump of the wheels on the ground.

April felt nervous and excited. It had been many years since her last trip to Castlewood, and she hadn't seen her cousins in all that time. She had been grateful that her aunt and uncle had come to her mother's funeral. They had invited her to come back and stay with them then, but she had refused, wanting to return to her work at the hospital as soon as possible.

Whenever she thought of her mother it was with such regret; Jenny Brookshire's had been such a hard life. Widowed young, always working at a menial job, Jenny had been so proud when April graduated and became a registered physical therapist. Somewhere a resentment lived deep within April against her aunt, for her mother's and her Aunt Elizabeth's lives had been so different.

Life's not fair – she knew that. Now she felt irritated by the cryptic note that she had been sent. She knew its short message by heart.

*Dear, dear April,*
*Come to Castlewood now, I must see you. I need you.*
*Aunt Elizabeth*

201

She couldn't imagine what this was all about; she had tried phoning several times and was told by Hannah, 'The Missus is laying down. The Missus is asleep – please come if you can.'

Finally she arranged for a leave of absence, booked the flight, and now was circling the airport in St Louis.

She wondered who would meet her. Would her cousins be there? She blushed with the thought of how she adored them, Kyle and Ryan. She loved them and the times they had spent while growing up. As a child she had day-dreamed about marrying one of them. They were so alike, yet different. If Kyle was nice, then Ryan was awful – or vice versa. In her memory she recalled the fun and mischief of all those wonderful summers of growing up.

On the ground, her small suitcase next to her, she looked through the crowd. It was Tom, grown heavier, his hair a shock of white, unmistakably his broad face looking through the crowd. His eyes passed hers and went on looking.

She came forward. 'Tom.'

He looked at her, examining her, noting the brown hair that curled about her heart-shaped face, eyes blue-leaning-to-violet. She had grown into a beautiful young woman. 'Miss April—'

'Yes, it's me.'

Awkwardly he withstood her embrace, took the suitcase. She almost had to run to keep up with him.

He opened the back door of the Mercedes, so she had no other choice but to get in. She would have preferred sitting in front so they could talk. He had established the division – clearly she was the guest and he the servant.

She leaned forward. 'How is everyone?' she asked.

'Fine, just fine.' A classic answer to a classic question.

Still talking to the back of his head, she went on: 'I mean Aunt Elizabeth. How is she, since the Judge's death? I certainly would have come to the funeral, but she didn't write till after.'

'It was private,' Tom said, 'just the Missus and the boys. She wanted it that way.'

'Oh.' April leaned back. It was awkward trying to talk to him from the back seat.

She directed her attention out the window. So much had changed. The buildings, the hotels, the roads . . . she remembered nothing on the twenty-minute ride until Tom turned onto the river road. The city had crept so close. It was only on this road that the subdivisions dwindled, as the road turned and dropped sharply, coming closer to the river. Only the swift blanket of trees, in the myriad of fall colors, sailing past them seemed familiar.

The city sounds faded, and you could hear the soft, gentle buzz of the forest.

On the right, the general store still stood. A dilapidated truck was there, with two men loading hay.

The orange, yellow and reds of the trees dazzled her, and she found herself searching the undergrowth for the familiar plant. It was the season for the ginseng.

On a tree closest to the road, a hand-lettered sign caught her attention: *No hunting*.

The road still dropped swiftly, and the tires of the Mercedes squealed as he came to The Crossroads.

To the left was the river; ahead of them the road said *Private*. Further down the sign still hung there, rustic, brown, swaying in the dusk. *Castlewood*.

She could see in the distance the old pool and the clubhouse, now a camp for disabled and disadvantaged children.

The car slowed and swayed on the road, which was rock, and through the pin oaks and scrub elm, April saw the house.

Gray stone, sturdy, meant to last forever. The ivy still clung to the stone, and in several places it threatened to cover the windows, which were unlit; only a weak light gleamed through the portico around the massive door.

It reinforced April's feeling that something was wrong.

She stood waiting nervously on the stone porch as Tom retrieved her bags from the trunk.

He opened the door, and they entered the hall. It was the same as she remembered; the quarry-tile floor, each piece cut in a beautiful, intricate design that fit into the next like a puzzle. Tiles from Italy. Above, the crystal chandelier, gleaming with a hundred tiny lights. The portrait of William and Elizabeth and the twins hung in its usual place to the right.

April felt a twinge of sadness. Uncle William not being here was something she'd have to get used to. She studied the portrait; it was familiar and dear.

'April,' Elizabeth called, and April turned to face her aunt. She ran to her and the two women embraced. The scent of lavender and lilac surrounded them.

Elizabeth pushed her gently away. 'Let me look at you, child.' She studied April's face with pleasure. Her niece's brown hair curled around the delicate oval face. It was the dimple in her chin that made her face appear heart-shaped. Her skin was a delicate baby-rose pink, her eyes violet-blue.

'You're positively beautiful,' Elizabeth pronounced. 'You were as a child. I so hoped you wouldn't outgrow it.'

April's cheeks flushed with pleasure and embarrassment. 'Thank you, Aunt Elizabeth.'

'Hush, my dear – you mustn't thank me for speaking the truth. Come along,' she took April's arm. 'We'll eat in the kitchen. The house is so big, so dark.'

April agreed, looking into the huge gloomy rooms on either side of them. The kitchen, in contrast, was warm and cozy.

'Hannah,' Elizabeth called. 'April's arrived.'

Out of the pantry, Hannah emerged, round and placid as ever.

'Welcome home, Miss.'

'Thank you,' April said.

'We'll eat in the kitchen,' Elizabeth announced, as she

pulled out the stout maple chair.

'Very well,' Hannah agreed. Her total discomfort at their presence in the kitchen was obvious. She dropped a pan, which startled them. The fire sputtered and they heard her plaintive 'Ouch!' as she burned her hand on the stove.

April could see why Elizabeth had chosen the kitchen. A fire roared in the fireplace and the warmth of the stove made the room cozy in its steaminess. The window-ledges were lined with potted plants, yellow flowers bloomed cheerfully on the dark windows.

It was impossible for April to broach anything personal with Hannah bustling among them. Then she wondered if this, perhaps, was the real reason her aunt had chosen the kitchen.

'Where are the boys?' April asked.

'Oh, Kyle is in Jefferson City. You know he has his heart set on being a Senator someday.'

April nodded. 'He'd make a good one. Kyle was always very diplomatic.'

Elizabeth beamed. 'And Ryan, of course, is in Africa. They'll both be here for Thanksgiving. You'll see them then.'

'Thanksgiving!' April exclaimed, her surprise making her direct. 'I won't be here for Thanksgiving. That's a month and a half away and I only have two weeks' leave.'

'Oh, I'll take care of that,' Elizabeth shrugged. She reached in the pocket of her robe and handed April a small piece of folded paper. It was then April registered that her aunt wasn't dressed. Elizabeth was wearing a silk robe over a gown.

'Are you ill, Aunt Elizabeth?' she asked, a small frown pleating her forehead.

'Not really. That's what it's all about,' she said, and pointed to the paper. It was a prescription.

'I'm only a physical therapist. I can't read prescriptions.'

'That's all right. That's what it's for. It's a prescription from my doctor for occupational therapy,' Elizabeth said, looking very pleased with herself.

Before April could comment, or question, the room became very still. Elizabeth stiffened visibly.

Tom, who was filling the woodboxes, dropped a log and was cursing softly under his breath.

April looked at Hannah, who glanced fearfully toward the windows.

Elizabeth jumped up and flung open the back door, peering out into the darkness. The 'Whoo, whoo' of an owl was heard clearly in the room.

'He's back,' Elizabeth said tersely.

'It might not be the same one,' Tom answered, as he grabbed the shotgun and went out on the porch.

The gunshot ricocheted through the trees and the woods.

Elizabeth shivered. 'I'm tired, and I suppose you are too, dear, with all that traveling. You could eat in your room.'

'Yes, I'm tired,' April agreed.

'Tom has put your things in your old room. Hannah can bring up a tray.'

It was the first time April noticed how old her aunt had grown. The slim shoulders were bent, and deep lines creased her forehead. She was still a handsome woman, her beige hair mixed with gray, small and slender, with the bearing of someone who has spent her life with the best of everything.

She reached for April's arm and they went silently up the back staircase.

At the bedroom door, Elizabeth reached for her. She crushed her tightly and said, 'I'm so glad you've come.'

April returned her embrace and lied, 'Me, too.'

April let herself into the room. It was like an echo of a familiar tune – parts of it well-remembered, while others seemed new and strange.

The canopied bed was fresh, with the white eyelet

covers. The French provincial furniture was placed as before – two chairs in chintz with tiny violets sprinkled among the fabric. The windows were done in Austrian shades, with pale satin drapes in the quietest of purple. It was a woman's room totally. White with all shades of violet and rose.

April seemed made for the room. She took off her jacket, kicked off her shoes, and felt the deep plush of the carpet. Shortly afterwards, Hannah knocked and swung open the door. She set the tray on the marble table.

'I'll be back for the tray later,' she said. A cloth in her hand absently dusted the table that was immaculate. Hannah was like that, plump, placid, forever in motion. It was hard to imagine her being still.

April ignored the food. 'Is my aunt ill?' she asked, searching Hannah's face for the truth.

Hannah looked down, not meeting her eyes. 'I don't think so. It's just that she's restless since the Judge's gone.'

April was all set to question Hannah further when it came again – the distinct 'Whoo' of an owl, somewhere close in the night outside the window.

Hannah, as before, was frozen, the dusting rag still.

'What is it?' April demanded. 'It's only an owl.'

'I know, Miss, but Miz Elizabeth insists it's the same one.'

'Which one? What do you mean?' April asked.

Hannah walked to the window and pointed. 'There in the tree, that banyan tree. It sat there every night for five nights and hooted. Then the Judge died.'

'Banyan tree?' April said.

'Yes. It's that same fool tree that Ryan brought from Africa or one of them foreign places he goes. It was that foreign tree the owl picked to sit in and hoot,' Hannah finished.

'There's lots of owls at Castelwood, Tom told you that,' April reasoned.

'I know, but Miz Elizabeth got something in her mind

'bout that tree. She had it cut down. Now the owl comes back just the same and sits on the stump.'

April took Hannah by the shoulders and looked at her honest, plain face. 'Hannah, that's silly. That's superstitious. You know that.'

The woman nodded. 'I guess so, but all that talk, it's Kack, with her silliness. I guess that got Miz Elizabeth that way.'

'What way?' April asked, lost.

Hannah's face looked closed.

'What way?' April repeated.

'Thinking that owl came back for someone else,' Hannah blushed. 'You better eat. Your food's getting cold.'

April sat down and took the lid off the silver tray. She was pleased to see it contained a simple savory stew, with hot biscuits and honey. She savored the honey, knowing it was from Hilltop hives. A pot of hot coffee, and fresh baked peach pie followed. The peaches were from the orchards – she could taste their freshness. She felt nostalgic eating Castlewood peach pie. When she had finished eating, she put the tray outside the door.

She went over to close the Austrian shades, and in the moonlight could see the raw stump of the recently felled tree. In the scrub elm beyond it was the distant shadow of an owl. Without meaning to, she shivered and closed the blinds.

April went into the bathroom and ran the steamy water. She unpacked the traveling case and took out her flannel gown. It was only October, but the old house had a chill, even though the radiators were warm.

She undressed and caught a glimpse of herself in the dimness of the mirror: her body white as marble, her hair agleam, and her eyes luminous as candles. She was slender, and tall, her figure in perfect proportions. The rosy pink of her nipples ... She stared at her image and thought of Ryan and Kyle. It was a mad insane moment, for she always forgot. She wished desperately that they weren't cousins.

She pinned up her hair; the soft curls struggled to be free.

She soaked in the huge, luxurious tub and tried not to think. The warm water relaxed her limbs and she almost dozed. The feeling that was foremost now was one of peace. She had come home. Though Hilltop was troubled, it felt like home.

When the water cooled, April climbed out and dried herself with the rough violet towel. It was then that she noticed the flowers in the vase on the marble ledge of the bathroom.

She leaned down and sniffed the redolent lilacs. Lilacs in October? She knew they had come from the greenhouse. The Judge had become an avid gardener after his retirement.

Her uncle had taken such pleasure in the greenhouse. He particularly enjoyed growing anything out of season.

She could remember several Christmases when the family had sent her plump juicy strawberries, grown right here in Missouri. She recalled the pleasure of eating them with the snow piled high against the windows in Ohio.

The lilacs now breathed their fragrance and made April feel sad and happy at the same time.

She put on the warm flannel gown, and catching her reflection again, saw that she looked about seventeen. Her gown loose and cosy around her made her feel young and hopeful.

She turned out the light and crept in among the thick quilts.

The moon was brilliant and cast shadows across the room. They seemed like the ghosts of yesterdays, and April felt herself stiffen and listen for the hoot that she was sure would come. It did not.

She tossed and turned, remembering other nights, other years, happy years when she was a child. She so loved Castlewood, its uniqueness, its traditions; even though the city crept closer on cat's paws, it remained unchanged, a special place.

April turned and her hand slipped under the pillow.

She felt the crispness of the wrapping paper, the unmistakable coil of a ribbon.

She sat up and turned on the light. She lifted the pillow and it was there – a pretty white package tied with a crimson ribbon. A small well of happiness bubbled within her. It had been a ritual since she was a child, whenever she came to visit. They had each given her a present, each and every one of them. There were always seven presents, from Uncle William, Aunt Elizabeth, Kyle, Ryan, Tom, Hannah and Kack. The presents were always hidden about the room.

April felt the same sense of elation now. She climbed out of bed; under it, a silver-wrapped present waited. Like a happy child she opened drawers, looked under cushions, behind the drapes, until she had found them all. Forgetting, she kept searching for the seventh one until, with a start, she remembered there would only be six now.

Happily she surveyed the stack of tiny packages. She tore at the silver paper, opened the slender box. The paper whispered as she held the elegant shaft of crystal aloft. The note was simple in his hand: *'I remembered you always wanted to catch a rainbow. I've done it for you. Ryan.'*

She put the obelisk of crystal on the table. The light caught it and the rainbow was hers, caught securely in the glass.

The next package was from Aunt Elizabeth. She cried when she saw the antique earrings and the matching necklace. Teardrops of amethyst – deep, deep purple – with a note from her aunt: *'To match your eyes.'*

She opened the box from Kyle. It contained an antique locket. She clicked open the scrolled cover, to see them as they were then, her two handsome cousins as children. His note in a bold hand said, *'I've done the impossible for you. I've given you yesterday.'* She understood perfectly, and looked into the smiling faces and remembered.

Hannah gave her make-up, gaudy and loud with a sweet note: *'For a beautiful lady'* and Tom a clumsy box containing Gardenia perfume with a crudely scrawled wish of good luck.

Last, she opened the package from Kack. Cradled in the box on a soft bed of dandelion wisp it lay there, the most perfect one she had ever seen. Its arms seemed to stretch upward, imploringly, its legs were widespread, with tiny grasping feet – and it had a wide portion of body. It was very old, one of the ones they believed to be the most potent. The twisted root looked like a tiny headless man. It was the perfect ginseng.

April lifted it out of the box, and dandelion fluff drifted away on an unseen breeze. She felt a thrill. How many times had she helped them gather it? The fun – the mystery of the sang-hunt . . .

Here in this room, it did seem mysterious, magical. In the box in a large scrawl Kack had written one word, *'Believe.'*

The owl hooted and sent a shiver through her.

She pulled up the shade and stared out into the moonlight. She held the manroot up before her like a cross and the owl flew away.

# CHAPTER 26

The scent of aftershave came to her, it seemed, as part of a pleasant dream.

The scent mingled with rum and maple pipe tobacco, and the smell of damp weeds invaded her senses. April felt a gentle yet firm touch on her wrist, and in the distance she heard the soft staccato of rain.

Whatever the dream was, it was far pleasanter than the one that had preceded it. She tried to turn over and burrow into the softness of the pillows, but the touch on her wrist restrained her. Her eyes flew open. The first thing she saw was the crystal chandelier above her.

*Castlewood.* She was really here. A pain throbbed in her head; she felt general discomfort in her whole body.

Her eyes focused, she turned to see him sitting by the bed. A shock of warm brown hair crowned his strong, angular face. His forehead was creased in a concerned frown.

His eyes, black and cool, searched her face, his firm hand still holding hers.

'April.' He called her name softly, with a familiar sound and pronunciation, yet his identity escaped her. His fingers clasped her wrist. She saw the barely perceptible movement of his lips as he counted. It was then she noticed the stethoscope around his neck. The realization that he was a doctor jarred her; she sat bolt upright in the bed.

Her lips started to form a question, but before she could

213

speak, his face broke out into a wide, reassuring smile. 'You're all right,' he told her. He took pleasure in searching her face. She had grown lovely, even in this condition. He took a man's pleasure in her tangled dark curls; he yearned to reach over and smooth them away from her satin face. Her dark eyelashes swept down over the startling violet eyes as she tried remembering, sorting it out.

'Bradley,' he said. 'Brad Estes. Dr Estes now.'

'Of course.' She reached forward to embrace him, but a pain jarred her, and she looked down at her shoulder instead. The flannel gown was torn in ribbons. She could see the angry scratches on her shoulder.

She flung the covers aside and saw that the bed was all muddy. Leaves were scattered all over the rug.

'What happened?' she asked, feeling frightened yet foolish.

'Remember what you used to do when you were a little girl and you were upset?' he asked, reluctant to tell her and placing hints so she might recall on her own.

'Of course – I *was* upset: the owl, Aunt Elizabeth, the nightmares ... have I been walking in my sleep?' She looked at his face for affirmation.

'I'd say, young lady, that you must have taken a hell of a walk in the woods. You're scratched from head to toe, and your feet are badly bruised and cut. It's nothing serious, however.'

April moved gingerly, feeling tenderness all over her body. 'It's good to see you again, Brad. So you're a doctor – I always guessed you'd become one. I remember the fallen robins, the injured squirrels, the possums.' She reached for his hand and turned it over to find the jagged scar. 'Yes, I guess you do remember the possum.' She laughed.

His eyes were warm as they reminisced. 'I remember you were always right behind me, bandaging them up, our poor charges from the woods. That is, when you weren't tagging Ryan or Kyle.'

April blushed and said nothing.

He ignored the blush and went on: 'Elizabeth tells me you're a physical therapist.'

'That's right. I took a leave because Aunt Elizabeth wanted me to come.' April stopped, not knowing how to word it. 'She said she needed me.'

'That she does,' Brad assured her. 'I'd say she needs you very much.'

'I have my work, my own life. I can't stay long,' April protested.

'You have your ties, too, of blood. She's your aunt, she has no daughters – and I'm sure she's always thought of you that way.'

'I know. What can I help her with? She very seriously showed me a prescription for occupational therapy. I told her I was a *physical* therapist. It's nowhere near the same thing – you know that.'

'That was really a private joke. When Elizabeth came with this ache and that pain, I jokingly wrote her that prescription, told her to get busy, find some new interests.' Brad put away the stethoscope and clicked his bag shut. 'I would say this little scare has given her something to do. I've been invited to stay for a late lunch or an early dinner, whichever comes first. She's ordering everyone around. She sent Tom out to look for blackberries. Hannah is fair near exhausted trying to keep up with Elizabeth as she keeps changing the menu.'

April stretched experimentally. 'Good, I'm glad you're staying.' She looked down at the bed. 'I've made a real mess.'

'Oh, your mess has been good for Elizabeth as well. She's moved all your things to another room, and you've given her something to think about.'

April laughed. 'I guess I'll have to do it more often.'

Brad nodded. 'I don't recommend it. For now, I'll ring for Hannah to run you a warm bath.' He reopened the case and handed her a small white bottle. 'Put this on the scratches. They're nothing serious.' He reached for the cord to call Hannah.

'Don't bother. I can run my own bath,' April said.

He stood up and she realized how tall and handsome he had gotten since those days when he came over to pal around with her cousins.

'I'll be in the library,' he said as he held out his hands. She reached for them and he gave her a pull. She leaped out of bed and stood a little unsteadily.

'Put this on the scratches,' he reminded. He picked up his bag and walked to the door. 'Kack is probably lurking around here somewhere with some potions of her own,' he warned.

April nodded in agreement.

'Kack is remarkable. You know, a lot of people have gone back to old-time medicine; nothing wrong with it,' Brad admitted.

He stood in the doorway, looking back at her. So little, so waif-like in her tattered gown. He was glad he had come. His heart quickened at the prospect of knowing her better.

April ran the water. She took off the tattered gown. The mirror was full of steam. She wiped it. She could see clearly now how many scratches marred her perfect skin. She looked down at her mud-caked feet. They ached.

She climbed into the soapy water, where an alarming stinging took place as the water touched her tender skin. She leaned back, trying to relax and let the warmth take out the soreness from her limbs.

She tried but could not remember clearly the nightmare that had sent her out to the dark woods. It was the same dream she had had as a child, of her cousin drowning in the river.

She heard a soft knock on the door.

'It's me, Miss April – Hannah. I'm changing the bed, and I brought your clothes. Miz Elizabeth picked 'em out. Your other things are in Mr Ryan's room. Miz Elizabeth thought you could sleep there till we get the rugs and everything cleaned.'

'Thank you, Hannah.' April called through the door. 'Sorry about the mess.'

'No trouble, Miss,' was Hannah's answer.

April closed her eyes and waited for the water to soak her clean.

It was fifteen minutes or so before she finally got out. She wrapped a small towel around her hair, and the large one sarong-like around her body. With relief, she saw that the scratches were indeed superficial, and already looked much better. Her feet, however, were swollen.

Although her bed had been freshly made, the rug was still full of leaves and footprints. A light rain beat at the window, and April went to the french doors and looked out.

The woods, for fall, looked incredibly green in some places, while the rain pelted at the other autumn leaves, forcing them to the ground. Behind the grove you could see the brown rushing water of the Meramec River.

It was a slender, narrow section that looked deceptively inconsequential. Yet April remembered the warnings and the somber times of the drownings. Many had been claimed by the river, for it was beset with deep, dark undertows. It always seemed strange to have it so close. That awful memory when she had almost drowned in its murky depths was very vivid.

She shivered as the picture of the drowned man could be recalled by just closing her eyes. Uncle William's lesson had been traumatic for her. It had brought on the nightmares that stayed with her for many years – the terror much worse, for in the dream, that dreadful corpse had been replaced by Kyle, no, Ryan – one of them.

April looked out into the autumn wetness of the day and wondered where she had gone walking in the night.

Among the trees, she saw a slight movement. April strained her eyes into the grayness of the day, then made out a figure standing there huddled in the grove of trees, looking up. A woman, dressed all in brown, a shawl wound tightly about her head.

It was Kack.

April opened the french door. She called out. Her voice was lost in the wind and carried back to her. She waved a hand and the figure moved forward, approaching silently through the trees. She came up the terrace stairs, and April pulled her in and shut the door behind them.

'Kack, I'm so glad to see you.'

The wet shawl fell off Kack's head. She looked just the same – her hair pulled back tightly from a face that was older but still smooth and brown, unlined. Only her hair showed her age, its strands of silver mating well with the black.

'I came when I heard you were hurt,' she said solemnly.

April laughed, remembering Brad's words. 'It's nothing,' she said.

Kack clicked her tongue under her breath. 'Sit, child, sit.' She ushered her to a vanity chair.

From under her skirt, she took out a leather pouch, and knelt and opened it. She unscrewed a jar and a fragrant odor of salve filled the room. Gently with her fingertip she smoothed an ocher potion on the scratches. April felt an immediate soothing sensation and gave herself up to the administration of Kack. They all trusted her; they always had.

It was when she lifted April's foot that she gave a quiet soft clucking. 'It is the bruise that we must fix.' She delved further into the pouch and lifted out a jar. It was filled with fluid, and clinging to the sides were small black leeches.

April gasped. She had never in her life challenged or questioned Kack.

'Here, child. Look outside. Count the raindrops. It only takes a minute.'

April obeyed, looking out the window. 'Count the raindrops' – how like Kack to say such an outrageous thing. She wasn't a child.

April felt the coolness as Kack applied the creatures to her bruised foot. She didn't know what she expected, but the pressure was relieved almost immediately. She kept looking away into the rainy afternoon.

Relieved, April heard the click of the lid as Kack put the things away.

'You're better now.' Her solemn face broke out into a shy smile.

'Thank you.'

Kack stood and gathered her wet things around her. She seemed anxious to go. She left by the french doors, went back into the forest, and April could imagine her threading her way back up the path to the cabin.

She shuddered as she thought of the leeches, but her feet looked better; the purple bruise had already faded.

She inspected the clothes Elizabeth had chosen from her suitcase: gray tailored slacks and a soft gray cashmere turtleneck.

She dressed swiftly. She chose only mascara. It enhanced her already beautiful eyes. She dabbed on soft pink lipstick.

The blower dashed her hair about, curling naturally and falling about her face like a delicate frame.

She put on the necklace – a single teardrop of purple. It caught the light and kept it prisoner. Next, the matching earrings. This old-fashioned amethyst set seemed made for her. It brought brilliant pinpoints of violet forth in her eyes. She looked radiant.

She took one last look at herself in the mirror and was satisfied.

Her arms and legs were covered; none of the scratches were visible.

She opened the door to the front staircase; already the house seemed different, more alive. The smell of cinnamon wafted from the kitchen, and a soft symphony played somewhere in the house. In the library Brad had made a large, cheerful fire.

Rabelay, old and weary, his thick yellow fur grown thinner, lay on the hearth. She went over to the old dog and patted his head. The warm brown eyes looked up at her and his tail wagged happily.

'Hi, boy. He must really be old,' she said to Brad.

'It's not Rabelay, it's his son, who is pretty old, too. You look very beautiful.'

'Thank you.'

'Shall we play chess, checkers, or just talk?' Brad asked.

'Let's talk. You always beat me at checkers and I don't know how to play chess,' she said truthfully.

'Brandy?'

She nodded yes, taking the chair nearest the fire. Brad sat across from her.

Her eyes wandered up and studied the painting above the mantel: two deer, a doe and her fawn, peeking out of the trees, a woodthrush on the branch above. April even knew the nook; it was Castlewood all right – the place near the big rocks.

Brad followed her gaze and said, 'The man's a genius. He is getting a worldwide reputation for being the finest wildlife artist alive. Ryan was always like that; he so loved them, the creatures. You could only paint like that if you really loved.'

April nodded. 'It's amazing how he captures and holds that one moment, even though it's gone.'

'He's coming home early, you know.'

'No, I didn't. Aunt Elizabeth said they'd both be home for Thanksgiving. I told her it was out of the question. I have my work,' April said.

Brad looked at her. 'This might be more important. She needs someone to wait on, worry about. Since William, she's lost, and those damn letters, they keep coming.'

'Letters?' April asked, puzzled.

'Yes. I guess she hasn't told you. A developer keeps

hounding her. Seems they want to buy Hilltop and build condominiums.'

'Condominiums?' April sputtered.

'That's the way Elizabeth feels too – outraged. But they won't leave her alone. They just think she's holding out, and so they keep upping the price.'

Elizabeth smiled through dinner. Hannah had outdone herself. The trout was perfect, as was the salad, asparagus and hot buttermilk rolls, and the blackberries were prime and sweet. The meal was perfection! Elizabeth coaxed them to eat as if they were children, and she enjoyed their eager talk.

It was good to have people in the house.

# CHAPTER 27

April enjoyed herself. She took long walks in the woods, and Kack had invited her to the sang-hunt.

For this she donned khakis and a thick sweater, and met Kack on the porch by the cabin. She was invited in for a brisk tea. Entering the cabin that was full of memories, she saw it was unchanged. Roots still hung drying in clusters and pots of herbs lined the window-ledges. In the back under the bookcases stood the perennial wicker cages. Rustlings from within assured April that, as ever, Kack had some small furry charges that were mending there.

Idly she browsed through the bookshelf. Surprise shone in her face as she read the titles. Here were all of the classics, as well as mythology of the world, the Bible, the Koran – and books on all manner of philosophy. The reading was eclectic. With new interest, she watched Kack pour the tea.

'You've some wonderful books.'

Kack nodded. 'The Judge was very generous. He encouraged me. Most of those, he gave me.'

Surprise and shame at the same time coursed through April. She hadn't realized that her uncle and Kack had been friends. She remembered the Judge as conventional, busy, staid; she could not envisage any rapport between them. She felt dismay at her own prejudice. She, and she imagined everyone else shared her view, had always thought of Kack as uneducated, ignorant and full of superstitions and quaint ways. A modern-day savage.

She looked at her with fresh eyes. 'Do you believe in precognition?'

Holding the tea in both hands, Kack slowly sipped. Nodding her head, she answered the girl cautiously. 'It's possible.'

April pressed for answers, wishing that Kack were more verbal. 'Do you believe in dreams?'

Still sipping, she nodded yes.

April now leaned forward, her forehead creased with anxiety. 'I mean, do you believe that a dream, a repeated dream of some event, can be precognition?'

'Yes, it can be that.'

'Oh, Kack,' April blurted. 'I've had the same dream for years. Then it went away, and now I had it again last night. I dream . . . I dream that Ryan – no, Kyle—' She stopped in confusion. 'I dream that one of them drowns in that horrible river.'

Involuntarily, Kack's hand went up and clutched her breast. Recovering her composure, she tried to ease the girl's mind.

'It's natural for you to fear the river, after almost drowning in it. I know the Judge meant well, when you were all children, but I'm not so sure he should have shown you one that had been claimed by the waters.' She reached across and patted April's hand.

'So you're saying it might be those things that are the basis for the dream?' April asked hopefully.

'Yes.'

They both felt relief and welcomed the exercise of walking, climbing through foliage, crawling under brush, seeking out the manroot.

When the sun was high in the west, they picked their way home slowly through the dense wood, dragging the full burlap sacks behind them.

Parting at the path to the cabin, they saw a rabbit loping up the worn track toward them.

'It seems tame,' April remarked.

'Yes, it's one of mine. The cages are not always secure.' She reached down and clutched the animal to her breast.

As April turned toward the house, she heard the soft humming, a happy uplifting sound, so unlike Kack. From that day forward, April discarded the name Kack and her image of the modern savage.

The woman was someone else.

She had always been Katherine – or maybe, when she was younger, even Kathy.

# CHAPTER 28

It was subtle and swift how quickly the house, the grounds had gotten their grip upon April. It reminisced of the times as a child when she expressed the longing to her mother: 'I wish I could stay here forever.'

The days were slow, easy. She grew interested in the greenhouse, which had been ignored since the Judge's death. She coaxed the wilted plants till small green heads peaked suspiciously out of the withered brown.

She found seeds and planted strawberries. How wonderful to have them ripe and luscious in the winter!

Always Aunt Elizabeth encouraged her to stay another few days, one more week. Finally, April called the hospital to extend her leave of absence.

Whenever she mentioned going back, Aunt Elizabeth burst into tears. 'You can't leave me now, dear. I need you. There's plenty to do. Why, the greenhouse – you've done wonders with it! April, hospitals are depressing. I know, child, you're a poetess at heart. I remember your mother reading me all those wonderful poems that you wrote when you were little. We have notepads in William's study. It seems with all the solitude it would be a wonderful chance for your poetry.' She finished, looking hopefully at her niece.

April realized the depths of her loneliness, and for the first time saw her aunt properly – as a spoiled, childish woman who couldn't bear to have the house empty. The luxury at Hilltop made it easy for April to give in. It was so different from her hectic, harried life. She had put herself through college and had managed on her own after Mother's death, but it wasn't easy.

So, sighing, she gave in, and happily Elizabeth began planning Thanksgiving. She was especially excited because Ryan was bringing from Africa a photographer from *Life* magazine, who had accompanied him on the safari.

'A fascinating woman, I'm sure,' Elizabeth pronounced. 'As for Kyle, perhaps he will bring someone from the Capitol – one of his political friends, maybe'

And, 'Good, good,' Elizabeth pronounced every time a new item arrived from St Louis. A silver punch-bowl – they'd need it for both occasions. New monogrammed napkins. The house would be full of voices, footsteps, music – it would be good. Maybe then she could drown out the humming that she heard at night, from within the green room.

Elizabeth spent the afternoons looking through catalogs, yelling from time to time, 'Hannah, quick! Come here!' Hannah would come and peer at the book on her mistress' lap.

'There, Hannah, look – isn't that marvelous? I think we need one of those. Well, on second thought, maybe two, in case we break one.'

Hannah carefully wrote down the numbers of each item that the mistress wanted to day. It gave Elizabeth something to do. She could listen out for the bell and then call down to the kitchen: 'Is that the bell, Hannah? Maybe it's a delivery!'

'No, it's Bruce about the brooms. He got locked out and came around front.'

'What brooms?'

'You know, ma'am, he makes them brooms. He's wantin' Tom to take him to Castlewood to sell some.'

'Oh, all right. But while Tom's there he could buy . . . he could buy—' she felt irritated with herself. There must be *something* they needed. 'Tell him they can go, as soon as I finish my list.'

She got the pad, wet the pencil-tip on her lips, saying aloud, 'There must be something we need.' She began thinking in earnest. Soon the pencil worked busily on the list. 'Hannah, it's ready!' Good, she felt satisfied there was something to do today. She would need to unpack the things when they got back, check the list; maybe the bell would ring and they would get a delivery today.

She sighed, then straightened up with purpose. She'd find April and send her outside to gather fall flowers or greenery – if nothing else, pretty leaves, for all the vases were empty. That just wouldn't do.

She went outside on the terrace and began calling, 'April! April, honey.'

# CHAPTER 29

The smell of food cooking began filling the house as early as 6 a.m..

Elizabeth had sent Tom to Castlewood twice. She had forgotten the cream for the frozen strawberries, and she was sure they needed more beer. 'Boys drink beer, don't they?' Her forehead knotted in concentration. She couldn't remember – did the boys drink beer?

She hushed Tom's protest about the stores not being open on Thanksgiving, especially this early.

'Nonsense, Tom, just knock. Kirby's Grocery – they live right upstairs. Tell them the Judge—' She stopped. It was a habit of many years – just mentioning the Judge had always got her what she needed. 'You know, Tom. You know what to tell them about the beer. Get Sheriff Mosley to ask them to open up. Run along, Tom – there's so much to do.'

Elizabeth rushed back and forth to the kitchen, peeking in pots, not sure what she was looking for, and anxiously asking Hannah, 'Is there enough room?'

'Yes, ma'am, there's plenty.' She nodded toward the kitchen table where the leaf had been put in to make it bigger.

Counting out loud, Elizabeth pointed, 'Hannah, Tom, Bruce and Kack.'

'Yes, ma'am, there's only the four of us.'

'Good, good,' Elizabeth exclaimed. 'It would be so

awkward. The Judge always insisted on her eating with us on special occasions.'

Hannah wiped her hands. 'Kack's more than welcome here. We have plenty of room.'

Satisfied, Elizabeth left the kitchen to inspect the dining room, which Hannah had prepared the night before.

The centrepiece waited. Elizabeth knew that April was planning something from the greenhouse. She better tell her pink would be best, to go with the rose damask curtains and the forest-green napkins. Yes, pink should be the dominant color.

Going to the hall, gently she called up the stairs, 'April! April, honey.' Getting no answer, she went back to the study and sat, leafing through her notebook, convinced she had forgotten something. She was the sort of woman who enjoyed the planning and preparation far better than the actual event.

When April awoke at eight and had eaten a quick breakfast, she went out to the back sun-porch to retrieve the centerpiece she had arranged yesterday.

The unheated porch had been a perfect storage place for the flowers, which looked crisp and fresh. They were primarily Thanksgiving colors – spotted orange day lilies, yellow carnations, russet and red mums. She was satisfied that the arrangement was perfect. She felt pleased at how appropriate it was, without being overdone.

Elizabeth, on seeing her carrying the arrangement into the dining room, followed her in. 'April, honey,' she began. April knew that tone. It was a request – no, not really a request – it was usually a quiet, whining demand.

Elizabeth sighed. 'It's real pretty. Fits the occasion all right.' She stopped the tilted her head from side to side. 'It's beautiful – don't get me wrong.'

April gave her an indulgent smile and said patiently, 'It's not what you wanted?'

Glad that the asking was over, Elizabeth moved to the drapes, picking at the cloth. 'Well, I thought pink or dusty rose or whatever the color is—' She rushed on, 'That one we'll put in the Judge's study. They all sit around and smoke in there. Why, with the Governor smoking those terrible cigars of his, I think that these flowers might still hold up.'

'The Governor?' April said quizzically.

'He's not the Governor anymore. He's not been for some years. He was a dear friend of the Judge's. I think he's taken to Kyle. Poor man, his wife died last year and he's getting on in years. It was mighty sweet of Kyle to invite him. Nobody should have to spend Thanksgiving alone.' Elizabeth reached over and carefully lifted the centerpiece and was off to debate where to put it in the study.

April grabbed a sweater and ran down to the greenhouse to cut new flowers, carefully selecting carnations and mums in ranges of pink. The greenhouse was now vibrant and alive under her care.

Within an hour, the new centerpiece was done.

'Perfect,' Elizabeth pronounced. 'You're so talented. How's the poetry coming?'

Rather than tell her she hadn't written any, April answered, 'Just fine.'

'You know about the typewriter in the Judge's study?'

'Yes.'

At noon both Elizabeth and April went upstairs to bathe and dress for the guests, as Tom was due at the airport in St Louis at one o'clock to pick up Kyle and the Governor. He would barely have time to bring them out and return to collect Ryan and his guest at three.

The Thanksgiving meal was planned for six that evening.

Under Hannah's capable hands, everything would be ready.

Two o'clock found both women dressed and sitting in the formal living room.

The peal of the doorbell startled Elizabeth, set her

nerves tingling. 'Darn that boy. I always give him an extra set of keys. I hope Hannah doesn't answer with her apron on.' The second impatient ring had April volunteering. She hurried to the hall.

She opened the door and Kyle, charming and vibrant, embraced her. 'Cousin April! How nice!' He held her at arm's length. 'Oh, you're a beauty all right. Mother said you were.' Graciously, he turned and introduced her to the rumpled old gentleman behind him.

April barely recognized the small boy grown so tall. Kyle was impeccable in an Italian gray silk suit. He was over six feet; a shock of wheat-colored hair fell across his forehead, and his eyes, clear and sparkling, appeared gray-blue. His jaw was angular and straight, his smile dazzling. He had the charisma of a born politician.

He led the tottering Governor into the living room. Before he was seated, the old gentleman was already searching in his pockets for the predictable cigar that Elizabeth had mentioned.

'Mother, how nice you look.' Kyle twirled her around, then grabbing her in a bear hug, planted firm kisses on her cheek. She blushed and was terribly pleased.

Patting her hair and smoothing her pearls, she led the Governor to the leather armchair by the fire. It was several minutes before she realized that she had to sit closer to him, for she was shouting and he still couldn't hear her.

Kyle had gone to the kitchen, untied Hannah's apron and lifted her off her feet and danced her around before putting her down before the stove.

'You're in high spirits,' Hannah laughed.

'Ah, woman, after a few bourbons I'll be higher still.'

'Mister Kyle, you don't need to be in any higher spirits.' She felt a twinge of nostalgia for days gone by that would never return.

He slapped her playfully on the rump and winked. 'Hannah, burn the turkey. I dare you. It would be worth it just to see Mother's face.'

Slapping a dishrag at him, she commanded, 'Git – now you git!' She loved it, the boys' teasing.

Like the perfect host, Kyle poured wine for the ladies and straight bourbon for the Governor and himself.

Looking from April to his mother, Kyle explained, 'The Governor's on the zoning committee for the county. Now that could be real helpful for the acreage.'

The older man nodded and sipped his whiskey, relighting the cigar that had gone out.

'Oh Kyle, later on I must tell you about the letters, the offers. That holding company – it upsets me so – keeps pestering me about the acreage.'

Her son's face grew grave. 'Mother, I don't want you talking to any of those people.' His jovial mood was gone.

'Oh, I haven't!' she exclaimed. 'I throw the letters away. Why, they have upped the offer twice.'

Like a sunbeam, his smile returned. 'How clever of you, Mother.'

Her face was puzzled and her voice trailed. 'But . . .'

He ignored her feeble protest and turned to April. 'I hear you've been a superb gardener and have Father's greenhouse in shape again.'

Modestly, April said, 'I've enjoyed it.'

Taking her hands, he pulled her up. 'You must show me. I'm from Missouri,' and the charming Kyle was back.

She grabbed a sweater and they walked down the brick path, crisp leaves crunching under their feet.

Once inside the greenhouse, the moist, heavy perfume surrounded them.

He pretended interest in the flowers; he snapped off a miniature rose, pink with a hint of purple. Reaching down, he trailed the velvet softness across her cheek. 'Almost as lovely as you.' His eyes smoldered, looking deep into hers.

Feeling uncomfortable with his intimacy, she turned and began rattling off the names of some of the new plants she had started from seedlings.

He touched her shoulder and leaned over her. She felt his warm breath on her neck, and if he hadn't been her cousin, she would have felt he was definitely making a pass at her. A smug smile sat on his face and he was amused at her discomfort. 'How long are you staying, little cousin?'

The word 'cousin' acknowledged their relationship; she felt better.

'I don't know. I've already been here longer than I intended. Your mother can be very persuasive.'

'It runs in the family.' She saw the mischief in his eyes.

He took her hand and she felt comfortable now walking with him.

'I hope Mother hasn't seated you next to the Governor at dinner. He's deaf as stone, you know. He's still part of the old establishment; he's been a big help. Why with Dad's old cronies, I'm a shoo-in for Governor, even Senator some day.'

'That's wonderful.' April squeezed his hand.

As they came up the driveway, they saw the Mercedes pulling in.

April shivered in the wind, holding her sweater closer. Ryan jumped out first.

The brothers embraced with much whooping, hollering and punching each other companionably.

April had a chance to quietly observe Ryan during the exchange. The twins were both the same height; Ryan's hair was shorter, leaning more to blond, his skin bronze. When he turned to her, it was the same square jaw, the eyes icy blue, and he gave her a shy smile reluctantly.

Then with recognition he burst out, 'April, of course!' He came and hugged her, rocking her back and forth. Holding her at arm's length, he looked deeply into her eyes. 'I'm so glad to see you.' They nodded, smiling at each other.

'Now, who's this?' Kyle's playfulness returned as he bent his head into the car.

Ryan, regaining his manners, helped Monica out of the car.

She was sleek, thin to the point of gauntness, tall, willowy, her blonde hair pulled severely back. She, too, was golden-bronze from the sun. She wore a stylish tight pants suit, cinched at the waist, her large dark eyes were immaculately made up and her jewelry was bold – huge gold earrings and on her arm, a jungle of bracelets.

She looked as if she had come off the cover of an exclusive fashion magazine. Her voice matched her appearance. It was low, soft, with a distant flat, bored accent.

In the house Elizabeth was pleased to see them. She brightened at the glamorous woman; she yearned to move away from the Governor, at whom she had been shouting for the last half hour.

Monica Mason was the well-known photographer who had been assigned to Ryan for his African trip. Together, they had produced the hundreds of slides from which he had worked when compiling the series of wildlife paintings for a company in New York, who would make numbered prints of his originals. It had been an important commission for Ryan.

Ryan was dressed casually in tan slacks and a V-necked sweater. Monica sat on the arm of his chair leaning possessively against his arm.

'Kyle,' Elizabeth said. 'Pictures – we should have some pictures of this occasion.'

Kyle looked across the room directly at Monica. 'With a world-famous photographer here? Mother, I'm an amateur, you know that.'

In the bored, flat voice Monica said, 'My equipment is in the luggage.' She continued caressing Ryan's arm, making it clear she didn't intend taking any pictures.

'Looks like I'm it.' Kyle left the room to get a camera.

The Governor, who had been napping, awoke with a start when the flashbulbs popped.

237

Kyle went about the room, taking random shots.

Elizabeth was pleased, as she liked looking at photographs and pasting them in the books.

Ryan extricated himself from the chair and Monica and made the drinks, and before they had finished them, Hannah announced dinner.

It was served early. Elizabeth would ask about that later.

Hannah served with a sly smile. If she had waited until six, the turkey would have been burnt to a crisp. Wouldn't Kyle have enjoyed that!

# CHAPTER 30

The dinner was perfection, and in the tradition of Thanks-giving, everyone ate too much.

They retired to the living room. Elizabeth implored April to play something for them. April looked through the piano bench and instead of selecting something classical, which she wasn't very good at anyway, she picked fun sing-along tunes.

Everyone was in a good mood, except Ryan. While the others sang in loud voices to *Row, Row, Row Your Boat*, he paced in front of the fireplace like a caged animal. He was furious when he asked his mother why Kack had been sent to eat in the kitchen. He was sure that she fibbed as she nervously twisted her pearls and avoided his eye as she told him, 'It was her choice, Ryan. She's uncomfortable around company.'

Ryan's scowl and the fact that he didn't sit had Monica miffed, so she zeroed in on Kyle. Taking the seat next to his, she draped her arm around him and they swayed rhythmically together as they belted out the songs.

The Governor dozed in the armchair. When the ash of his cigar dropped onto his vest and smoldered, Ryan was the first to smell the burning cloth. He dashed his drink onto the spot, which woke the old man up.

Elizabeth felt obligated to take him upstairs and show him his room. She was sure he would burn the house down before his visit was over.

Monica glanced sideways at Ryan to see if he had

noticed her obvious attention to his brother. Kyle kidded her – pretended a big leer – and offered to show her his photos. She accepted, telling him she would like to see his collections.

They went upstairs to the room addition that was Kyle's. Over the years, none of his equipment or things had been disturbed; Hannah merely cleaned and dusted the boys' rooms during their absence. When they returned, it was as if time had stood still. Nothing had changed.

Monica leafed through the albums of photographs. She grew excited when she saw the series he had done on Kack.

'These are wonderful! She looks like a savage. You know the hippies today pretend they are so back-to-nature – it's so artificial. But this woman, she's absolutely genuine. Oh Kyle, do you think she'd let me do a series on her?'

'Not a chance. She doesn't know I've taken half of these.'

'What's she doing here?' Monica asked, holding forth a blown-up bronzetone.

'Sang-hunting,' he replied.

'The composition is fantastic on this one. What's sang-hunting?'

'It's ginseng. It grows profusely in these woods and she gathers it.'

'What's this one?' She held up another photo of Kack ministering to a tiny doe. 'These are fantastic. Oh Kyle, I must talk to her. I could do such a wonderful series on this woman. Who is she? I mean, is she an employee?'

'No, just one of Father's – I don't know what you'd call it – he just allowed people to stay. I've no idea how she got here. She was Ryan's and my nursemaid when we were babies. I don't think he ever thought of her as an employee. It was before Bruce. I don't know how he got here either.'

'Who's Bruce?'

240

Kyle sifted through the photographs and found a poign-
ant one of Bruce sitting in the shed, working with the
brooms.

'He's blind, you know.'

'These are wonderful, too. I have to be able to work
with them. Why, the setting of these fantastic woods – it's
so picturesque. Their faces . . . God, Kyle, do you see her
cheekbones? Marvelous!' And she studied another picture
of Katherine.

'Well, don't get all excited, honey. She'd never let you.
I told you she never knew I took these. Her ancestors
were Indian, and she's full of superstitions about mirrors
and pictures, and images that steal the soul or something.
But Bruce – he's no problem. Shoot away. He'd love the
attention.'

'What did you take these with?' Monica was all business, asking about F stops and light and which camera.
Kyle opened the cabinet and handed her the Leica.

She turned it over and over in her hands. 'I've never
seen a camera like this,' she said.

He smiled. 'I guess not.'

'What do you mean?' she asked, puzzled. She was a
professional; she had worked with cameras most of her
life and had never seen one quite like it. 'It's backwards,'
she pronounced finally.

'I know. It was custom-made. My daddy knew how
frustrated I was as a kid – all cameras are made for right-
handed people. I'm left-handed.'

'Oh,' she smiled. 'How clever.'

'Yes – he had it made specially in Japan. I must say I
took my best pictures ever with that camera.'

He was tired of the talk. He shut off the bright lamp,
mixed them a drink and came to her smiling. 'Enough of
that,' he said, pushing the pictures away carelessly and
setting down her drink. He asked, 'Are you my brother's
private stock?'

'No,' she answered simply.

241

He drained his glass, his face red and flushed. 'Are you a match made in heaven?' he teased.

'No,' she answered again.

'You've been in the jungle with him for six months. Did you and he—' His voice trailed off.

'Yes – and I've been here with you a half hour.' She leaned forward and reached for him.

Elizabeth saw the Governor to his room and like a good hostess she rushed back downstairs, but everyone was gone.

Feeling a headache coming on, she went back upstairs to her room and opened a window. The sharp air cleared her head a little and she fell asleep.

After Kyle and Monica disappeared, Ryan and April grabbed their coats and went for a walk. The night was clear and cold, the moon as bright as daylight.

'I'm sorry about – about . . .' April began, not sure how to put it.

'You mean Monica? Oh, we're just friends. I'm rather amused at how competitive Kyle and I still are. He probably thinks I care. In the morning he'll feel like a louse.'

April was relieved. 'You seemed so angry, I thought—'

'No, it wasn't that. It was Mother's putting Kack in the kitchen. Father always insisted she eat with us on special occasions.' April nodded, and they walked along the bank of Kiefer Creek and the water rippled silver.

'How is she?' he asked.

'All right. I went sang-hunting with her. Of course she treated me, not satisfied with Bradley, or should I say Dr Estes.'

He stopped and turned to her. 'Treated you?'

'It was one of those stupid nightmares. I went sleep-walking outside and got pretty scratched up.'

He took her hand. 'I remember you did that as a kid. Did you ever try to seek treatment, maybe a psychologist? It can't be good for you. I thought you might outgrow it.'

'Oh, I did outgrow it,' April explained. 'I haven't done it for years. I had that same awful nightmare – the two seem to go together.'

'You wanna tell me about it? Sometimes talking can help,' he offered.

She bit her lip. She couldn't tell him that it was he whom she dreamed about. In a small voice she said, 'The nightmare's about someone drowning in the river. I get terrified and then I find myself – no, I shouldn't say find myself, as I don't remember the sleepwalking. I get back somehow or they find me. It's scary,' she ended.

'I know.' He squeezed her hand. 'Daddy and his lessons. He sure taught us something. Most lessons have a price. I'm sorry.'

He began to reminisce about happier times. 'Remember the gypsy?' She smiled and he chuckled out loud. 'She spit in Kyle's hand. God, he never forgot that.'

The night grew chillier so they turned around and started back to the house.

'How long are you staying?' he asked.

'I don't know. Your mother was very persuasive, and I sense she really is uneasy about those phone-calls. If not Hannah, then she has me answer the phone when those developers call.'

'They have been a bother,' he agreed. 'I'm staying for a bit. I'm putting Monica on the plane Sunday. I'll be going back and forth to New York about my next series, but I'll be here to put those developers to rest.'

'That's wonderful. What's the new series about?'

'Well, it's pretty much the opposite of the African commission. There I was working with exotic animals, rare and endangered species but this new one's called *Backyard Wildlife*.'

She looked puzzled.

'You know,' he continued. 'Rabbits, possums, racoons, hawks, owls, the animal life we have around here. The wildlife that stays even when civilization encroaches upon their territory.' He looked around at the dark woods. 'I can't wait. I love those guys. It's also kind of a new departure for me as an artist because up until now most of my commissioned work has been for paintings but this time they want sculptures. They want to do a series of porcelain figures to produce in limited editions. I've always loved sculpture and enjoyed doing it but it's different when you're getting paid. It's a challenge though.'

She nodded. 'That's exciting. I'm real glad for you.'

He didn't mean to monopolize the conversation, so he asked about her. 'Mother said on the phone that you might be helping out at the camp at Castlewood?'

'Well, it's really her idea. They don't bring the kids out a lot in this weather. I'm sure they could use a volunteer physical therapist. I'm just reluctant to get started with them as I don't know how much longer I'll be here.'

'Is there some reason you couldn't stay?'

They reached the porch and paused before going in.

'I can't take such an indefinite leave. The hospital needs to know when I'm returning. They've been very patient.'

'I didn't mean your job so much. Is there a special someone?' He paused.

'No, there's no one like that in my life right now, and with Mother gone, a girl has to earn a living.'

'I know,' he said. 'I'm sorry about your mother. Kyle and I were backpacking in Italy, so we didn't hear until we got back. I'm so sorry we weren't there.'

'It's OK. The Judge and Aunt Elizabeth were very supportive. In fact, your mother pleaded – I guess I should say badgered – she was insistent that I come to Castlewood even then.'

Ryan opened the library door, shivered, and put a log on the glowing embers. 'I think we could use a nightcap to warm us up.'

They spent the next hour remembering childhood times. Both went up to bed pleasantly weary from the long day.

# CHAPTER 31

Saturday found Elizabeth stuck with the tiresome Governor again. Indeed, she was afraid of leaving him too long, for his careless smoking gave her something to worry about. She listened to his stories of political campaigns and victories, and more than once he asked when the Judge would be returning.

'The man's positively senile,' she complained to Hannah, 'but if Kyle needs his help, then we must do everything to keep him happy.'

Kyle smiled and winked at his brother over breakfast. 'She's really something, that Monica. She was all over me last night and now she wants me to give her the grand tour. Apparently she's keen on doing some photographs. She has something in mind for Bruce, but Kack is who she's really interested in. So, do you mind, little brother, if I kidnap your girl?'

Ryan shook his head, drained the last of Hannah's coffee and replied, 'Of course not. Be my guest. I've just spent the last six months with her so you show her around. I'm relieved.'

'She wants to photograph Kack.'

'Oh, you know that's impossible. You know how she is. She's proud and pleased about my artwork, but in a way that superstitious stuff about images scares her.'

'Yeah, I know.' Kyle went off to get the jeep. He'd show Monica the countryside first. They could worry about photography later.

Kyle enjoyed the day. Monica and he caused some excitement in town. She was dressed in a short khaki skirt, knee-high boots, and a leopard-skin print top. Her hair was pulled back into a sleek bun, and huge ivory earrings matched the thick bracelets on her wrist. She had Big City written all over her. Her cameras slung over one shoulder, they stopped occasionally when she found a scene she pronounced 'quaint'.

Kyle spun the jeep around the town square. 'See the petition? My Daddy's gonna be there, lookin' over this good town.'

'Really?'

'Yep. My mother's commissioned a bronze of the Judge – a life-size statue. She wanted Ryan to do the work but he couldn't. He felt he was too close – couldn't get the right perspective, so she hired the next best thing, an artist from Chicago.'

Monica looked around the simple town. 'You're important folks around here, aren't you?'

'Yeah, I guess you'd say that.'

She reached over and ran her long nails down his cheek. 'I wouldn't think you'd enjoy being a small-town boy,' she teased.

'It's OK for now, honey. I got long-range plans. For now I'll just be the big fish in a small pond.' He gunned the jeep, squealing the tires like a teenager.

The patrol car parked on the side street made ready to follow and give out a ticket, but when the cop noticed it was the jeep from Castlewood, he turned out the light and resumed reading his girlie magazine.

Monica was pleased with their day. She felt she had gotten some wonderful middle-America shots.

'I can't wait to see my pictures,' she said.

'We could develop them at Hilltop, although I'm not sure if there are enough chemicals.'

'That's OK. I'm heading for New York Monday. I'll do it when I get back.'

Manroot

---

They drove through the crisp dusk, up the bumpy road, returning in time for dinner.

Elizabeth was puzzled. It seemed Ryan's girl was being monopolized by Kyle, yet her other son didn't seem to mind.

Bradley was invited to dinner. He came early, bringing some imported wine and flowers for Mrs Reardon. She was grateful to Bradley, for he sat next to the Governor at dinner and shouted answers in the old man's direction. Hannah, bless her heart, made his after-dinner drinks doubles, so the Governor retired early.

After dinner, Bradley and Ryan played chess by the fireplace. April watched, trying to learn. First she sat on the arm of Ryan's chair, then Bradley's.

Elizabeth opened one of the new records she had gotten from a record club that she had recently signed for, and put it on the stereo.

After a few minutes, Kyle questioned, 'Mother, what is that?' He walked over, turned it off and looked at the label. 'It's one of those new phony composers – minimalism, or whatever you call it.' He replaced the record and took Monica's hand. 'Let's get some air.'

He led her into the cold night, walked by the bushes, following the path. She moved close to him.

'It's spooky, but nice,' she said. They passed by the cabin, where the kerosene lamp glowed rosily in the window. They saw her, Kack, holding a skinny black hare, smoothing its sleek fur; her voice hummed a melody, sweet and haunting.

'Kyle, I must – I simply *must* – photograph her.'

'We'll see,' he promised as he took her hand, leading her away from the cabin, down the path toward the river.

They sat on the bank; she shivered as he kissed her, caressed her until she no longer felt cold.

They made love there under the stars. It reminded her of other times, back in Michigan when she was a teenager, before she had become the sophisticated, famous photog-

247

rapher. He was a pleasant distraction for her weekend in the sticks. It was eerie, for being with the brothers was good.

The next day started out badly; everyone was grumpy and out of sorts. Monica sat on the sun-porch filing her nails. She was angry at Kyle; he hadn't gotten her permission to photograph the Indian woman. Instead, she had worked with the blind man. She found herself disgusted; Bruce constantly dribbled saliva down his chin. While being remarkable in his ability to work, she was piqued that she didn't get to photograph the woman. If Kyle really wanted to, he could have arranged it. After all, she was just a servant or something.

They ate a light lunch. Elizabeth chattered vacantly. Ryan and April tried to keep the conversation going, but it was a dismal failure.

They heard the squealing of tires in the driveway and a crash of metal. Tom had hit the brick wall. Without even looking at the damage to the car, he arrogantly strode into the house, his walk uneven.

They heard him arguing loudly with Hannah in the kitchen.

Later, he came into the library, stood in the middle of the room and like a small boy trying to remember a recitation, began, 'The Judge, he promised Hannah and me the ten acres west of the cabin.'

April blinked in surprise. She dropped her needlepoint on the chair and quickly left the room.

Monica still felt vicious and angry, but knew she had no right to stay. She got up as well and left.

When the door closed behind them, Ryan asked, 'What's the problem, Tom? What's eating you?'

'The Judge promised that land to us.'

Ryan looked towards his mother. 'Was it in the will?'

Kyle answered for her. 'No, the will left everything to Mother and the trust for us to begin on our thirtieth birthday.'

248

Elizabeth looked around, not understanding.

Tom stepped forward, his Adam's apple bobbing with nervousness. 'He must have told you about it, ma'am. He must have said something.' His words were a desperate plea.

'Well,' she wrung her hands helplessly. 'I left stuff like that up to the Judge.'

Tom's frustration over all the years bubbled forth. His head swam with liquor. He knew, he'd always known they'd be cheated out of it after all.

'But ma'am—' He stepped closer to her, swaying, his breath heavy with drink. 'He must have—'

'Stop badgering her, Tom. She said he didn't, so he didn't,' Kyle barked.

'All these goddamned years we worked for you. She knows goddamned well he said it.' Tom's voice rose with anger.

'You're talking out of turn,' Ryan said.

They all looked at Elizabeth. She had shrunk in size; she looked like a small, helpless child sitting in the big damask chair. Her shoulders heaved with crying.

'I thought it was only relatives who argued over an inheritance. You're only—' Kyle stopped himself, glad he hadn't use the word *servant*.

Tom's mouth worked, as fury coursed through him. The word relative was singing in his brain. The old hidden truths came rushing out. 'Yes – only *relatives* fight about inheritance,' he hollered. 'Not *bastards*, dirty *bastards*. Some whore's bastards floating down the river – to cheat Hannah and me out of what's ours.'

The scream started in Elizabeth's throat – high, shrill, like an animal in agony. '*No, no!*' Her sons turned to her. She jerked, convulsing in the chair. The scream only ended when Ryan slapped her cheek.

Tom escaped, bumping into the table, sending a tray of glasses clattering to the floor.

'What's he talking about, Mother?' Kyle dropped to his knees, pulling her hands away from her face.

She sobbed and gulped, unable to speak.

Ryan's face blanched white, yet he patted her shoulders softly.

'Mother, answer me!' Kyle ground out, no longer gentle. 'The election – they pry, they find out everything. Tell me! Tell me what he's talking about!'

Kyle handed her a drink. Ryan gave her his handkerchief.

It was ten minutes before she could speak.

'It's true,' she said. 'We both wanted you, we loved you,' she pleaded, wanting forgiveness.

'Oh God,' Kyle said. He paced, running his hands through his hair. 'Next year, when the campaign starts, they probe – they snoop. Who else knows about this? Who was the doctor, the lawyer?'

'They've passed away,' she said.

'So it's them–' he pointed toward the kitchen. 'They're the only ones who know.'

She nodded a silent yes.

Kyle finally stopped pacing. God, he wanted a drink. The tray lay smashed at his feet.

Elizabeth got up and walked out of the library and went up to her room, still crying. Everything went wrong without the Judge. How she wished he were here.

The brothers sat in silence, staring at the flickering fire. Occasionally each stole a glance at the portrait. They didn't belong in it according to Tom. The portrait was a lie – the two handsome parents with the nameless boys from nowhere. Yet they could not doubt the evidence of their own eyes. They were the Judge's sons, through and through, but which whore was their mother?

Suddenly Kyle remembered. 'The Governor – where is the Governor?'

With all the screaming and shouting, had he heard anything? No, the old fool was deaf as a stone and senile to boot. He was scheduled to leave for the Capitol in the morning. Kyle had best remember his manners. He left the library, looked through the rooms. He found Hannah shaking and crying in the kitchen.

'The Governor?'

Drying her eyes on her apron, she answered, 'He didn't hear anything. He's been in his room for hours.'

He gave Hannah a withering look and left the room without a word.

Kyle hoped Tom would be sober enough in the morning to drive the Governor to the airport. He felt annoyed that now he had to go along, too: he couldn't trust Tom to be alone with him.

Scheduled to leave early, the Governor paused in the hall talking until Elizabeth thought he would miss his plane. He took her hand, kept calling her 'my dear' and thanked her repeatedly for the wonderful weekend.

Tom moved from foot to foot, holding the door open, while the cold air blew into the hallway. Elizabeth nodded as he rambled on. 'You must be very proud. Fine son you got there, talented young man. He'll be Governor someday. Impeccable breeding – impeccable background. You must be very proud.'

His compliments made her forget the cold draft. The old man seemed bent on praising Kyle; it pleased her so much.

Tom cleared his throat more than once. Finally, it occurred to the Governor that he should be going. 'It's a shame I missed the Judge, my dear. Give him my regards,' he said in farewell.

Elizabeth nodded. 'I will.'

At last Tom led him out to the car where Kyle had been waiting, the old man mumbling, 'Impeccable, impeccable young man.'

Monica was aware of a family feud brewing; she heard the angry voices behind the closed doors. She really wasn't the least bit interested. After all the time spent in

Africa she was ready for the big city – lights, parties, fun.

Both brothers seemed to be caught up in whatever this family argument was about. Kyle's mood was foul; gone was the teasing, fun guy. He lost all interest in her.

It was boring, sitting here in the sticks. She packed and told Ryan she needed to return to New York now. He shrugged his shoulders, called Tom to drive her. She had forgotten about both brothers before she reached the airport.

The house was pervasive with gloom. April starting packing as well. When Hannah saw this, she told Kyle and Ryan.

Hannah was calm now, for she had apologized for Tom to the Missus in front of the boys. She begged to stay, saying they had nowhere else to go.

The family were uncomfortable at her obsequiousness. They assured her that this was the couple's home and no one wanted them to go anywhere. Yet it was awkward, now that they knew how Tom really felt.

Ryan went up and asked April to remain. They needed her; Elizabeth needed her. She consented, not really knowing how she could help.

On Tuesday, Kyle and Ryan went over all the papers and bills.

'The accounts are in piss-poor shape,' Kyle grumbled.

'She's not much good at managing,' Ryan agreed, referring to their mother.

'Managing? It's outrageous the things she buys! She orders everything, and it's really mounting up.'

'About the will – why would the Judge promise them something and not make it legal?' Ryan mused.

'I don't know,' Kyle answered. 'It's straightforward enough – everything goes to her, except our trust fund. Somebody better put the brakes on her. She's spending a fortune on junk and the bill just came for the statue – fifty thousand dollars! After that's paid, she's practically broke until the annuities come in.'

'Maybe April can do something with her,' Ryan suggested.

'We'd better talk to her. I'm glad April's staying. I've been going over the bills. Maybe we should consider selling.'

Ryan was surprised at the suggestion.

'I've been thinking,' Kyle continued. 'Mother's almost seventy. How about one of those condos in St Louis – you know, the Kindo complex. That has a restaurant, beauty parlor, shops – and nurses on the premises. With Tom feeling that way, we can't count on them staying forever.'

'No, you're right. I still can't believe the Judge left everybody high and dry – Hannah, Tom, Kack, Bruce. What did he think would become of them?'

'I don't know,' Kyle smirked, his natural sarcasm revived. 'I think he was a better gardener than lawyer.'

'Well, I've still got the series *Backyard Wildlife*. Let's let it rest for now. I'll be staying around for four or five months. We'll work it out later.'

'OK, but you better put a stop to her crazy spending. You know, I wonder what she would have said if she knew their offer was ten million on the property?'

'You've talked to them, the developers?' Ryan asked.

'Yep. Seems they got some big plans. It won't hurt them to wait awhile.'

They closed the checkbooks, put the papers away. Kyle stayed a few more days. He wasn't anxious to get back to Jefferson City. He felt tainted, he felt dirty. His ego had withered and he felt almost paranoid that people knew he was a phony, a fake. When he returned to the Capitol, he was quieter, less confident. His political acquaintances started to worry. The charisma that had been his had dimmed.

# CHAPTER 32

Ryan traveled back and forth to New York until the details for the series on the wildlife sculptures were settled. On his return to Hilltop he was pleased to see that things had pretty much settled down.

April was brilliant. Somehow she had interested Elizabeth in doing an auction for the handicapped club at Castlewood.

They had scoured the closets and gathered together all the unnecessary items Elizabeth had purchased. April had her working on the catalog. For once she was interested in giving away instead of acquiring. The auction was planned for the next month and Hilltop was a beehive of activity. Kack had donated several beautiful hand-made Indian rugs, fifty jars of preserves, and Hannah had coaxed her to donate some ointments as well. Kack was very modest about her remedies.

Ryan was relieved to see that the women had their own projects, as he needed time and solitude to begin his series. He would need to spend many hours in the woods observing the creatures that he would sculpt, as well as a time-lapse camera placed in certain habitats so he might have correct models to work from.

Happily he donated some original paintings from his last wildlife series to his mother's auction. This gift changed the whole tone of the event.

An honorary luncheon was arranged as a preview; Elizabeth was asked to speak. Nervously she practiced to

April and Hannah. Her three-minute speech was very appealing.

Ryan saw all of this, and one day when April came up to the studio for the original paintings, he stopped her.

'I'm so grateful,' he said.

'For what?' she asked, puzzled.

'What you've done with Mother. She's come out of herself, and as for her doing a speech – why, she couldn't wipe her nose without the Judge, you know that.'

April nodded. 'She is rather pleased with herself.'

Ryan looked down at his hands; he didn't know how to put it. He wanted to tell her how he felt. 'Sit down, April, I want to talk to you. I never meant to diminish you when I asked you to stay – it's like I was saying your life, your work wasn't important. I didn't mean that. It could seem like I was telling you that. It's just that the family is so torn up right now. Why, I saw Kyle – he's drinking too much, and I've got a deadline—'

She hushed him. 'I never felt that. In fact, I'm very excited about an important project of my own. I'm writing a book!'

'That's wonderful,' he exclaimed. 'Mother always called you the poetess.'

'No, it's not that kind of a book. I got interested in Kack's remedies, and I've been tracking down some of her ointments, checking with Bradley – he arranged lab-work for me. You know, Ryan, some of her things are right on target – they contain ingredients that medical science documents are right. This whole movement of holistic medicine – it's fascinating.'

'Bradley's been helping?'

'Oh yes. I'm seeing a lot of him. He's become almost a co-author. You know how he always admired Kack.'

'You're seeing a lot of him?'

'Yes.'

For the first time he became aware of April as a woman. Her face was flushed with excitement, her eyes sparkled.

She was beautiful. She was not his cousin; they were not related. He looked down at the clay to cover his confusion.

# CHAPTER 33

All the newspapers covered the luncheon. Elizabeth was so proud. She clipped the articles and asked April, 'Instead of Mrs Elizabeth Reardon, should they have referred to me as Mrs Reardon, wife of the late Judge?'

'No,' April corrected her. 'This has nothing to do with the Judge. It's something you're doing.'

Elizabeth blushed. She wasn't accustomed to doing anything. She had lived her life basking in reflected glory.

Her happiness was short-lived as Kyle came out over the weekend.

'Why all the publicity?' he stormed.

'Why, dear, it's my auction. People are interested,' she said proudly.

'They're interested in Ryan's paintings, you mean. What a dumb thing to donate along with Kack's preserves – paintings worth thousands of dollars! See how they mention Ryan – and then go on to mention me and my work in Jefferson City? I don't *want* publicity now!'

Ryan tried to calm him. 'It's over and done with.'

'With him in the house,' Kyle nodded toward the kitchen, 'he could blow the lid on this thing any day now.'

'He won't,' Ryan said, 'and if he did, what's the difference? Children are adopted every day.'

Kyle didn't answer. He sat drinking in the chair, staring up at the picture. He saw that they had the Judge's chin, nose, jaw ... they were the Judge's sons, all right. He didn't doubt that – but who was their mother? The media would have a picnic with this story: *'Found floating in the creek – two modern-day Moses.'*

Kyle's visits were painful. His deep depression did not seem to lift; he made everyone in the house uneasy.

The auction went very well; Elizabeth was pleased. April began looking for a new project that would interest her. She herself was spending a lot of time with Kack; the laboratory documentation on the remedies was very positive. Their book, *Holistic Country Ways Remedies*, was coming along nicely.

Ryan had completed four of the sculptures for *Backyard Wildlife* and their molds had been sent to the studios in Germany where the limited edition of porcelain would be produced.

The first sample arrived back that morning for his approval and he unwrapped it carefully, hoping they'd gotten the finish right. Ryan had selected the paints and the glazes himself and provided detailed instructions about how and where they should be used, but he had still been worried. Color and shading were so important, so central to these figures and he knew that the finish would either make them or break them.

The first figure was a rabbit and after unwrapping it, he could not contain his joy. He had to share it with someone. He heard the tapping of the typewriter keys. He knocked at the studio door.

'Come in,' she called, and the keys still rattled.

'April, sorry to disturb you. I just had to share this with someone.'

'It's OK,' she said as she got up from the chair, stretched and came over to him. 'I wasn't being creative. I was only typing.'

He had placed the porcelain on the table.

'It's exquisite,' she said. 'Why, I seem to see its chest moving. It's so real – it looks like the one that Kack always carries around.'

'It's good, isn't it?' he said, asking for approval.

'It's better than good – it's beautiful. It looks alive.'

'Thanks.' He hugged her in his happiness. 'I shouldn't be so insecure. I love working in this medium but I'm not as confident as I am in painting.'

He started to release her, when he was suddenly filled with the soft scent of her. He looked into her eyes and saw her lips were parted. Her breath was shallow and warm. He knew she felt it, too.

Softly he kissed her. The kiss deepened and she clasped him closer and closer.

They drew apart. She looked down at the statue between them.

He turned and left the room; she saw him go through the french doors and head for the woods, walking rapidly. He needed to think now that he had come to see her as a person, as a desirable woman. He had erased that old image of little April as his cousin.

# CHAPTER 34

April sat at the plank table with Kack and the papers piled high in stacks by categories.

'This is the apple cider vinegar and honey chapter, Kack. Look it over and see if I've omitted anything.'

Katherine studied through the typed pages carefully; seeing all the words there gave her an odd feeling. These were her remedies. She knew they worked. Over the years she herself, Hannah and many others had tried them and obtained relief.

Now she rubbed at her slightly swollen knuckles, which were aching. 'It's living by the water,' she said in answer to April's unspoken question. 'Still, this recipe morning and night gives relief.'

Her concentration in reading allowed April to study her closely. She saw that Katherine had an odd, natural beauty. Her face remained smooth and unlined, her hair, pulled back and braided atop her head, was still a warm auburn colour with few silver strands. It was her clothing – dark, obscure, loose, that hid a still-youthful, slender body. The clothing gave a false impression of age.

April had always been fascinated by her.

A rustling from the cage that stood in the corner interrupted Kack's reading. She got up, opened the door and took out the small feline, making a soft murmuring sound in her throat that seemed to calm the animal.

Returning to the table, she kept the kitten enclosed in her apron.

'A kitten?' April questioned.

'Of sorts.'

April rose and came around the table to see. She reached down to stroke the tiny creature that shivered. She noticed the pointed, tufted ears, the small spots.

'Is it a bobcat?'

'I think a mixture,' Kack answered.

The cat looked up at April with large slate-colored eyes that glittered like marbles, and hissed loudly.

'He's hungry,' Katherine said.

'We've done enough for today,' April said. 'You've checked that section. We're almost done with the entire manuscript.' She stacked the papers and prepared to leave.

The small hare that had sat quietly at Kack's feet under the table now began a frantic race around the cabin. The cat's presence had set it in motion with fear.

April closed the door of the cabin, leaving Kack to attend to her small charges.

Coming up the path April met Ryan, who was returning from an afternoon in the woods. He was laden down with sketchbooks and a full camera bag.

'Looks like you've been busy,' she said.

'You, too,' he replied, noticing her stack of papers.

'Yes, the book is almost done. I'm having Kack check through the last chapters now. It's amazing what she knows without any formal training. Why, she even knows reflexology. Some of her headache remedies deal with massage, which works on the reflexology concept of the body having meridian lines that connect with other organs.'

'I'm surprised at you,' Ryan said. 'With a medical background like yours, some of these unorthodox remedies certainly must be frowned upon by the medical profession. How do you incorporate both in your beliefs?'

'I have an open mind. I'm convinced that some of these ideas are not quackery. Brad has also come around. Of course he's not sharing some of these beliefs with his colleagues. With all these tests the lab is growing very curious.'

They had reached the patio door; both shifted their bundles. Ryan tugged at the door.

April's papers suddenly slipped. The wind took the loose sheets, whirling some away.

'Damn,' she muttered. Ryan opened the door, put their things inside the room and skipped after the papers, some gleefully dipping up in the breeze like wayward kites, some caught in the bushes and brambles.

Both of them whooped and hollered like two kids as they jumped up in the air catching the swirling sheets.

Finally they searched the bushes for stragglers. April crawled through the brambles to secure the remaining two pages.

Ryan flopped down on the carpet of leaves, breathless. 'Do you think we got them all?' he asked.

She sat down next to him, sorting the papers. A concentrated frown wrinkled her brow.

He studied her. She was very beautiful. This observation struck him again as fresh knowledge. She was April; he had known her forever. The knowledge again came to him. She wasn't his cousin, she was just a beautiful, desirable woman.

Looking up, she saw in his eyes what he was thinking. All the love she had always felt for him spilled over.

Together, in a synchronized movement, they reached for each other.

The kiss was tender, full of respect, liking and a new-found passion.

They drew apart. April looked down, blushing.

He reached over and took her chin, gently nudging it until she looked up at him.

'I know it's hard to realize that we have every right to feel like this.'

Again they merged. Kissing, caressing, they lay back in the softness of the leaves and he said her name over and

265

over. 'It's OK, it's OK for us to feel like this.'

She played none of the games of the reluctant female – it was he who pulled away and sat up. 'We'd better stop,' he said. 'I can't be trusted.' He offered his hand, pulled her up, and while walking toward the house, picked the leaves from her tangled curls lovingly.

At dinner they stole glances at each other. April felt her cheeks burn.

The next day they went to St Louis. Ryan had finished another sculpture, a squirrel this time, and he needed to take it to the studio where the molds were made. As they drove to town he explained this process to her and she listened attentively.

'They'll take an impression of the squirrel, a sort of negative made out of rubber. I know it sounds simple but molds can be tricky especially with something so small, so detailed. This place has been great so far but they better keep it up. I want perfection.' He glanced toward her and smiled and repeated the words: 'I want perfection. I demand it!'

'Don't we all?' she teased.

Like all lovers, they found everything exciting – the shopping, a Chinese dinner. Later in the movies he put his arm around her and they sat close in the dark like two starry-eyed teenagers.

Returning from St Louis, April sat close to him in the jeep. The bumps on the road brought her jarring into his body.

'I guess you'll have to tell Bradley,' he said, and glanced toward her.

'Tell him what?'

'About us,' he said.

'I guess you'll have to tell Monica,' she answered, fishing for information.

'Wait a minute.' He pulled the jeep off the side of the road. The motor died and he turned to face her. 'Is that jealousy I hear?'

They reached for each other, the questions lost in their embrace.

'I feel sixteen,' he said, 'parking on the road to neck.'

They both laughed and clung to each other.

He started the car, looked ahead and cursed as headlights blinded him on the narrow road. 'Dimmers – use your dimmers, idiot,' he said to the passing car. 'We should announce it soon. We must tell Mother tonight.'

'Tell her?' she quizzed, determined to make him ask.

'Of course. We've got to let her know that we're in love and want to get married.'

'I don't recall being asked,' April teased.

Once again he pulled off the road, and turned to face her. 'I love you, April. I know you love me.'

'You're right, I do.'

They reached for each other, feeling that they could never get enough. Their love was so special, for in addition to passion they felt a long-standing liking for each other.

'We'll get married soon, just tell me when,' he coaxed.

'I couldn't stand to make the gypsy wrong.'

'The gypsy?'

'You remember, the gypsy. She said I would marry you!'

'Of course,' he laughed. 'She also mentioned Kyle. Maybe I've got competition – more than just Bradley.'

'Don't be silly, Bradley is just a friend.' She leaned over and laid her head against his strong shoulder as they drove the last few miles home.

With her eyes closed, she seemed to see clearly the old woman's face, her wrinkled brow and piercing black eyes, and involuntarily April felt frightened. It was strange that her prediction, unlikely as it was, was going to come true . . .

# CHAPTER 35

Elizabeth was delighted with the news; their plans seemed perfect. They would stay at Hilltop until the *Backyard Wildlife* series was completed. Ryan felt that the series would go quickly as the animals in question were those he had known intimately all of his life.

April would have time to finish the book and look for a publisher.

'After I'm finished with the series, we'll take a year off. We'll travel anywhere we want to go – Paris, London, Rome. We'll do it – we'll do the world,' Ryan promised.

They laughed and clung to each other like two happy children. The future lay in front of them, mapped out golden with promise.

Elizabeth set about in a fury, ordering books on bridal gowns, conferring with florists and caterers.

'Mother, slow down. We haven't actually set the date. I'm not sure April wants all this fuss.'

'Of course she does,' Elizabeth scolded. 'Every girl wants a beautiful, special wedding that she can treasure all her life. Why, your father and I had ten bridesmaids and dozens and dozens of white roses, and the catering. Besides, Jenny would have wanted it.'

He shushed her. 'We'll see, Mother.' He left her rushing up to the attic to unpack her own wedding dress in case April wanted to wear something antique.

Later he apologized to April. 'I'm sorry Mother's making such a fuss. I hope you don't mind. She's always said how she wanted a little girl.'

'I don't mind. It's nice. At a time like this, I miss my mother.' Tears welled up in her eyes.

'I know,' he comforted her. 'If you can stand it, so can I. I guess we can afford to take two weeks off after the wedding. I thought maybe this island in Florida might be nice for a honeymoon.'

April glanced at the brochures of Sanibel and Captiva. 'It looks wonderful. The sun, the sea. We'll need the quiet and solitude after this mammoth wedding.'

Kyle came that weekend.

After dinner when they all went into the study for coffee, Ryan announced, 'Kyle, as your big brother, I've got something to tell you.' April came over and sat next to Ryan on the love seat. He took her hand, saying, 'April and I are going to be married.'

Ignoring the information, Kyle echoed, 'Big brother? We'll never know who's the big brother here, will we, Mother?'

Elizabeth looked down and began crying softly.

'Oh, come on Kyle. I thought you'd be happy for April and me.'

'It's fine,' he said, and getting up he went to the side-board and poured himself a bourbon. Neatly he threw the drink down and poured another.

Trying to cover the awkwardness of the situation, Ryan continued, 'We've settled on May twentieth.' He looked toward April, pleading for it to be OK.

She smiled and nodded her consent.

'Of course I want you to be my best man. Maybe you could persuade the Governor to stand in and give April away.'

'What? What did you say?' Kyle shouted.

'Mother thought we could have the wedding here, one big blow out, then we're off to Florida.'

'No, no, you can't do that,' Kyle exploded in a rage. Pacing up and down he stopped in front of Elizabeth. 'You stupid old lady.'

With that, Ryan leapt from the chair and stood in front of his brother, his fists clenched, anger making a tic jump under his eye.

'You can't talk to her like that. You're drunk. We'll discuss this when you're sober.'

'No,' Kyle roared, 'we'll discuss this now.' He glared at Elizabeth, his face a mask of fury. 'I know what you want, you foolish old lady. You want a big to-do, those society-page photographers falling all over themselves. You dimwit, don't you realize someone will remember April? They'll remember she's supposed to be our cousin.'

With that Ryan swung a hard punch. Kyle staggered back drunkenly and finally crashed into the table and fell on the floor.

'April, fetch Tom,' Ryan ordered. 'I need help to get him up to bed.'

After the men had taken Kyle upstairs, April went over to her aunt and put an arm around the frail, shaking shoulders.

'He's been drinking,' she apologized.

Elizabeth looked up, her eyes swimming with tears. 'He's nasty about it when he's *not* drinking. He badgers me constantly to repeat the story over and over – how the twins were found in a hollow log floating in the creek. He demands descriptions and details and he gets furious if I forget something or tell it in another way. He keeps questioning – was there a note, clothing, anything? I find myself always almost telling him about—' She stopped mid-sentence and wiped her cheeks and said she had a headache and was going up to bed.

'The teeth, the teeth,' she muttered to herself as she climbed the steps. She must watch herself; she must never tell Kyle about the teeth. Oh, how she wished the Judge were here. William would have known what to do.

Ryan put on a record. April and he continued to sit in the study sipping after-dinner drinks.

'God, how he's worried about it. God knows I think about it sometimes, but Kyle is almost paralyzed with fear that someone will find out.'

April nodded and remained silent.

Ryan paced the room, went to the french doors and looked down to the cabin. He saw the soft orange light from her windows: *in that instant, he knew.* If it were true, how much worse for Kyle, Kyle who needed respectability, lineage and family ties that were above reproach.

He turned back into the room.

'It's Katherine, isn't it?' she whispered.

He nodded and came to her. They held each other, their hearts beating in time.

'He's my brother. I can't bear to see him hurt.'

'I know,' she said.

'I can't bear to hurt you, either. I don't know how important the wedding is to you?'

'It's fine,' she assured him. 'I was only going along with all the fuss because your mother – Elizabeth,' she corrected herself, 'because it seemed so important to her.'

'How's the City Hall in St Louis look to you?' he asked.

'Romantic!'

'That's what I love about you – you have a vivid imagination.'

They took their blood test; three days later they were married in the City Hall, with hired strangers for witnesses.

They packed, took the plane for Fort Myers, Florida, and began their wonderful honeymoon.

On their return, both threw themselves into their work, happy and fulfilled.

# CHAPTER 36

Elizabeth never mentioned the wedding. She showed a renewed interest in scrapbooks, carefully pasting in yellowed newspaper articles concerning the Judge. She kept every news item to do with Ryan and his artwork. Kyle, too, filled the pages with small blurbs and boring articles about state legislation in which his name was mentioned.

She never referred to the humiliating, hurtful incident concerning Kyle. Rather she babbled incessantly about the boys' escapades as children, forgetting that April was as familiar with some of them as she was.

A New York publisher sent the good news that April's book had been accepted. Secretly, April had Kack's name added to the publication. After all, the book was really hers! The editors requested that she send Kack's photo as well as her own. She ignored this for she knew it would be impossible.

Excitedly, she went to the cabin to tell Kack of the book's acceptance. She found her in the small patch of garden that was alive with flowers. Kack was on her knees, patting a mound of dirt. Her shoulders heaved with sobs, and her tears dropped to the earth.

Hoping to turn away and not be seen, April was caught.

'He died this morning. Little rabbits do not live very long,' Katherine said.

Dropping down beside her, April patted her shoulder comfortingly. 'Which one was it?'

'Mine, he was mine,' she said simply. 'A special one.'

April assumed it was the one she had tamed – the little one she carried in her apron and that went hopping behind her like a faithful dog. Most she did not tame; Kack had always lectured Bradley that wild animals were wild animals, and not meant to be pets. You should mend and tend them if they were sick or injured, she said, then release them back to their natural habitat.

They huddled together in silence, and when Kack was composed, April told her of the good news.

'That's wonderful. Come, we should have some ginseng tea.' Together they went into the cabin.

As they talked, Kack felt a sensation of doom. April and Ryan were too happy, too lucky. It was like she and William had been, before the magic wore itself out. Today the rabbit had died.

She listened to April's happy talk of the book, the series . . . All was going so well. April mused about the places she and Ryan would see on their year-long trip.

Still Kack shivered, brooding on the death of the rabbit and the peculiar wilting of the ginseng in the forest this year. Only yesterday the birds had gathered in the trees and chattered nervously. She tried to quell her fear of omens.

Ryan's insistence on taking her to the studio to see his finished statues made her even more uneasy; the sight of the life-like hare, possum, the raccoons, and all the others in the series gave her goosebumps. Her flesh crawled. She knew a primitive fear: now that her son had captured them in such life-like forms – had he stolen something from them?

Ryan worked at a feverish pace, but the work had come easy until now. His deep bond with the creatures had made it so. He was pleased, for he felt that these tame, small, everyday animals were just as important and beautiful as the exotic ones he had painted in Africa.

Last in the series was the tiny, almost extinct owl. He had studied pictures of the bird and had sat for many hours quiet as a stone, in the dark, and watched as the owl came to the bent sycamore to drink from the river. Even he, with his intimate knowledge of the woods, could not discover its nesting grounds. He only knew where it came to drink.

Ryan did not feel comfortable with the background he had on the owl. He needed to get closer; he needed to study every movement, every quiet posture.

April felt his frustration. He had come to the end of the series and now the work went badly.

'I need more photographs – a whole series of them. I just feel so tired, so looking forward to our trip, that I mustn't rush. I mustn't cheat by doing inferior work now. I'll set up the time-lapse camera tonight.'

They were both looking forward to Kyle's weekend visit. Things had been better since the outburst. Kyle felt guilty at having cheated them out of a big wedding and so he made a great effort to be warm and charming to everyone. Elizabeth had forgiven him. It seemed he was back like he used to be. Things in his life were going well – or so he told them. Secretly, however, he brooded.

He was due to run for Governor next year; the political machine was behind him and he was confident. Yet he worried about the shadow that followed him.

Ryan had planned on talking to Kyle this weekend about Mother, the house, what should be done about the help . . . He had given a lot of thought to it all, since after their extended trip, he and April were to move to Florida permanently, to live on Captiva.

On their honeymoon they had both fallen in love with the romantic island, with its stories of pirates who kept women captive there, and the talk of buried treasures. The Ding Dong Sanctuary was the place Ryan felt closest to God. The fantastic wildlife, birds that migrated there, the creatures – alligators, fox . . . and the beaches alive with shells . . . As two people so very much in tune with God's creation they could think of no other place where they would rather spend their life than among nature's generous bounty of plants and animals on that island.

Kyle's visit went well. He teased Hannah, presented his mother with a sapphire locket to match her eyes, and brought fresh lobster flown in especially from Boston, as he knew it was Ryan's favorite food.

Elizabeth watched fondly as the boys played ball in the clearing next to the patio.

Such handsome boys, so athletic. As they jostled and played on the lawn they reminded her of the Judge when he was young. He had been like that – fun, exuberant. Tears filled her eyes. She missed him so. If she was honest, she had never cared for the physical part of her marriage, but the Judge was a thoughtful man, and after the unsuccessful pregnancies he had not bothered her with that sort of thing again. She had never worried about it, just felt relieved that that part of their marriage was over. Now she missed the feeling of protection he had given her. She still had Kyle. He would make her feel safe; he would have power like the Judge. She relished the thought of being the mother of a Senator, of the Governor . . . Like Kyle, her dreams were bigger. Ryan, too – he brought her honor. His fame was something she tasted like a sweet chocolate on her tongue.

Elizabeth went to bed early that night, happy and content.

Ryan cautioned April not to wait up for him as Kyle and he needed to talk, and resolve some family business.

They retired to the library. Ryan was cautious as he did not want to taint the bond of love and companionship that they had again achieved.

He cleared his throat. 'Kyle, April and I have decided we want to move to Florida after the trip.'

'Great, it sounds good, little brother.' They both gave a chuckle at the 'little brother'. It was a game they had played as children. They had always badgered Elizabeth as to which one was born first. She had pretended confusion and would name first one then the other, then shake them both off, saying 'I don't remember. Childbirth is painful – you're not really awake for it.' Later when they had grown up, they never thought to ask. Now they knew they would never know.

'I'm worried about Mother. What will she do, roaming around this mausoleum?' Ryan said.

'I agree totally. I'm sure the developers are still interested.'

'Well, Kyle, I didn't meant to actually sell the property. Why, with the trust funds coming due, if we sold, we'd give it all to the Government anyway.'

Kyle leaned forward. 'What do you have in mind?'

'I've given it a lot of thought, and I've also talked to Tom and Hannah. It seems the Judge definitely promised them those ten acres west of the cabin.'

Kyle nodded thoughtfully.

'The cabin,' Ryan continued, 'has been ˙ack's for as long as I can remember. We could give her that strip of land.'

Kyle was silent.

'Then,' Ryan trod softly, 'as for the house – we could donate it to the blind, and that takes care of Bruce.'

'Neat package! Well done, as the English would say. Sure.' Kyle rose and paced. 'Mother gets her reward, the Judge finds another philanthropic charity named after him. It won't do my career any harm either.' It sounded as if he agreed; anger and indecision kept him from saying more.

Kyle poured two drinks; the brothers held their glasses up, clinked them, and he said solemnly, 'To the future.'

They drank in silence. Finally Ryan said, 'About Mother. I thought that condo you described in St Louis sounds perfect. The house being donated to be named after the Judge will please her. Even now, she makes Tom drive her into town once a week to see the statue.'

'I guess she loved him in her own way, whatever that was,' Kyle said sarcastically.

The silence was split by the hoot of an owl.

A. N. Steinberg

'Damn, I forgot,' Ryan said. 'I had Tom string up the extensions. I need to set up the time-lapse camera.'

'He's your last one in the series?' Kyle questioned.

'Yep. He's it, and I must say he's been a lot of trouble. I can't seem to get it right. I just need some good natural pictures.'

'Well, come on, let's go. I'm the photographer around here, little brother, remember?'

'It's so dark, we'll be tripping around out there,' Ryan cautioned. 'Your suit – you better change.'

'I'll get the equipment.' Kyle went upstairs, changed into khakis and a warm flannel shirt, and came down carrying the camera bag.

The cool night air hit the brothers and cleared their heads from the liquor. They walked the familiar path to the fishing tree, occasionally pushing aside the thorn-bushes and cursing loudly when they got pricked. They argued companionably over who would set the cameras. 'I know the angles I want,' Ryan stated.

'Who's the photographer in this family?' Kyle retorted.

Their loud voices carried in the still night. When they arrived at the tree, they saw the owl sitting high in the branches.

'Damn. Damn,' Ryan muttered as he flew away. 'Don't know if he'll return tonight.'

They set about untangling the electric leads, found Tom's extension waiting. It was a dark night. The moon entered and exited the clouds as they drifted quickly in the wind.

Someone said, 'Ready?'

With that word, the lead dropped and hit the water. Brilliant colors sparked and lit his figure like the Fourth of July. The last sound was his body dropping in the water.

'*Oooh-ooh-ooh.*' The terrible hoarse, agonized cry split the night. Kack sat up in her bed, fear catching in her throat. She heard the soft beginnings of the Oh mu's moan.

278

She jumped up, clutching a robe, and grabbed the creature. She put the drops in his mouth to still his fear and ran along the dark banks of the river, her heart beating fast with fear. She knew one of her sons had died!

Tom, who had been setting mole-traps, ran to the tree. He unplugged the cord and restrained the struggling man, who was screaming hysterically, 'Kyle Kyle! My brother! I've got to try—'

He managed to wrench himself away from Tom's grasp and dove into the black water.

'Come back, Mr Ryan. It's too late. He can't be alive now – the electricity,' Tom shouted.

Kack knelt down in the marsh, hidden among the cattails. She knew that what Tom said was true. She heard the shriek of the Oh mu. She crouched down and waited.

# CHAPTER 37

It was a private funeral. Elizabeth could not bear to face anyone; her grief was too profound. Inside the bronze box that was put in the earth next to the Judge lay her unfulfilled dreams. She would not be the mother of a Governor or a Senator. She cringed within herself, and like a woman who cried often at small things, she sat grimly through her son's funeral, her eyes dry.

Ryan seemed a broken man. He repeated over and over to April, 'It's my fault. We shouldn't have gone there that night. It's my fault. I had no right to ask him. Why, oh why did I even mention it?' he moaned.

'He was a photographer; it was logical to mention it,' April reasoned.

In their sorrow, they did not realize that Kack had not been seen since the death.

She had locked the cabin, drawn the shades, and everyone in their private sorrow did not interact with each other.

April was afraid. She remembered the dream; she was uneasy with the knowledge. The beloved land, house, woods – all seemed ominous now, threatening, cursed.

She forced herself to console Ryan, who sat for hours in the studio looking at his hands and the lump of clay that was to become the owl.

The house took on a cast of mourning; it seemed gloomy, cold, even though the summer came.

Tom and Hannah were hushed, serving Elizabeth in her room. They noticed the strain between the young couple as they sat in silence at the dinner table.

Summer turned to fall. Elizabeth never left her room any more. She grew frail. Her son's passing, as well as her husband's, made her passive; she wanted nothing! It was as if the small childish woman had already fled and left a dry husk behind.

April, too, suffered terribly.

It was after seeing Ryan for so many days sitting immobile in the study staring at the blob of clay that she spoke. 'Ryan, please, please, seek help. Bradley knows a fine psychiatrist. This guilt is eating you up alive.'

'What do you know?' he screamed at her. 'You never had a brother – a twin. Kyle was part of me.'

She retreated, leaving him sitting alone in the studio until it was dark, when he would shake himself and leave the room, his work still undone.

The agency called, wrote, and after six months they demanded to know when the final figure would be completed.

'Hell, I don't know,' Ryan screamed over the phone. 'Maybe never.'

April worried when the agency eventually threatened to rescind the contract, making it null and void. It had been drawn up for a dozen pieces; only eleven were ready.

Every night for the past week Ryan had taken the gun and gone out with Tom to hunt for it, the owl, but tonight they came back successful. Ryan's voice could be heard laughing, a high, hysterical laugh. He stayed in the library drinking until April came down to see if he was all right.

Tom stood outside the door; he'd had his suspicions, but now he was sure. He had watched Ryan all night, loading and reloading the gun with his left hand.

'What is it?' April whispered to Tom.

'The owl. He shot him.'

Relieved, April stepped into the room. She wasn't prepared for what she saw.

Ryan had laid the bird upon the desk. With the garden

shears, methodically he had cut it apart bit by bit. The burnt flesh was acrid in the room, smoking in the fireplace.

April turned away, revolted, and fled back up to the bedroom. It was sickening, but maybe he had cleansed himself of some of the destructive guilt.

It was late, very late, when she felt his body crawl into bed. Roughly he pulled her to him. He kissed her harshly until she felt her lips bleed. He smelled of warm blood – she tried not to gag – and of whiskey and sweat. His fingers bit into her flesh and he made no attempt to arouse her, but roughly mounted her, and with a body full of white-hot anger, he punished her for half an hour.

She arose, went to shower, and found bits of the creature, small slimy particles, gleaming wetly on her breasts. She studied her face in the mirror and saw, stuck to her bleeding lip, a small feather.

She gagged, vomiting into the basin until she was so weak she could hardly stand.

She stood under the hot shower shivering with fear. He needed help, he desperately needed help, but how could she make him get it? Elizabeth was no use; she couldn't confide in her. Bradley was a doctor. How humiliating. How could they force him if he didn't agree?

Finally cleansed, she tiptoed into the bedroom. The soft night light shone on him as he slept, uncovered, spread-eagled. She saw shimmering in the light soft globs, pieces of the flesh and intestines from the bird, on his body.

She opened the french doors, stepped out into the cold night and stared up at the star-filled sky and mumbled a silent prayer.

It was a movement in the dark that caught her eye. She strained and saw Kack sitting at the edge of the forest, her knees drawn up, her arms closed around them. Her face looked up, offering itself to the moon and starlit night. Next to her the cat circled around and around, his leash growing shorter.

# CHAPTER 38

When Ryan returned from the lawyers in St Louis, his scowl told April that all had not gone well.

She waited for him to speak, as his touchy moodiness was something she could not gauge any more.

It was after dinner; Elizabeth ate downstairs and had retired early. Ryan morosely drowned his third scotch before he told her, 'The contract's airtight. They don't have to pay a cent, even though they have the eleven pieces and are presently marketing them – the bastards!'

'I'm sorry,' April said.

'I'm not. I'm damn mad that they'll make a fortune off the series, and they don't have to pay me a red cent.'

She came over and sat next to him and patted his hand.

Restlessly, he moved away, paced the room. His words spilled forth in a gush. 'I've decided to sell the property. I checked on that condo complex for Mother. It's ideal, restaurant, beauty parlors, shows, stores, nurses and doctors in the complex if needed. I thought maybe we'd get her a companion.'

April gasped in surprise. It wasn't like him to go ahead with decisions without even talking to her.

'Have you thought of the others – Hannah, Tom and Kack? And Bruce? Where will they go?'

He still paced restlessly, an angry pulse throbbing in his cheek. 'I'll pay them off.'

'Oh,' she answered, knowing he was in no mood to talk reasonably.

She finished her drink and went up to bed. It was hours before he came up. She lay stiffly next to him pretending to be asleep.

April was surprised when the next morning, without any warning, he told Hannah at breakfast: 'I'm selling the property, Hannah. You and Tom should start making other plans.'

Hannah dropped the platter in surprise. April saw the tears in her eyes as she hurriedly tried cleaning up the toast. When she brought in a fresh platter several minutes later, her eyes were red and she did not look at them.

April was furious at how coldly he had broken the news to the faithful woman. She took her coat and went walking in the woods. It had been eight months since Kyle's death and nothing would ever be the same. She sat on a log and looked around and remembered happier days. She yearned for her husband to face his guilt and grief so they could go on with their lives.

She had left him in the library going over the bills, writing the checks. It was clear he was not open to discuss anything.

He was annoyed when Tom interrupted his paperwork. 'I need to talk to you, Mr Reardon.'

Ryan looked up, surprised, for he had never been called Mr Reardon by Tom.

'Al right, come in,' he said. He finished writing a check.

Tom closed the door softly. Now he was sure he wasn't crazy. He had seen it again and again, that telltale left hand, and now he *was* sure – absolutely sure *Ryan wasn't Ryan*.

With an unaccustomed familiarity, Tom helped himself to a drink, sat down, put his feet on the coffee table, leaned back, and with a satisfied smirk on his face said, 'I'm here to talk to you about the ten acres west of the cabin that was promised to Hannah and me by the Judge.' He thought he was fair; he could have asked for a lot more and got it.

* * *

April was pleased to hear that he had been generous with Tom and Hannah; she wondered what arrangements he would make for Kack. Still, his foul mood prevented her from discussing anything controversial with him. The past nine months had deteriorated their marriage to such an extent that she wondered if they would ever be close again.

They slept like strangers, stiff and uncomfortable next to each other. When Ryan had been drinking, he came to her rough and uncaring. She began to dread his touch.

It was the night that he reached for her and she pushed him away that his anger flared. He held her against her will, pressed her lips tightly until she couldn't breathe.

'Stop,' she commanded.

He ignored her and roughly caressed her breasts.

'Stop it,' she breathed, and attempted to get free.

This resistance seemed to excite him more. She writhed and struggled beneath the weight of his body. Anger, and for the first time fear, overcame her. Ryan was her husband but she felt she didn't know him any more. She struck out at him. Without realizing it, she raked his face and saw the lines of blood rising where she had scratched him.

'Ryan, stop. Please, Ryan.'

Her pleas further enraged him. With her arms now pinned beneath his body, the unbelievable happened. He grasped her throat with his hand to quiet her, and continued. She felt faint. Her beloved Ryan was raping her.

It seemed a second; it seemed an eternity. It stopped. He rolled over, and she could not even sob. He was sick; something was terribly wrong with him and she knew no way to fix it.

He rose and showered, and when he came back into the bedroom, he was smiling and touching his cheek.

'You were like a little wildcat, honey.'

She couldn't believe it. There was no apology, no explanation. Once again she experienced a deep fear of him.

She felt lost, for she knew of no one whom she could tell. Maybe Bradley . . . but she'd have to find the courage to tell him. Somehow, some way she had to get help!

After she had showered, she examined her face in the mirror. It was bloated and a faint bruise had appeared on one cheek. Clear red marks glowed angrily on her throat where his fingers had hushed her protest.

She entered the dark bedroom and heard the even sound of his light snoring. Taking her robe, she went out on the terrace. In her mind she mumbled a confused prayer. 'Help me, help us. Dear God, I don't know what to do.'

There on the edge of the forest, she saw the figure as she had seen her before.

*Kack!*

In the night she knelt, her face again offered to the stars, and April felt that Kack in her own way, to her own God, was also praying.

# CHAPTER 39

The complimentary copies of the book arrived. This revived April's spirits and she went excitedly to the cabin to show one of them to Kack.

Kack made them both some herb tea, then sat at the table smoothing the cover of the book and carefully turning the pages, handling the book as if it were a rare treasure.

'They work, you know,' she said proudly.

'I know,' April answered softly. 'I wouldn't have wanted to put the book together if I didn't believe in it.'

Kack stopped at a particular page. 'This one,' she said, 'should be helpful today in this troubled world. Comfrey, marigold leaves, apple cider vinegar – it quiets and cleans the troubled mind.'

As she finished the sentence, she looked up and caught April's troubled eyes. It was a bold, knowing look.

In that moment, April knew. Here was someone she could tell. Without expecting to, she burst into tears, laid her head on the table and sobbed.

In her wisdom, Kack didn't go to her, did not implore her to stop. She knew these cleansing tears were the release from pain and confusion that she needed.

Finally, when April could not cry any more, she lifted her head, dried her eyes and apologized.

'It's all right. Sometimes that's the only remedy that works.' Kack looked down at the page and said, 'But for a deeply troubled mind there are other things that cure and can heal.'

April knew she was referring to Ryan. Slowly, in a muddle, she began talking – describing how different, how unthinking, how cruel he had become.

Kack let her talk, urging her on; she gave no opinion and no advice.

It was when the girl was talked out that Kack finally responded, speaking in halting sentences. 'You believe in my remedies – you've shown me that by writing this book. There are other remedies, too, secret ones. There is one I cannot share with you, but I know in my heart it would heal Ryan.'

April's eyes lit up with hope. 'Kack, you must help me. You must help him. I know you love him. He suffers so, and in his suffering, he hurts others.'

'Then you must do as I say.' She reached into her apron. 'Tonight, pour this into his drink. It is not harmful; it will only make him sleep.'

April reached for the small vial. She trusted her. She knew Kack loved Ryan; she knew Kack would never hurt him. If it were only superstitious mumbo jumbo, what did it matter? Yet she had proved that the woman knew things beyond medical science – natural things. Maybe, by some miracle, she *could* help . . .

After agreeing to the conspiracy, April walked back to the house, her hands deep in the pockets of her jacket, her fingers touching the vial. Here, out in the sunlight, it seemed crazy to hope that Kack could restore him. She was tempted to fling the little bottle in the bushes, but it clung to the bottom of her pocket like a burr.

That night, Elizabeth joined them for dinner. She was a ghost of herself. Ryan spoke of a lovely condo in St Louis and what fun she would have decorating it. She nodded politely and cocked her head and seemed to be listening for distant voices. They were not sure if she really understood when Ryan told her of the imminent sale of the property.

April was puzzled by Ryan's behavior toward Tom. She

heard him mutter under his breath, 'Bastard.' Tom these days seemed so out of character – brazen and often rude. It seemed peculiar, as he should have been pleased now that Ryan was going to honor the Judge's promise and deed him the ten acres.

Elizabeth's conversation at the dinner table rambled on, mixing up the here and now with happier yesterdays. After her brandy, Tom assisted her up to bed.

The others watched television in the library. Ryan's face was flushed, his eyes feverish, as if he looked right through the screen. April suddenly felt a rush of fear, and her fingers curled around the vial that was hidden in her pocket. When he went to put another log on the fire, she hurriedly uncapped the small bottle and poured the few drops of liquid into his drink.

Ryan came back to the love seat, reached for his glass, and with a swift swallow, finished the remains of his drink. She nervously watched his face for signs that he knew something was amiss. He gave none.

Reaching for her hand, he held it absentmindedly.

'Let's go to bed,' she said. The words held promise.

'All right.' He shut off the TV and followed her up the stairs.

He undressed quickly. She went into the bathroom and sat on the edge of the tub waiting. How long would it take? She didn't know. She delayed for what seemed a long time, then cautiously opened the bedroom door a crack. He was asleep.

He lay across the bed, his features at rest, mouth open slightly, his breathing slow and even. His face was so dear to her. She yearned for him as he had once been. She loved him deeply. If only this cancer of guilt that gnawed at him could be conquered.

Going to the french doors, she saw Kack waiting at the edge of the woods. The dark figure moved forward, the quiet slap of Kack's tread on the terrace stairs an alien sound in the night.

Under the cape, April saw the movement. A small rabbit emerged, jumped to the floor and began to hop across the carpet. A canvas bag, redolent with spice, was deposited next, and beneath her other arm, April saw that Kack held a second animal.

'Go,' Kack ordered. 'Go, and do not come back till morning.'

An urge to stop the craziness swept over April. Her husband needed a psychiatrist, not this black magic or whatever. It reminded her clearly how far she had gone; she was without hope.

'Go,' Kack ordered loudly now, for she felt the girl's doubt. Laying her bundles on the floor, she took April's arm and led her to the door and closed it after her, turning the lock with a final click.

April stood outside. It was too late; she had allowed it. She knew it was crazy. She went to the green room, took two sleeping tablets and quickly fell into a dreamless sleep.

Kack's hands shook as she lit the candles. She had done this before. It was different; she had loved the Judge, so she had saved him, to touch, to hold, to love in the small bundle of fur. The flame flickered in the room, which grew fragrant with the scent of bayberry. She shuddered as she watched the rise and fall of his chest, this alien thing that lay before her. It did not house Ryan's soul – no – his soul was here in her hand, waiting under the soft fur. She dipped a finger into the jar of burnt ash, drew it on his chest – a large yawning entrance.

He stirred, a soft murmur in his throat.

With trembling fingers she painted a small mouth on his forehead, the lines enclosing the pineal eye.

His eyelids fluttered and were still.

She waited: only the soft sound of the rabbit thumping across the floor could be heard. The creature sensed the importance of the moment. When she reached for him, gently pressing his body to the floor, the rabbit's nose quivered. He strained to understand. The meat cleaver gleamed in her upraised hand; her eyes caught his and begged him to be still. The rabbit blinked, and in that moment swiftly the sharp edge crushed down through the soft fur, through the thick pile of the carpet, and lay wedged into the wood floor.

The sound of the Oh mu rose from the severed head.

Kack held her ears and rocked back and forth gently on her heels. She watched only one thing. The opening she had drawn on her son's chest.

Her hands against her ears could not exclude the sound. The Oh mu searched. She heard its moan above her, behind her, until it settled like a gathering of dust on the satin ruffle of the bed. It slithered under the cover, creeping slowly onto the warm flesh.

His chest heaved. The mouth of ash worked violently – sinking in momentarily to puff outward. The movement went on. The mouth seemed to breathe. A violent pop was heard and the body began to tremble and thrash about the bed as if fighting an invisible intruder.

Katherine took the sleeping cat and stood at the head of the bed and watched the struggle. Her son quieted. She leaned closer, placing the cat's loose mouth near the pineal eye. A small blister formed, quivered, and then burst. The cat inhaled deeply. Katherine held her breath; she felt the subtle wind, a stench, fill the room. It flowed stream-like, inward, and the cat arched as he became the unwilling host.

She peered fearfully at the human face as its stiffness dissolved. The mouth softened, a tear slid from under a shuttered lash, the cheeks bloomed and like the sand – the hourglass shifted. She sobbed softly, gratefully, for Ryan was back and sleeping peacefully; the exchange perfect.

'Forgive me. If there is a God, forgive me,' she murmured. 'It is worse than the forbidden rug; I deserve to lose my sanity and my soul.'

She cradled the sleeping cat and cried into its fur.

She stayed until the first light of day, putting the remains of the rabbit into the canvas bag. She dreaded the moment when the other creature would awake.

It was as she prepared to leave that it stirred. The cat's eyes blinked stupidly. It rose on wobbly legs, circled the room and stopped before the mirror, where its tail switched back and forth with a newfound anxiety.

A paw reached out gingerly and touched the mirror. Its eyes met those in the glass. Recognition – fresh knowledge. It let out one agonized roar.

Kack gathered the leash and struggled with it. It tore her flesh, scratched her arms. She welcomed the pain; she deserved it. Before she had the cat subdued he had managed to fish the rabbit head out of her bag and savagely devoured it while her stomach heaved with disgust.

She was the caretaker.

He was hers to guard forever until he died a natural death.

# CHAPTER 40

Ryan awoke; April was not there. When he rose, his head was muddled and thick, a pounding headache beginning behind his eyes. He went toward the bathroom, stepped on the freshly scrubbed area of rug. The wetness on the soles of his feet made him recall the frightening dream he had had that night. It had been so vivid, the sensation of drowning . . . Remembering, he began gasping for breath.

April entered the room and felt alarmed at his appearance. His eyes were wild, his face flushed and feverish.

'What's wrong?' she asked, fear hammering wildly within her. She was so foolish for having allowed Kack's interference.

He sat down in the bedroom chair. 'It was a dream so frightening, so real. I dreamt that I had drowned.'

She went to him and held his shaking shoulders. 'It's OK, darling, it's OK,' she repeated, talking and shushing him like she would a frightened child. She held him. They stayed like that for a few minutes.

'I'll shower; maybe it will clear my head,' he said.

'Good idea – maybe it will. Bradley's dropped in. I invited him to stay for lunch, but not if you're not up to it . . .'

'That's all right. It's Saturday – is Kyle coming this weekend?'

A shiver ran up April's spine. She had been so foolish – first the blood on the rug and now this. She had been crazy to let Kack try her superstitious magic.

Ryan still looked at her quizzically. 'Well, is he coming this weekend?'

She ran from the room down to the library. In a rush, she spilled out all the horror to Brad – how Ryan had changed, how he was abusive. She even told him between sobbing of the rapes. She admitted she had allowed Kack to conduct some sort of secret ceremony, and now, this morning, Ryan was asking her if his brother was coming this weekend.

'It sounds like some sort of amnesia brought about by guilt. Denial is very common. Denying Kyle's death is just another way of handling his emotional pain,' Bradley explained. 'Twins are closer than most brothers, so there's a tighter bond.'

'He needs help,' April pleaded. 'Please Bradley, please find him help.'

'I will. I know a fine psychiatrist. I can phone him now.' But he aborted the call as they heard Ryan speaking to Hannah in the hall.

Bradley drew in an audible breath of surprise at Ryan's appearance.

'Hi, guy,' he greeted him nervously.

'Long time no see. Hi, yourself.' They could see the effort this mundane greeting cost Ryan, for he immediately lowered himself into the nearest chair, his body sagging into the brocade.

'I'll see to Hannah,' April said, looking at her watch. 'I guess we'll call it brunch.' She backed out of the room, closing the door softly behind her.

With a feeling of shame, she pressed her ear to the door, but its thick oak only allowed unintelligible sounds to filter through. She could not make out the words. She did not leave until she heard the harsh sound of her husband weeping.

Good, she thought. Maybe with Bradley he could talk, he could say out loud what he was feeling, allow the painful grief to come out.

She went to the kitchen feeling somewhat relieved. Bradley was a doctor; he would know what to do. Hannah made her tea. Silently, she sat at the table sipping it slowly. Her teaspoon doodled in the spilled drops on the oilcloth. Later, when Hannah wiped it clean she saw the doodles were a series of small crosses.

'God help us, Hannah. God help us all.'

Ryan told Bradley of the dream. 'It was crazy – it was so real. It was a dark night, the moon was hidden behind clouds, and Kyle and I were out by the sycamore. I'm not sure what we were doing there. We weren't kids – we were grown up. It was like now.' He hesitated and put his head in his hands, his face now hidden by the thick strands of sandy hair falling through his fingers.

Bradley drew in his breath sharply. Denial. Ryan's denial now making the reality into a dream.

'It was lightning,' Ryan continued in a hoarse whisper. 'No, not exactly lightning. Something was flashing and popping, a light – a force, that's it – an unknown force seemed to knock the wind out of me. The water was cold as I felt myself falling, falling.' He looked up, his eyes wild and full of fear. 'I knew I should swim, but I couldn't. Something was holding me still. It was like I was paralyzed – the awful suffocating, the water killing me slowly . . . it took so long.'

He looked straight at Bradley, his eyes searching deep into his friend's. 'In the dream, I died.'

Bradley rubbed his chin. 'As far as nightmares go, that's a doozie.' Totally professional now, he went on. 'I'll get my bag out of the car. You won't deny a friend a chance to show off?'

Returning with his bag, he found Ryan still limp in the chair. After taking his blood pressure and checking Ryan's heart, Bradley knew he had to be persuasive. He sat down opposite his old friend and pulled his chair closer.

'Ryan I think you're suffering from some form of amnesia. This dream you've just told me about is really the true circumstance of how Kyle died. It's almost six months ago now. People deny what they cannot bear, like the death of your brother, your twin. One always feels some sort of guilt. A checkup and rest and some sessions with a good doctor is what I recommend.'

'*Kyle is dead?* My God – you mean he's dead and *I can't remember it?*' Ryan gave a howl of anguish. The world, his life, this day swirled about him in confusion. He stood up and walked to the mirror, moving stiffly like a person in shock. He stared at his own face searchingly, as if seeing it for the first time. 'Dead,' he thought. 'How can he be dead and I not know? We were twins – we shared everything. *I should have known!*' Tears slipped down his face. It was dream-like to be told that the shadow, his other self was dead.

'I cannot believe it,' he said, sinking down heavily in his chair. 'How did it happen?'

Brad chose his words carefully. 'It was almost like your dream; he was helping with the time-lapse camera. Remember the owl? You needed to photograph the owl. Kyle slipped, the lights, the water . . . he was electrocuted. It was over in a heartbeat. He didn't suffer.'

Ryan shook with grief and confusion. His dream had been so real that he felt it, the dying – oh yes, it *was* suffering. He had felt it, every agonizing moment of it, in his dream.

'Kyle dead? I can't believe that Kyle's dead,' he repeated, and even as he murmured it he could not really remember Kyle clearly. It was as if his twin had been some sort of appendage of himself . . . Ryan put his head in his hands and sobbed quietly.

After a time, Brad went over to him. 'There, there,' he said, and awkwardly patted his old friend's shoulder.

Bradley knew of a good psychiatric hospital in St Louis

and Ryan had begun his sessions with Dr Wendt. The doctor came highly recommended, with the bonus of his being an authority on twins.

Ryan found the sessions a catharsis. When he talked of childhood times, his eyes often brimmed with tears.

'Doctor, I loved my brother, yet at times I hated him and sometimes I felt like I was him and he was me. I know this doesn't make any sense, but I felt we were the same person – and our sameness was a burden to us both.'

'That's understandable,' commented Dr Wendt. 'I've heard this sort of thing from other twins. Did your parents encourage your sameness?'

'Oh no. My father was furious when Mother tried dressing us alike. The second set of clothes was sent to the church for their annual rummage sale. He encouraged our different interests. He often said that he didn't want to make the same mistake that his father had made, of forcing us into molds that didn't fit.'

His hands held before him, fingers in a tent, Dr Wendt nodded.

Silence sat between them. Finally, Dr Wendt asked, 'At this time, Ryan, can you remember the events on the night your brother died?'

Thoughtfully, Ryan rubbed his jaw. 'I remembered it in the dream, but – but—' He stopped. 'Now I'm not really sure what is the dream and what really happened. In my dream it was I who died!'

'I see.'

'I still do not recall the actual accident,' Ryan admitted.

'But you've come to terms with reality. You accept that your brother drowned that night. I think I've explained why you might have blocked it out.'

Days turned into weeks, weeks into months, and always April lied to Elizabeth. 'Ryan's in New York. He can't get away. He sends his love.'

The silent woman would nod, not believing her. They had all gone away, she was sure of it.

With the deed in hand, Hannah and Tom could have left, but didn't.

'So much trouble,' Hannah muttered. 'Such happiness and now so much trouble.'

Tom was silent. He couldn't be sure now. He had been certain of what he had seen the night that Kyle died, and equally certain of what he had seen that night when they shot the owl, but he had never told Hannah any of it. Now he began to doubt his own memory.

'Is he better?' was the eternal hopeful question Hannah would ask, each time April returned from the hospital.

Eventually, Dr Wendt felt he could do no more. He arranged for Ryan's release from the hospital.

Rested, his mental state much improved from the sessions, Ryan went home to Hilltop.

April filled the house with flowers; she spent hours on her hair, her nails. She needed to look good for her husband, now that she had him back.

She had never spoken to Kack since that night, although she had seen her walking in the woods or sitting on the porch, the huge cat at her feet. She felt a need to do so now. As she approached the cabin, the animal that was tethered by Kack's chair, growled.

Kack saw her. 'Wait – he is not tame.'

April stopped and was alarmed as she saw the struggle that ensued. The cat snarled, clawing at Kack. A towel was thrown over him and she took him inside the cabin where the sound of thrashing continued.

Kack reappeared alone, rubbing an ointment into her hands where the cat had clawed her.

'He's better. He's coming home,' April said simply.

Tears welled in Katherine's eyes. 'Prayers are sometimes answered,' she said softly.

They sat together on the porch, watching the sunset. Neither of them spoke. They shared a silent communion, each grateful that he was spared.

# CHAPTER 41

Ryan was thinner and pale. He walked often by himself in the woods. It refreshed him, renewed him. Eagerly he went to his studio and the last statue, the owl, was finished. If possible, it was the best of the series.

April was happy. Secretly, she would sometimes watch him sleep, his face in repose, so dear to her, yet strange. Wherever he had retreated, he had come back to her and was whole.

They discussed the property, and she agreed with his decision. They had enough money already. The trust fund had doubled with Kyle's death, and the successful series had clients clamoring for Ryan's services, so there was no real advantage in selling Hilltop. They would lose any profit to taxes.

They went ahead with the original plans – donating the house to the 'indigent blind', providing the codicil that Bruce would be a lifetime resident.

They deeded the cabin and its acreage to Katherine. Elizabeth had recovered miraculously, for she saw in Ryan that he was left to bring her honor. She would bask in his fame.

The selfish, spoiled child in her was revived. She took pleasure in selecting furniture, drapes, new things for the condo on the river. Strangely, she did not seem sad to leave Hilltop – it was not the house of her memories any more. Ryan was surprised that the only object she wanted to keep from a houseful of possessions was the portrait

301

of the Judge and herself with their handsome sons. It was hung in due course above the marble mantel in the condo, the only reminder of another life. A companion was hired for her. She embarked on an new life. The balcony at the condo had a marvelous view of the Mississippi River. She had traded one river for another.

Hannah and Tom said their goodbyes, Tom feeling guilty, for in his pocket he held the check for the acreage. He had sold the land where a factory would soon stand, billowing smoke and ruining the landscape. He deserved this money, he believed; he and Hannah needed the cash. Hannah did not share his satisfaction. She had premonitions that their money would not bring the happiness her husband had always imagined.

With everything settled, Ryan and April still lingered. The Society would not be ready to occupy the house for several weeks. The stillness and empty rooms grew heavy. They did not want sadness to overwhelm them.

Ryan at times held one of his statues in his hands, trying to grasp happiness, to make the world stand still. What time would he have chosen? Would he have chosen one summer's day long ago – with Kyle and he and April? Yes, he had loved her even then. Would he have picked the day that he knew he loved April? Yes, he could have picked that day . . .

He thought of Kyle, and the emptiness, that feeling of being incomplete still stayed with him. It was like a forgotten tune that danced in his head now and then.

He had no heart for travel now. His hands ached physically with the need to create. It was still that childish whim – to make time stand still. The porcelain rabbit before him lived just as it had the day he created it.

Now, the wildlife on the island called to him. He felt the urgency to give those creatures immortality.

April seemed to know without his saying so. In the night as they clung to each other, she whispered, 'Let's go to the island.'

# CHAPTER 42

Ryan, or April and Ryan, went back at least once a year to Hilltop. The responsibility of Mother and Kack and their charities were things they attended to.

Ryan felt annoyed that after all these years Kack still did not have a telephone.

'Who would call me?' she reasoned.

It was with a great deal of haggling, finally lying to Kack, that they managed to have the cabin improved. Ryan told her that county ordinance demanded indoor plumbing, electricity etc. It was the least he could do for her. Five years ago when they had moved to Florida, Ryan offered to buy a house for her in New Mexico, but she refused.

'No. It's better to dream of a place remembered, what was pleasant, and forget what was not. That place lives as a pleasant memory, but this is my home now. I have Bruce – and who would gather the ginseng?' She clocked the seasons, periods of her life. It gave her purpose, the annual harvest.

The inconvenience of not being able to call her when they came to St Louis was annoying. This time, Ryan came alone and unannounced. He did not send a letter to say he was arriving. He wanted to tell her the news in person.

The annual visits were short, consisting of a few hours spent on the porch beside her, or if the weather was inclement, sitting inside the cabin, where the ghost of a thousand memories sat with them. Unused to company, her life spent virtually alone, Ryan sensed that a touched hand, the brief embrace, was all she could endure.

Always, they urged her to come visit or live with them in Florida. Always, she seemed pleased and would agree. 'But not now, maybe later.' They all knew she would never do so.

Today, Ryan's meeting with the Board of the complex had been tedious, involving him with so many trivial details. After that, he had gone to issue a check for the upkeep of the statue of the Judge with the city council. His next errand was at the Home for the Blind, where he settled a few outstanding things with the director.

Errands completed, Ryan noticed that his driver had fallen asleep. The man was slumped in the car, his hat pushed back, snoring loudly. Silly to awaken him to drive the short distance to the cabin.

In the dusk, he started down the path that took Bruce to the cabin every Tuesday. The crunch of fall leaves under his feet filled him with nostalgia. As he followed the rope, a sense of satisfaction filled him. He had done well; the Judge would have been pleased. He had taken care of them all. In the end the Judge's money had created so much good.

As he fingered the stiff envelope in his jacket, Ryan wished with all his heart that his father could have been here to share his joy at this special time in his life.

Coming up to the porch, he saw her silhouette in the chair, her back to the road, her face to the beloved woods.

He noticed her head drop, then right itself. She was asleep.

Quietly he walked up the steps, unaware of the eyes watching him.

The shadow under her chair could have been a basket of yarn, fall apples – any number of things. He paid no mind to it.

Then, possessing agility that belied its age, fueled only by hate, the creature leapt high in the air. Its long claws

304

ripped each of his cheeks, and the sound of a banshee shrieked in his ears.

She awoke, as the tugging of the lead upturned the chair. She fell, tangled in the leather.

Ryan pushed and punched wildly at the thing, his own ankles now entangled. He was jerked viciously, off-balance, then fell, landing on his back! Putting his hand before his face, through the latticework of his fingers, those eyes stared into his. The film on the aged cat's eyes lifted, now clear gray like the aggie marbles he and Kyle had treasured, and they stared into his.

A high keening sound echoed: it was Katherine. Before the cat leapt away, it snapped at Ryan's protective fingers. He felt a burning pain, and as he struggled to get up, saw with horror a vacant hole pumping dark blood where his little finger had been.

'*Ai-eee, ai-eee!*' The unearthly sound was still issuing from Kack's throat, her face turned up to the sky. The scream finally died, and in an ordinary voice, like that of a frontier mother summoning her child in from the dark, she called, '*Kyle! Kyle!*'

During his phone calls to April he sounded plausible; she didn't suspect anything wrong, or ask him why he prolonged the visit. Ryan mumbled something about the Board, the charities and some minor matters he had to attend to for Elizabeth.

He was released from the hospital in two days. He gave thanks that it was his left hand. Kyle was left-handed; he was not.

The unfortunate accident created intervention; the authorities were informed and they were obliged to find the animal. The possibility of rabies had to be addressed.

When Ryan went back to Hilltop to tell her, Katherine panicked.

'Ryan, they mustn't shoot the creature. They mustn't!' she repeated, over and over.

'I'm sure they won't. I think they'll keep him, when

he's caught, and look for signs. Rabies, you know.'

The bandage on Ryan's hand was a badge of guilt for her.

She made him sit at the table, and as she brewed the ginseng tea, her heart was like a heavy stone in her chest. She had to tell him the truth, but would he believe her?

'I'm so sorry,' she said. 'It isn't—'

'No, I'm right-handed. It won't interfere with my work.' He rubbed the injured hand along his trousers. Curious how badly that phantom finger throbbed.

The cabin seemed eerie in the lamplight. She still used the oil lamps instead of electricity.

She sat down opposite him. She must make him understand.

Seeing the worry on her face, he reassured her with, 'It will be all right. They'll find him.'

'No, I must find him, for if they shoot him—' Her voice dropped '—if they kill him, it will be an untimely death that releases an unfinished soul – the Oh mu . . .'

Ryan remembered that strange word. He had heard her speak of it before.

She leaned forward, her dark eyes glinting in the lamplight. 'You must believe, Ryan. You must believe in things unseen. They do exist.'

He nodded.

She reached for his hand. Hers felt cold and clammy squeezing his.

'My grandmother told of its existence – the Oh mu – the unfinished soul. It comes from those who die too early – those who are murdered or commit suicide, or who die in an accident, *unfinished* – not left to term.'

He nodded.

Satisfied that he understood, she went on: 'And there are other unseen things that *do* exist.'

The phantom finger throbbed.

'Twins,' she cried in a whisper. 'Twins are not always real twins. Sometimes it's like a mirror, or an illusion. You see two, when there is only one . . .'

He listened, feeling afraid for her. Was he responsible, leaving her here alone, murmuring to her animals, cooking potions, myths becoming reality . . . Eccentric, that's what they had always thought, but this showed it could be a lot more serious.

She sensed his thoughts, his doubts a real presence in the room. Clasping his other hand, the bandaged one, she pulled him closer so he *had* to look at her. With dread he gazed into those eyes that glittered like a dark mirror.

'Sometimes it is nature's mistake,' she said, willing him to understand. 'There can be two beings, yes – two, but with *only one soul*.'

Her voice, that singsong chant from his youth, when he was overcome by that mysterious illness, the wasting, the fading, IT WAS THIS VOICE.

'It's OK, you're calm, you're fine . . .' Her dreamy voice was creating the slow liquid relaxation within him.

'There was only ever you, Ryan. Like an hourglass, it shifted between you – first one, then the other, shifting like the sand . . . You know, Ryan, you felt it. There was only ever you – and the Shade.'

From far away, he heard her voice. It filled him.

'That night, Ryan, he was behind you – the Shade, this illusion we saw. Remember the feel of his hands as they pushed you? Of your paralyzed limbs as you hit the water and were electrocuted?' She paused, her breathing ragged. 'The terror you must have felt, your soul screeching and calling, seeking. I came to you by the cattails with a new rabbit then – warm, so warm. You found him sleeping. You crawled into the shelter of him. I kept you safe. You were safe here with me, waiting.'

He nodded as one in a trance.

'Transference. I wasn't sure how I did the transference.'

# CHAPTER 43

She found the cat herself. His lead had tangled on a stump. The fire in his eyes had died; embers glowed weakly there. He was safe. She reached for him, felt the quivering of his flesh.

Three days of terror he had endured out there. Between the slats of the cage, he had looked out, dreaming of freedom. The mirage of freedom stretched so far; the years of confinement, shrunk so much.

NOW HE WAS ONLY AS GOD HAD INTENDED, A CAT.

The comfort of her arms, the humming in his ear – *safe*. At last he was safe.

Dead was the rebellion, the struggle quieted. Warm milk, to doze on the coverlet, it was enough. The physical house had grown old, the dampness of the woods caused pain.

It was better to be safe, warm and safe in the cabin. Liberty had expanded from two feet of the wicker cage to the fifteen feet of the cabin. It was enough. On the porch, he sat beneath her chair, no collar, no lead to restrain him.

She was at peace; it was finished. Someone, somewhere, if it was written, would punish her. This one – the son – was not her sin. It was as she had told him: there was only one. It had always been so.

The other, she was certain, *was* a sin. She walked down to the mound and put a single dandelion on it. The small rabbit that had housed William for her, and had surely turned to dust by now . . . it was her sin. That day in the green room, she had decided that she could not bear to let him go. That was her sin, for now she understood that she had him always: he was part of the earth, the leaves that fluttered, the dandelion that bloomed, the wind that caressed her face. All these were as important as one another. None had a greater value. This was the oneness of the world.

She felt the cat's head resting on her feet. This, too, was finished – ended. He was now simply an old cat.

The other – the Shade – had dimmed, dissolved, gone back to unknown, unseen places. She was at peace. Her son, her only son, was restored, complete!

# EPILOGUE

Over coffee at the condo, Ryan spoke to Brad. He arranged for the doctor to visit his mother once a month; also, without seeming official, to call on Kack.

'She's gotten far more eccentric than I realized,' he explained.

'She always was,' Brad defended. 'If she's not a danger to herself or others, what's the harm?'

'I guess none. Brad, she's gotten some funny ideas about twins . . .'

'Oh? What do you mean?'

'Aw, it's impossible to explain – just nonsense.'

'Unfortunate about the accident,' Brad sympathized as he looked down at the bandage.

'Yeah.'

'Does she have any more animals that could present a danger?'

'I don't think so. The cat's been caught. She claims it's OK. It's been checked by the vet and there are no signs of disease, just normal wear and tear. He thinks the animal won't be around much longer. It is pretty old.'

'That's good.'

Ryan looked at his watch. 'It's getting to be that time. I'll go tell Mother goodbye.'

'That your bag?'

'Yeah. I only have one. I didn't plan on staying this long. Thanks for offering the lift to the airport.'

'It's nothing.'

When he was ready to leave, Ryan turned back on impulse to look at the room. Feeling the envelope in his pocket, he knew he'd never tell her now. He tossed it into the fire, where flames licked at the corners of it until superstition overwhelmed him and he jerked it out, one corner partly seared. The fire flared up again and shadows danced on the wall. Looking up at the portrait, he saw the Judge and Elizabeth. Between them stood one handsome boy aged about ten. *A trick of the light*, he told himself. Shoving his left hand in his pocket, he rubbed with his remaining three fingers and thumb the birth announcement of his own twin daughters.

# ABOVE THE EARTH, BELOW THE EARTH, THERE'S NO DEATH MORE HORRIFYING

# GARY GOTTESFELD
# ILL WIND

When a massive earthquake uncovers a large Indian graveyard in Beverly Hills, forensic expert Wilhelm Van Deer – known as 'the Dutchman' – is confronted by more bones than he can cope with. But he soon realises that some of the remains are not as old as they should be, nor the manner of death as straightforward as first appears.

Digging deeper, he comes across weird underground passages and strange paintings of giant centipedes. Somehow these discoveries are linked to mysterious deaths that occurred over twenty years earlier, but there are powerful anonymous people now determined to keep their dark secrets buried for ever.

When the chilling murders begin anew, the Dutchman sets out to catch a maniac – an elusive psychopath obsessed with a grotesquely unusual method of killing...

**FICTION/THRILLER   0 7472 4168 6**

# A selection of bestsellers
# from Headline

| | | |
|---|---|---|
| THE LADYKILLER | Martina Cole | £5.99 ☐ |
| JESSICA'S GIRL | Josephine Cox | £5.99 ☐ |
| NICE GIRLS | Claudia Crawford | £4.99 ☐ |
| HER HUNGRY HEART | Roberta Latow | £5.99 ☐ |
| FLOOD WATER | Peter Ling | £4.99 ☐ |
| THE OTHER MOTHER | Seth Margolis | £4.99 ☐ |
| ACT OF PASSION | Rosalind Miles | £4.99 ☐ |
| A NEST OF SINGING BIRDS | Elizabeth Murphy | £5.99 ☐ |
| THE COCKNEY GIRL | Gilda O'Neill | £4.99 ☐ |
| FORBIDDEN FEELINGS | Una-Mary Parker | £5.99 ☐ |
| OUR STREET | Victor Pemberton | £5.99 ☐ |
| GREEN GROW THE RUSHES | Harriet Smart | £5.99 ☐ |
| BLUE DRESS GIRL | E V Thompson | £5.99 ☐ |
| DAYDREAMS | Elizabeth Walker | £5.99 ☐ |

*All Headline books are available at your local bookshop or newsagent, or can be ordered direct from the publisher. Just tick the titles you want and fill in the form below. Prices and availability subject to change without notice.*

Headline Book Publishing PLC, Cash Sales Department, Bookpoint, 39 Milton Park, Abingdon, OXON, OX14 4TD, UK. If you have a credit card you may order by telephone – 0235 831700.

Please enclose a cheque or postal order made payable to Bookpoint Ltd to the value of the cover price and allow the following for postage and packing:
UK & BFPO: £1.00 for the first book, 50p for the second book and 30p for each additional book ordered up to a maximum charge of £3.00.
OVERSEAS & EIRE: £2.00 for the first book, £1.00 for the second book and 50p for each additional book.

Name ........................................................................................................................

Address ....................................................................................................................

..................................................................................................................................

..................................................................................................................................

If you would prefer to pay by credit card, please complete:
Please debit my Visa/Access/Diner's Card/American Express (delete as applicable) card no:

| | | | | | | | | | | | | | | | | | |
|--|--|--|--|--|--|--|--|--|--|--|--|--|--|--|--|--|--|

Signature ......................................................................... Expiry Date .........